ONE SUMMER IN MONTE CARLO

JENNIFER BOHNET

Boldwood

First published in Great Britain in 2021 by Boldwood Books Ltd.

Copyright © Jennifer Bohnet, 2021

Cover Design by Debbie Clement Design

Cover Photography: Shutterstock

A CIP catalogue record for this book is available from the British Library.

Paperback ISBN 978-1-83889-094-0

Large Print ISBN 978-1-80048-593-8

Ebook ISBN 978-1-83889-095-7

Kindle ISBN 978-1-83889-096-4

Audio CD ISBN 978-1-80048-541-9

MP3 CD ISBN 978-1-83889-225-8

Digital audio download ISBN 978-1-80048-539-6

Boldwood Books Ltd
23 Bowerdean Street
London SW6 3TN
www.boldwoodbooks.com

For Eve Page, who loved her visits to Monaco. R.I.P. Mum. xxx

'Nanette, this has been the perfect day. I'm so glad you agreed to be our wedding planner. You've done an amazing job. As for this place,' Vanessa gestured around, 'it doesn't get any more romantic than this. Ralph and I can't thank you enough for finding it,' and Vanessa hugged her friend tightly.

The two of them were standing in the grand entrance hall of Dymond Park Hotel, the eighteenth-century manor house that a far-seeing local hotelier had bought and turned into the most aspirational wedding venue in South Devon. Once the home of a local aristocrat, the house stood at the end of a drive lined with tall silver birch trees, today though, their branches were bare of the silvery leaves which rustled in summer like tinkling water. The private chapel, set in the middle of a snowdrop-covered field, with views tumbling down the Devonshire countryside towards the distant River Dart sparkling in the late-afternoon winter sunshine, had proved to be an ideal venue for Vanessa and Ralph's winter wedding.

Nanette smiled at her friend and employer. 'I must admit to being worried about organising your big day. It's been such a long time since I've done anything like it.' She paused. 'I did wonder whether I was still up to it.'

'You did a great job. No question about it,' Vanessa said.

'You were a beautiful bride,' Nanette answered.

'Right, enough of this mutual admiration society. I need to talk to you urgently.'

Nanette looked at her anxiously. 'Can't it wait until you return? You are only away for the weekend. Incidentally, you have to leave in about ten minutes,' Nanette said, glancing at her watch. 'Surely Ralph must be wondering where his new wife is?'

'He knows I'm with you. It's important for me to talk to you before we leave. I have to ask you something.' Vanessa glanced at Nanette. 'You know that Ralph has got this big filming project lined up in the Amazon?'

'He was telling me it's his biggest project yet,' Nanette said, remembering how enthusiastic Ralph had been earlier. 'He's really passionate about this film, isn't he?'

'He wants me to go with him. We'd have a week's belated honeymoon in Brazil and then I'd become part of his team filming the documentary in the rainforest.'

'For the whole of the five months?' Nanette looked at her friend wide-eyed. Personally, she couldn't get her head around the prospect of spending such a long time in a rain forest away from civilisation.

Vanessa nodded.

'How do you feel about being away for so long? What about the twins and your business – Oh,' this, as realisation dawned. 'You want me to step into your shoes while you're away?' Nanette took a deep breath. 'Looking after the twins, fine, I'm used to that, but running the business? I don't think I could do that.' Nanette shook her head. 'Organising today with the help of your office, is one thing, running your business in your absence, would be totally different.' Vanessa ran a highly successful PR business with clients ranging between official government bodies, small businesses and the media. Nanette looked at Vanessa anxiously. 'You know I haven't done any office work since...' She shrugged and didn't finish the sentence. 'I did think after organising today, I'd ask you if I could come in and do a regular stint in the office to help get me back into the swing of things, but being in charge—'

'No, no, I don't want you to run the business,' Vanessa interrupted. 'Caroline is more than happy to look after that side of things for me – she's been taking on more responsibility recently anyway. But I do want you to carry on looking after Pierre and Olivia for me.'

Nanette gave her a relieved smile. 'Of course, I'll look after the twins while you're away, no problem. But five months is a long time. What happens if there's an emergency? Do I have full responsibility? What about Mathieu?' Nanette couldn't help but think about Mathieu, the twins' father. Surely, he should be the one taking care of the nine year old twins while their mother was away?

There was a pause as Vanessa fiddled with the sprays of freesias pinned to her wedding dress, before she sighed and looked directly at Nanette.

'I know it's a huge ask, but I need you to look after the twins in Monaco.' Vanessa held her hands up in a conciliatory gesture as Nanette looked at her aghast. 'I know, I know. You vowed never to go back and I promised you wouldn't have to.' She hesitated before continuing. 'Mathieu has agreed to have the twins live with him for six months provided you go too and look after them like you do here for me. He says he's too busy to become a school-gate dad.'

Nanette turned away and watched silently as an all-enveloping mist began to rise from the river and drift up towards the chapel and the hotel. The afternoon was turning cold as the last rays of sunlight vanished. Damp air began to swirl around them as the reassuring presence of the old chapel became an eerie outline as the mist swallowed it up. Nanette tried unsuccessfully to suppress a shivery shudder of apprehension at the very thought of returning to Monaco. Painful memories of the place she'd pushed into the darkest recess of her mind began to swirl into her consciousness.

'Can't Mathieu come over here?' she said, turning back to face Vanessa. 'I'll willingly look after the twins here.'

Vanessa shook her head. 'Apparently not. He says it's impossible for him to leave the country for so long right now. He's got some sort of business deal going through and needs to be there.' Vanessa placed an arm around Nanette's shoulders. 'I realise I am asking a lot. I know how difficult it will be for you to even think about returning and if you can't face it, I will understand. So will Ralph,' Vanessa said. 'But please, will you consider the idea while Ralph and I are away this weekend?'

Nanette sighed. 'Okay, I promise I'll think about it. I'll even run the idea past Patsy and see what her reaction is, but I'm ninety-nine per cent certain it will be the same as mine. A big fat, no way.'

* * *

After the happy couple left for their weekend on Burgh Island, staying at the iconic art deco hotel situated there, Nanette scooped the twins into a waiting taxi and headed off to the station to catch the train to Totnes, where the three of them were spending the weekend with Patsy, her older sister. With only ten months between them, and both inheriting their mother's dark auburn hair and brown eyes, they were invariably taken to be twins themselves. Sibling rivalry was something that simply didn't exist in their world and they'd been inseparable growing up. Later, separated by their choice of degree courses – Art History for Patsy and Business Administration for Nanette – they'd still talked daily via Skype and quickly signed up to WhatsApp. Patsy had used her degree to obtain a job with the National Trust and had worked as a curator for them in several of their properties. Nanette, who loved to travel, had soon found herself working in the high-octane world of Formula 1 motor racing – to the delight of her father, who'd loved the sport.

When their parents died in a boating accident seven years ago, Patsy and Nanette had consoled each other and become even closer, if that were possible. After Patsy met and married Bryan, a Devonshire farmer, and settled into her role of farmer's wife like a born countrywoman, she'd insisted that Nanette regarded Blackberry Farm as their family home. 'Until you get married, of course, and have your own home.' But that had never happened.

As the train sped through the Devonshire countryside, with the twins both playing games on their iPads, Nanette gazed unseeingly out of the window, deep in thought. One question and one question only kept running through her mind. Dare she return to a place that still haunted her dreams? Going back to Monaco would open up old wounds, remind her of what she had lost. Vanessa would surely understand if she told her there was no way she could return.

They'd met on the very first day of the Business Administration course they had both signed up for and struck up an instant and lasting friendship. They'd been through a lot since they'd known each other: job hunting, Vanessa's marriage, the birth of the twins, the divorce from Mathieu and now her wedding to Ralph. Not to mention Nanette's own major life trauma that

Vanessa had helped her survive. Patsy was Nanette's sister and best friend, but Vanessa had become more than a close second.

Nanette was happy with her life the way it was these days, although if she was honest with herself, she was living an easy life, a half-life in truth. She was safe and secure doing a job with people she loved but with little excitement. So different to the one she'd worked hard for when she was younger, before it had been cruelly snatched away from her three years ago.

Pierre and Olivia were nine now and soon wouldn't need her constant presence in their lives, but mentally she'd consigned her need to decide about her future until they were older. Vanessa's request today though had set her mind racing and her thoughts spinning out of control. Nanette sighed. She'd talk to Patsy about it. See if she thought going back was a possibility – or even a good idea.

Patsy was standing waiting for them on the platform as Nanette shepherded Pierre and Olivia off the train.

'Hi. Everything go according to plan? Good. You look like a princess in that frock, Olivia. Did you enjoy being your mum's bridesmaid? Of course, you did, silly question. And you, Pierre, how are you doing? You look very smart in that posh jacket. The car's parked right outside. We should be home in fifteen minutes. I expect you're looking forward to your supper – or did you fill up on wedding goodies?'

Simply listening to her, Nanette felt breathless. She was always amazed at the speed at which Patsy spoke and sometimes found it difficult to get a word in, let alone answer any questions.

'It was a lovely wedding. Such a shame you couldn't be there. Vanessa sends her love. How are you? Any news? I think you've put on weight since I last saw you,' Nanette said quickly, when Patsy finally took a breath.

'I'm fine. My news can wait until later. Talking of weight – you could do with putting on some, you're scrawnier than ever,' Patsy said, with sisterly bluntness. 'I hope you are eating properly – or has organising the wedding stressed you out?'

Briefly, Nanette wondered what Patsy's news was likely to be as she answered her sister. 'I'm fine.' She glanced across at her sister as the twins ran ahead to the car. 'I need to run something past you later. Need your advice.'

Patsy gave her a quick concerned look. As they reached the car and she unlocked it, the twins clambered in and did up their seatbelts. 'Okay.'

She was really looking forward to this weekend break. She probably was stressed, she realised. Life recently had been busier than she'd become accustomed to for the past three years and she was tired after all the excitement of planning and organising the wedding. The twins always enjoyed themselves on the occasions she looked after them on the weekends Vanessa had to travel for business and she brought them down here. They would disappear for hours at a time, exploring the woods and surrounding fields and helping Bryan around the farm, while she and Patsy did sisterly things. Fifteen minutes later, Nanette sighed happily as they turned on to the farm lane.

'How's Bryan's mum? Enjoying her new home?' Nanette asked, as they passed a pristine bungalow at the top of the farm track.

'Think so, but you know Helen. Drove Bryan mad for the first week or two, wanting shelves put up and cupboards moved, but she's finally got it as she wants, although the kitchen will never be right – it's far too small! And, of course, she'll never like living there as much as she enjoyed the farmhouse, even though she moaned for years it was too big and draughty. She'll be joining us for lunch on Sunday as usual, so you are sure to hear all about the drawbacks of having to live in a modern bungalow.' Patsy smiled at her sister.

Once the twins had been fed and settled in their rooms, and Bryan was in the study working on the farm accounts, together Nanette and Patsy went into the sitting room to make themselves comfortable for a sisterly chat.

'Glass of wine to toast the happy couple?' Nanette asked, holding out the bottle of champagne Vanessa had insisted she take.

'A small glass,' Patsy said. 'I shouldn't really, but I don't suppose a sip will hurt junior, Aunty.' She grinned mischievously at Nanette.

'Oh, congratulations,' Nanette said, jumping up to hug her sister. 'That's your news? I'm going to be an aunty. You and Bryan must be so thrilled. I know you both longed for a family. When's it due?' She quickly pushed away the tiny shaft of jealousy that pierced her heart. Her time would come, wouldn't it?

'Late July, early August. No definite date yet, but knowing my luck it will be right in the middle of haymaking. Can you be here? I really, really want you around. Helen is already threatening to move back to help out. Promise me you'll tell Vanessa you need to be here. You can bring the twins.' Patsy looked anxiously at Nanette.

'I'll be here,' Nanette promised. 'Even if Vanessa is still paddling her canoe up the Amazon.'

'Vanessa's going up the Amazon?' For once, Patsy seemed speechless.

'Yep,' and Nanette told her sister about Ralph's wish to make his new wife part of his film team. Patsy took it for granted that Nanette would be looking after the twins whilst Vanessa was away.

'The three of you will all be able to come down regularly. Oh, I'm really beginning to look forward to the next few months.'

Nanette shook her head. Perfect time to tell Patsy about Vanessa's request. 'Afraid not, Patsy. Mathieu has agreed to have the twins to live with him in Monaco while Vanessa's away.' She took a sip of champagne before adding quietly, 'The only condition is that I have to go with them.'

Patsy's eyes widened in incredulity. 'You're not serious? I know it's nearly three years ago and you've supposedly recovered from all the trauma, but are you sure you are strong enough mentally to face things out there? You're bound to meet up with certain people; certain situations are going to bring back painful memories.'

Nanette nodded. She also knew how village-like the Principality was, with its own drumbeat of gossip sweeping down the well-heeled streets. 'I know. My first reaction when Vanessa mentioned it this afternoon was no, no, no.' Nanette swirled the wine in her glass thoughtfully. 'Vanessa's been so good to me – I owe her so much. I'd feel as though I'd let her down if I don't agree. I know she desperately wants to go with Ralph.'

'I'm sure she'll understand if you say you can't do it though,' Patsy said. 'Surely Mathieu could find someone local to help look after the twins for a few hours each day after school. Doesn't his father, what's his name, Jean-Claude, live nearby? I'm sure he'd be delighted to have some bonding time with his grandchildren. Personally, I don't think you need to go at all.'

Nanette was silent for some seconds before looking at her sister. 'I was thinking, coming here on the train, that maybe I do need to go – return to the scene of the crime, as it were. Being airlifted out so quickly left a lot of questions that in my mind have never been answered. There were also a lot of people I didn't get to say goodbye to.'

'Not many of them have been in touch with you since though, have they?' Patsy demanded. 'Not even he, whose name shall not be mentioned unless I'm blaspheming, despite insisting he was acting in your best interests at the time.'

Nanette flinched. 'Perhaps by going I can finally close that particular chapter of my life and begin to look to my future. I can't be Vanessa's housekeeper-cum-childminder forever, the twins are growing up,' she said quietly.

Patsy shook her head. 'Oh, Nanette. If you feel like that, I don't know what to say or suggest. I just don't want you being hurt again. I'm afraid you'll find going back a lot harder than you expect. Could you cope with any recriminations that might occur? If you do go and things get too difficult, promise me you'll come straight back here, with the twins if necessary.'

'Where else would I go?' Nanette said quietly. 'The thing is, what do I do if I don't agree to take the twins to Monaco? I was so shocked I didn't think to ask Vanessa what would happen if I said no. What if I refuse and the twins go to Monaco anyway, where does that leave me? My job and my home will have disappeared. I'll have to find somewhere else.'

'Oh, come on, Nanette. Vanessa has always treated you as part of her family. That's not likely to change,' Patsy said. 'She'll probably offer to find you a job in the office. She's certainly not going to throw you out on the street.'

'I guess you're right.' Nanette sighed, looking at her sister. 'Are you all right? You look a bit pale,' she asked, concerned.

Patsy put down her virtually untouched glass of champagne. 'Excuse me – don't know why it's called morning sickness, mine comes morning, noon and night,' and she disappeared in the direction of the bathroom. 'Back in a mo.' An ashen Patsy reappeared a few minutes later. 'If you don't mind, I'm going to go to bed. We'll talk more tomorrow.'

2

Nanette followed her sister up the stairs, deciding to have an early night herself. Unpacking the suitcase in her familiar bedroom tucked away in the eaves of the farmhouse, she remembered the weeks she'd spent here with Patsy mothering and fussing around her after the accident. An accident that she herself remembered little about. All she could recall was the physical and mental pain she'd suffered on the flight back from Monaco, when both her body and her successful career lay in tatters. Her dreams of marriage and a family were all shattered too.

Vanessa had visited several times. On one visit, a couple of months after the accident, she'd arrived with a proposition.

'You're looking better than the last time I saw you,' she'd said.

'Considering I was still black and blue and various bits of me were swathed in bandages, that's not so hard.' Nanette had smiled. 'How are the twins? Your business?'

'Pierre and Olivia are fine and the business is really taking off,' Vanessa had replied. 'Mathieu has taken them to Disneyland for a few days. He was a lousy husband, but I have to give him credit – he does try to be a good father. I just wish he hadn't decided to live in Monaco permanently. It makes access a bit complicated.' She'd glanced across at Nanette. 'Have you made any plans for your future yet?'

Nanette shook her head. 'No. I'm trying to find the courage to face the world again, but I just don't know where to start. My body has been battered and broken, I don't have a job and my savings are rapidly disappearing. So, do I get fit before I start to look for a job to get back on my feet? Or do I stay here with Patsy and Bryan and try to find work locally. Or what?' She'd looked helplessly at Vanessa. 'On top of it all, I feel such a fool.'

'Hey, you're not a fool. You were holding down a very busy and stressful job when the accident happened. If Zac Ewart had an ounce of decency in him, he'd have supported you, made sure you had a job to go back to, not dumped you before the case came to court. Honestly, Nanette, I can't believe he behaved as he did. Talk about putting the boot in when you were down. You were engaged, for goodness sake. He should have stood by you.'

Nanette had bitten her lip as she'd listened to her friend and vainly tried to stop the tears flowing down her cheeks. It was what she'd expected to happen too. Instead she hadn't heard from her erstwhile fiancé since she left Monaco. Although she had seen the headlines about the accident, calling him a hero and her a reckless driver.

Vanessa, instantly contrite, had put her arms around her friend. 'Nanette, I'm sorry. I didn't mean to upset you. It's just I get so mad on your behalf.' There'd been a pause before she'd continued, 'How do you feel about moving to Bristol and coming to work for me?'

Nanette had looked at her in surprise. 'You need a PA for the business?'

Vanessa shook her head. 'No. Caroline is doing a great job.

What I need is a housekeeper and someone to help with the twins. I know it's not what you're trained for, but maybe a complete change for a while would be good? I have a very busy few months coming up and I need someone at home I can trust to look after the twins and generally take care of things.'

'You're not offering me a job out of pity?' Nanette had asked.

'Definitely not. I'm trying to juggle home and work and I'm desperate for some help. Being a single mum is difficult enough without trying to start and keep a business afloat. I need you, Nanette.'

'What happens about getting the twins to Monaco to visit Mathieu? I couldn't face taking them there. I can't do the school run either now I've lost my licence,' Nanette had added quietly.

'Mathieu will have to collect them. We'll sort something out so you don't have to go. As for the school run, we're only ten minutes away. Much better for them to walk anyway. I can't pay you a fortune, but you'll have your own room, your keep – although you'll be in charge of the cooking! I thought it would help us both – you to get back on your feet and recover from recent events, and me, because I will have someone I can trust utterly while I concentrate on this business and make it work.'

'Maybe we could try it for a couple of months? See how things work out,' Nanette had said thoughtfully. 'Have to warn you though, I'm not a brilliant cook.'

'Great,' Vanessa had said. 'School starts next week, so how d'you feel about coming back with me tomorrow? You can settle in and have a few days to organise a routine.'

Patsy had fussed over her like a mother hen for the next twenty-four hours, worried that she wasn't ready to leave the sanctuary of the farm, but pleased that there was to be some purpose in her life again.

The couple of months' trial had gone quickly and Nanette,

finding she enjoyed a domestic working environment more than she'd thought possible, had happily agreed to stay on permanently. It was certainly less stressful than her previous job as a PA to a Grand Prix racing driver. She adored looking after the twins and running the house, especially when Vanessa was away on one of her frequent business trips. It was like having her own home and children, something she'd always wanted – had imagined having by now, if only things had turned out differently.

Mathieu visited frequently, much to the twins' delight. Separated and divorced when the children were still tiny, he and Vanessa had managed to remain friends despite their differences and both did their best for the twins. Pierre and Olivia were now so used to the way their lives were divided between both their parents and England and Monaco, they simply accepted it as the way their particular family worked.

Things had, of course, changed when Vanessa met Ralph eighteen months ago, but everyone had been careful to make sure the twins were happy and knew they were loved by both their parents. Today's marriage ceremony would serve to cement their own happy nuclear family. Nanette loved the three of them and was already very fond of Ralph. He and Vanessa were so right for each other.

The sudden switching on of an outside light, flashing a beam into the room, brought Nanette out of her reminiscing and back to the present. She glanced out of the window to see Bryan, the happy father-to-be, on his way across the farmyard to do his final night-time check of the animals in the barn. Earlier, the twins had helped him fill the hay racks and now, as Bryan opened the barn door, Nanette caught a whiff of the hay and the acetic smell of contented cows chewing the cud.

Thoughtfully, Nanette drew the curtains and went to finish her unpacking. Could she really turn her back on everything

Vanessa had done for her and refuse to help out? Besides, if she didn't agree to take the twins to Monaco, where would that leave her? Patsy, she knew, would welcome her with open arms if she decided to move in and live on the farm permanently with her and Bryan. But soon they would be their own little family unit, and she dreaded the thought of morphing into the aged spinster aunt who just existed without a proper life of her own.

Patsy was right when she said Vanessa treated her like family, but relatives had fallen out over less and Nanette dreaded the thought of losing contact with Vanessa and the twins simply because she refused to go to Monaco and face up to her past.

Nanette sighed. It was such a big unexpected decision to have to take and so little time in which to consider all the options, to get her thoughts in order and to make the right decision. She could only hope a good night's sleep would help clear her mind and in the morning she would be nearer to having the answer. If she managed to sleep at all that was.

3

The smell of freshly percolating coffee greeted Nanette as she made her way down to the large kitchen on Sunday morning. Patsy was busy pushing sprigs of rosemary and gloves of garlic into a large leg of lamb ready to roast for lunch.

'Hi. Did you sleep well? The twins are helping Bryan feed the baby calves. Help yourself to coffee. You know where the cereals are. There's plenty of bread for toast. Can you pass me the pot of honey please? I want to drizzle some over the lamb. I'd offer you bacon and eggs, but I can't stand the smell of bacon cooking at the moment.'

'Coffee and toast will be just fine. I'll do the vegetables for lunch afterwards, shall I?' Nanette asked as she handed her sister the honey.

'Thanks. Helen always insists on bringing the dessert so I don't have to worry, she says. More like she doesn't like my pastry! I thought we could go for a walk after lunch – maybe take the twins down to the lake. Helen always likes Bryan to take her on a tour of the farm on Sunday afternoons, like they used to when Albert was alive.' Patsy sighed. 'Honestly, Nanette, sometimes I could strangle the woman, but she does mean well, I suppose. I thought when she finally moved out, things would be better. She'd get an independent life again. Leave Bryan and me to our own devices a bit more.' Patsy shook her head. 'Nothing's really changed. She's still up here every day on some pretence or other and Sunday lunch here every week has become something of a ritual set in stone. Not sure how I'm going to deal with all the "grandmotherly" advice that is sure to be heaped on me. That's why I need you here as an ally when junior arrives.' Patsy glanced at her sister. 'Any closer to deciding what you're going to do about Vanessa's request?'

Nanette shook her head. 'Still mulling it over. Maybe the walk this afternoon will clear my head and I'll be able to think straight.' She certainly hoped so. As she'd expected, sleep had evaded her for most of last night and she'd tossed and turned for hours trying to reach a decision without success.

* * *

Helen arrived just as Patsy placed the roast in the Aga and immediately queried whether it would be cooked in time.

'I always had the meat in the range by ten o'clock at the latest. Ready for lunch at one on the dot. Still, you young things abhor routines, don't you? Mind you, once the baby arrives, you'll soon change your tune.'

'Helen, it's lovely to see you again,' Nanette said quickly before Patsy could respond to her mother-in-law's criticisms. 'How's life in your new home?' She couldn't decide whether Helen's prickly nature had got worse since she'd handed over the farmhouse to Bryan and Patsy or whether the woman had always been so... so prickly.

'Different to what I've been used to, but I'm settling in nicely, thank you. Once Bryan finishes off a couple more little jobs, I'll be really organised. Ready to devote my time to helping Patsy with the new addition.' Helen slanted a look at Nanette. 'How about you? Your memory completely back to normal now?' she asked briskly. 'I saw a picture in one of the Sunday papers recently of – oh, what's his name? Your ex-fiancé, anyway. Had a blonde on his arm. Said something about him being newly single again and playing the field. Zachary – that's his name.'

'I saw that photo too,' Nanette said quietly. 'As for my memory, I still have no recollection of certain things people tell me happened three years ago – maybe it's for the best,' she added, forcing a smile in Helen's direction. 'Otherwise I'm fine. If you'll excuse me, I'll just go check on the twins.' Leaving the kitchen, Nanette mouthed an apologetic, 'Sorry – I'll see you later,' at Patsy before closing the kitchen door behind her.

After a slightly strained lunch, Nanette, Patsy and the twins went for their planned walk down to the lake at the far end of the farm, with the twins running ahead.

'I'm sorry Helen assumed your memory had returned to normal,' Patsy said quietly. 'And mentioned you-know-who. I know you find both difficult to handle.'

Nanette shook her head wearily. 'Don't worry. I wish my memory of that evening would return, but I'm beginning to believe it never will now. As for Zac, well, I can't hide from news about him for ever.' Opening a heavy farm gate so that Patsy didn't have to climb over as the twins had done, Nanette said to her sister, 'Actually, I think Helen's comments have helped me make up my mind. I can't run from the past for ever, so' – she took a deep breath – 'I'm going to tell Vanessa, yes, I will go to Monaco. At least Mathieu will be around if there are any problems with the twins and he'll be a friend for me too.'

That night, though, the nightmares that had taunted Nanette for months, years, after the accident returned with a vengeance.

Nanette could feel the wind tearing at her face as she frantically skied faster and faster down the mountainside. Adrenalin flowed through her veins as she heard the noise of the avalanche behind her gathering speed, devouring everything in its way. Her lungs forced a terror-stricken scream into the air. She couldn't die like this, she...

'Nanette, Nanette, wake up. You're having one of your nightmares,' Patsy shook her gently.

A shudder went through Nanette's body as she came to.

'Here, have a sip.' Patsy handed her a glass of water. 'What was it this time? Another monster breaking into the house? An earthquake?'

Nanette shook her head. 'No. I was caught up in an avalanche.' She took a sip of the water as Patsy regarded her thoughtfully.

'It's been ages since you've had a nightmare.'

Nanette nodded. 'I know. I was hoping they'd finally finished,' she said, her body still racked with shakes.

'The therapist was saying only last month that it was a good sign I'd gone for so long without one. Wonder what interpretation she'll put on tonight's little episode?' Nanette added through chattering teeth. 'It was horrible.'

'The stress of planning the wedding? Or maybe the thought of returning to Monaco?' Patsy said, giving her sister a concerned glance. 'Are you cold? Shall I get you a hot-water bottle?'

'No, thanks. I'll snuggle back under the duvet in a moment and I'll soon warm up.' Nanette smiled at her sister. 'You go back to bed. Remember your condition. Don't want you with dark circles under your eyes tomorrow, or rather today.' She glanced at the bedside clock. 'I'm sorry I woke you.'

'If you're sure you're OK,' Patsy said. 'I could stay with you for a bit?'

'I'm fine. Go back to bed,' Nanette ordered. 'I'll leave the light on for a bit.'

Patsy glanced anxiously at her before leaving and pulling the door closed behind her.

Once she was alone, Nanette sat on the edge of the bed and took some deep breaths, trying to get her shaking body under control. It was never easy to banish the apprehension and terror that the nightmares brought.

Sitting there, watching a moth seemingly mesmerised by the bedside light, flying frantically round and round, Nanette's thoughts flitted about in a similar manner over her latest nightmare.

These terrifying dreams had been an irregular part of her nights for nearly three years now. Ever since the car accident in which she – and Zachary Ewart – had nearly died.

The therapist, whom Patsy had persuaded her to see when the nightmares began in the weeks after the accident, had been right when she'd said they would happen less and less as time went on. Tonight's nightmare, though, had been truly terrifying. As bad as any she'd ever had.

Slowly, as she sat there, the shaking stopped and the feeling of devastation retreated into her subconscious. There had been an extra dimension to the nightmare tonight – something that had lingered as she'd woken up.

As she'd hurtled down that slope in the path of the avalanche, screaming in terror, she hadn't been alone. A shadowy figure had been alongside, urging her on.

'*Faster, faster. Remember, remember...*'

Remember what? Despondently, Nanette replayed the nightmare in her mind, trying to come up with some positive memory from the episode, but her brain refused to co-operate.

Wearily, she slipped under the duvet and reached out to turn off the bedside light. Hopefully the rest of the night would pass peacefully. Now the decision was made and she was going to return to Monaco, she would need all her strength to get through the memories the coming weeks and months were sure to throw at her. She could only pray that she was making the right decision for her, but, in truth, what else could she do?

4

Returning to Vanessa's with the twins after their weekend stay at Blackberry Farm, Nanette caught up with the usual chores that were involved with looking after Pierre and Olivia. Vanessa and Ralph returned late the same day, with Vanessa shooting an anxious, enquiring look at Nanette. Nanette smiled at her and nodded before saying, 'We need to talk about it.' But it wasn't until the evening of the following day that she had the opportunity to talk properly to both Vanessa and Ralph.

The three of them were having a late supper around the kitchen table and Vanessa was saying how much she'd enjoyed their weekend on Burgh Island.

'The hotel was wonderful. So luxurious. And its spa treatment room, sheer bliss,' Vanessa sighed happily. 'I haven't ever been spoilt in quite the same way, even in Monaco. Something I could get used to, I warn you.' Vanessa smiled at Ralph, who gave her an amused glance.

'I think the Amazon jungle will soon bring you back down to earth,' Ralph said.

'Ah,' Nanette said, pushing her supper plate away and picking up her still half-full glass of red wine. 'About that.' She took a mouthful before placing the glass back down on the table and looking at Vanessa. 'First, are you still certain Mathieu and Jean-Claude can't manage without me being there?'

'Mathieu is adamant that he's got too much on over the next few months for him to guarantee being available on a day-to-day basis. Jean-Claude, I know, will step in and help, but he's busy with his business too. And, honestly, I'd feel so much happier if you were looking after them while we are away. You're such a constant in their lives already. And I trust you to put them first whatever the circumstances.'

Nanette took a deep breath. 'For you and the twins, I will go with them to Monaco and look after them. I can't say I truly relish the idea of returning there but...' And she gave a resigned shrug.

Vanessa was on her feet and rushed round to hug Nanette. 'Thank you, thank you – I know it's been a difficult decision for you. I promise you Jean-Claude will do everything to make your stay as easy as possible, even if Mathieu is away on business a lot,' Vanessa said. 'I can't thank you enough for agreeing.'

'Neither can I.' Ralph quietly added his thanks to Vanessa's. 'A toast, I think? To Nanette, for Monaco, and to us, for the Amazon.'

Nanette smiled her acknowledgement of the toast as they all clinked glasses. Inwardly, though, she was terrified and fighting an overwhelming urge to shout out – I was joking. I didn't mean it. I can't possibly go back to Monaco.

And she definitely didn't have an answer to the other major, panic-stricken thought going round and round in her mind: *What have I done?*

* * *

After a couple of weeks of frenzied preparations, Vanessa and

Ralph departed for Brazil, leaving Nanette with no option but to fly to France with the twins.

As the plane lost height in preparation for landing at Nice Côte d'Azur airport, Nanette caught a glimpse of the famous giant pyramids complex on the Baie des Anges, in Villeneuve-Loubet. Built to resemble waves, standing seventy metres high above sea level, the apartment blocks overlooked a marina and the Mediterranean Sea. A sight that so many times in the past she'd been happy to see as she'd returned to Monaco after being away working. Today though, she didn't feel the happiness, just a flood of unwelcome memories.

By the time the plane touched down some minutes later and taxied along the landing strip that ran alongside the edge of the sea, Nanette had taken several deep breaths. For better for worse, she was back in the South of France.

The Mediterranean sparkled under a warm March sun and she remembered how in the past returning had felt like coming home, and she'd always felt content to be back. Not today though. Today she was a bundle of apprehension, wondering what she would be forced to confront in the coming days and weeks. Whatever the next few months had in store for her, she prayed that the turbulence of her past wouldn't intrude into the future.

She undid her seatbelt and began to gather their things. The twins were already on their feet, excited at the prospect of the next part of the journey. Normally transfer to Monaco for them was via tram from the airport and then a train from Nice, but as a special treat, Vanessa had arranged a helicopter flight for the three of them.

Walking through the arrivals hall, Nanette put on her large sunglasses. She knew from experience that there was always the odd photographer, or even a group of paparazzi, lurking around the airport in the hope of snapping someone famous on their way out to the helicopter pad for transfer to Monaco. She knew she was unlikely to be of any interest, but hiding her eyes and obscuring her face behind the dark glasses made her feel better.

It wasn't the paparazzi who greeted her, though, as she walked towards the helicopter check-in desk: it was a large billboard advertising the Monaco Grand Prix in May.

But it was the smaller poster featuring a film-star-style close-up of the man regarded as the local hero, with the words 'Is this Zac's year?' emblazoned over it that took her breath away. Seeing Zac's familiar face smiling out at her made Nanette want to do the impossible: run and catch the next flight back to the UK and safety. Impossible though; she'd given Vanessa and Ralph her word. She just had to spend one summer in Monte Carlo, as she'd agreed, and then she need never return again.

Turning her back on the poster and trying to shut the images and the memories it invoked out of her mind, Nanette handed over the flight reservation tickets to the desk clerk.

'Great,' Pierre said excitedly. 'We'll be here for the Grand Prix. Do you think Dad will be able to get us some passes for the pit lane?'

'I shouldn't be surprised,' Nanette said, with a sinking feeling. She'd totally forgotten their time in Monaco would clash with the race. That a certain person would obviously be in town. Pierre, being a typical boy, would naturally be fascinated by the racing cars and their drivers and would want to go out and about at race weekend to see as much as possible.

'Well, I don't want a pass,' Olivia said. 'I hate the noise those cars make. It hurts my ears.'

Inwardly, Nanette agreed with Olivia. Not because of the noise, but the last thing she wanted too, was a ticket to anything that involved contact with Zachary Ewart. Maybe Mathieu would

be around at Grand Prix time and would take Pierre down to the
pit lane while she and Olivia stayed well away.

The twins clambered happily into their seats in the helicopter, leaving Nanette to sit alongside the pilot. As the turbines
screamed and the rotors beat the air, the helicopter took off in a
rush of noise, and Nanette took several deep, steadying breaths.

The pilot glanced at her sympathetically. 'First helicopter
trip? You look a bit nervous. It's only fifteen minutes.'

Nanette shook her head. 'No. It's not my first trip, but I am
nervous.'

Staring out through the window at the coastline that had once
been so familiar to her, Nanette didn't add that it wasn't the flight
she was nervous about, but the fact that she was returning to
Monaco.

After landing at the helipad in Fontvieille, a downtown extension of Monaco which had been built on land reclaimed from the
sea, Nanette and the twins took a taxi to Mathieu's apartment on
Boulevard Albert 1er, overlooking the old port. As the taxi took
them through one of the many tunnels that made their way,
mole-like, under the Principality's roads, Nanette remembered
how surprised she'd been the first time she'd arrived by the exis-
tence of this underground road system, hewn out of the rocks that
lined the walls. She'd never suspected such a labyrinth of tunnels
under Monte Carlo even existed.

Within minutes, they were back above ground and the taxi
was stopping outside Mathieu's apartment block. Moments later
and the twins were knocking on the door of his ninth-floor
apartment.

To Nanette's surprise, it was Jean-Claude, Mathieu's French
father, who opened the door to them.

'Bonjour mes petits and welcome,' he said, hugging the twins
before turning and giving Nanette a light kiss on each cheek.

She liked Jean-Claude and they had always got on well on the few occasions they'd met, although secretly Nanette wondered how on earth he could really be Mathieu's father. Older brother, yes, but father? He simply did not look or behave old enough.

'Where's Daddy?' Olivia asked, disappointedly.

'He'll be here later, ma petite,' Jean-Claude said. 'He has to take care of some business this afternoon. You two can take your things through to your rooms while I show Nanette hers. Lemonade and biscuits on the balcony in ten minutes.'

Once the twins were safely out of earshot, Jean-Claude turned to Nanette hesitantly.

'Mathieu offers apologies, but something came up that he couldn't get out of. He hopes to be here later this evening. In the meantime, I take care of things. Help you settle in, give you keys and things. I stay tonight in case he doesn't return.' Jean-Claude picked up Nanette's suitcase. 'You haven't been to this apartment before, have you?'

Nanette shook her head. 'No, Mathieu had a place up near the casino itself the last time I was here. It was a lot smaller than this one.'

'Come on then, I show you around.'

The apartment, with its five bedrooms, all with en-suite bathrooms, a large sitting room with doors opening out on to the balcony, was as sumptuous as any Nanette had ever been in. Fleetingly, she wondered how Mathieu could afford such luxury, she'd never really known what sort of business he had, but maybe Jean-Claude, who she knew ran a successful wine business, had helped him out.

Her own room was charming – with a mixture of French Provençal furnishings blending in with some more modern pieces, its own balcony with a view out over the harbour and a bathroom with marble and gold fittings.

'It's a very grand apartment,' Nanette said slowly.

Jean-Claude smiled. 'I have the feeling having the twins living here permanently for a few months rather than simply visiting will turn it into more of a home. Now, I'm sure Florence will have tea and biscuits ready on the balcony. We join the twins?'

'Who is Florence?' Nanette asked, as they made their way back to the sitting room.

'Mathieu's housekeeper.'

Nanette turned and looked at Jean-Claude in surprise. 'But that's partly what I thought I was here to be. Mathieu doesn't really need me if he's already got a housekeeper and you to help.'

'You're here simply to look after the twins – organise them when they are not at school, including evenings and weekends, of course.'

'That's still going to leave me with an awful lot of time on my hands,' Nanette protested. 'With nothing to do.'

Jean-Claude didn't answer. He simply raised his eyebrows at her quizzically. 'I'm sure you find plenty to do once you settle in. Merci, Florence,' he said as the housekeeper arrived with a tray. 'We manage now.'

Distractedly, Nanette accepted the cup of tea Jean-Claude handed her.

'Vanessa and Ralph got away all right yesterday?' Jean-Claude asked.

Nanette nodded, forcing herself to focus. 'The twins and I went to Heathrow to wave them goodbye at the crack of dawn. They should be sleeping off their jet lag right now. Vanessa said she'd try to phone tonight to make sure everything was OK this end.'

'Netty, Pierre wants to play with his computer game and I want to watch television in my room,' Olivia said. 'May we?'

'Half an hour,' Nanette agreed, and smiled as the twins dashed away.

'Nanette, I need to talk to you,' Jean-Claude said. 'To explain something.'

Nanette looked at him in surprise.

'I have to be honest with you. I don't say anything in front of the twins, but I think you have the right to know. It's extremely unlikely that Mathieu will be here tonight.'

Nanette waited as a clearly unhappy Jean-Claude ran his hands through his hair.

'I've spent most of this afternoon with my lawyers,' he said, 'trying to sort things out, but...' Jean-Claude shrugged unhappily as he looked at her. There was a pause before he added, 'Mathieu hasn't been delayed by business: he's been arrested.'

5

Three days later, Nanette was enjoying a coffee and a croissant at one of the cafés that edged the La Condamine Monaco flower and vegetable market, when her mobile rang.

'Hi, Patsy. Everything all right?' she asked quickly, as her sister's number flashed on the screen.

'Yes. Just wondering how you are. Texts are all very well, but I need to hear your voice. I start to worry when we don't actually speak to each other. I wonder what you're not telling me,' Patsy said.

'Sorry. My silence wasn't deliberate, it's just that things have been a bit upside down here since we arrived, but everything's fine here now.'

'What do you mean now?' Patsy demanded. 'What's happened? Are the twins all right? Are you?'

'The twins and I are fine.' Nanette hesitated. 'Mathieu wasn't here when I arrived. He'd been arrested.' Quickly, before Patsy could draw breath, Nanette continued, 'He's out now. They kept him in for twenty-four hours before releasing him on bail. He has to report back once a week.'

'What's he done?'

'I don't know exactly. Something to do with his business,' Nanette said. 'Apparently all he said to Jean-Claude was it's nothing to worry about and that he'd got it sorted.'

She didn't add that Jean-Claude was furious with his son for not asking him to put up the bail money. Instead, an unnamed foreign business associate had stood surety. Privately, Nanette thought it sounded more than shifty but she'd kept those thoughts to herself and decided not to mention the incident to Vanessa when she got in touch. Mathieu himself was acting much as normal, which she took as a good sign.

'I'm sorry I haven't rung you before, but as you can imagine, trying to occupy the twins and keep the news of their father's arrest from them hasn't left much time for anything else. Thankfully, Mathieu has taken them to Marineland in Villneuve-Loubet today to give me a couple of free hours. Jean-Claude is organising an extra computer for them, so they'll be able to follow Vanessa and Ralph's progress from this weekend.'

'Have you heard from them?'

'Only a quick text to say that she'd tried to phone last night but couldn't get through for some reason but they've arrived safely in Brazil and are enjoying themselves. Their honeymoon will be over next weekend when they fly up into the jungle and meet up with the film crew ready to begin filming the documentary.'

'When do the twins start school?'

'Monday, so that's something else we've been busy doing: sorting clothes, buying books and stationery and backpacks big enough to carry everything. Honestly, the amount of stuff they have to carry on a daily basis is unbelievable.'

'What about you?' Patsy asked. 'How are you coping with being back in Monaco? Met up with anyone from your past yet?'

'If you mean, have I seen Zac, the answer is no. How's your morning sickness?' she asked, deftly changing the subject.

'Slowing down, thank goodness,' Patsy said. 'I'd better go – Helen is about to arrive and if she realises I'm on the phone to you, I shall get a lecture about wasting Bryan's hard-earned money on foreign phone calls – even though its WhatsApp!'

'I'll ring you at the weekend,' Nanette said, laughing. 'Take care.'

Thoughtfully, she put the phone in her bag and looked around her at the colourful scene. Local housewives and Filipino servants with raffia baskets were busy doing their daily fresh vegetable shop and Nanette could see the walkway up to the palace was crowded with tourists.

It was hard to believe she was back here. If someone had told her last year that she would be living in Monaco again, her immediate reaction would have been outright disbelief. The scars were still too sore then to even contemplate returning. Now, having settled in, and despite the problems of the last few days, Nanette was beginning to enjoy being back. The Principality had always been a special place for her and she'd been sad everything had fallen apart in such a horrendous way.

She realised after she'd finished talking to Patsy that she'd forgotten to tell her about last night when Mathieu had taken her out to dinner after the twins were in bed and Florence was babysitting. Partly to apologise for not being there when she arrived and simply, 'Because I'd like to,' he'd said, with a disarming smile when suggesting it. The evening, though, had ended on a strange note.

The small family-run bistro he'd taken her to was a familiar one, hidden in one of the back streets, away from the tourist haunts. Nanette had pushed the thought of the last time she'd been in there with Zac away and tried to 'live in the moment', as all the self-help books advised, rather than let that memory cloud the evening.

'I'm so glad you decided you'd come with the twins,' Mathieu had said, as they'd waited for their first course to arrive.

'Can't understand why you wanted me here really,' Nanette had replied. 'Florence lives in, and Jean-Claude seems more than happy to help look after the twins.'

'Vanessa thought it was important for Pierre and Olivia to have some sort of continuity in their lives. They are used to you looking after them when Vanessa is away. It certainly makes things easier for me, knowing you're in charge.' He'd smiled at her and added, 'And it was definitely less of a worry for me earlier in the week, knowing that you were here with them.' There was a slight pause before he had said quietly, 'I have to confess to an ulterior motive too. I also hoped we could get to know each other better. That perhaps you could stop thinking of me simply as the twins' father and we could become better friends.'

The waiter arriving with their starters at that moment had spared a surprised Nanette from responding. She hoped becoming better friends was all that Mathieu had in mind. There was no way she'd even think about getting involved with him. He was her best friend's ex-husband, for goodness sake. Thankfully, Mathieu had changed the conversation to more general things once the waiter left them.

'It's the Tennis Masters Series soon,' he had said. 'I remember you and Zac used to play a lot. I've been offered the chance of a couple of tickets for the opening day, would you like to come with me?'

'Oh please,' Nanette had replied, ignoring the flicker of pain at the mention of Zac. They had been passionate about tennis, both playing and watching. To actually go to a Tennis Masters match would be wonderful. Zac had always been tied up with racing by April when the event happened and had never managed to schedule it into his programme.

'Good. I'll confirm the tickets before I go away next week.'

'Business trip, or pleasure?' she'd asked.

'A trip to Switzerland on business,' he had said quietly. 'So long as the authorities don't prevent me leaving.'

'Are they likely to?' Nanette had looked at him, trying not to show her worry but not wanting to pry.

Mathieu had shrugged. 'I'm hoping they'll realise they've made a mistake in the next couple of days and everything will be sorted out. I'm not the man they want.'

'Do you know who is?' Nanette had asked quietly.

Mathieu had nodded. 'Oh yes.' But he'd said no more and the subject had been dropped.

As they had finished their meal and prepared to leave, the restaurant door opened and a couple entered. The man, a burly figure in an expensive black coat and wearing a trilby, immediately came over to Mathieu. The two shook hands and chatted briefly, but it wasn't until the man said, 'Mathieu, who is your charming companion?' in a foreign accent that Nanette recognised as Russian, that Mathieu, reluctantly it seemed to Nanette, had introduced her.

'Boris, this is my children's nanny. Netty, this is Boris, a business acquaintance.'

'Aw, come now, Mathieu, more than a business acquaintance since last week. Remember how I help you with your little difficulty?' Boris had turned to Nanette, briefly acknowledged her with an abrupt 'Bonjour, mademoiselle,' and turned his attention back to Mathieu. Nanette couldn't help but overhear Boris's next words. 'Tell Zac I need to talk to him urgently.'

Mathieu had nodded in reply before placing his hand in the small of her back and gently pushing her towards the door, saying goodbye to Boris.

Knowing the way society in Monaco worked, Nanette was not surprised that once he'd learnt she was a mere nanny, Boris had ignored her. As far as he was concerned, she was just a servant and not important enough for him to bother with.

The question, though, was, why had Mathieu introduced her as the nanny, complete with the childish name the twins called her, when earlier he'd intimated he wanted them to get to know each other better. He must have realised he'd effectively precluded her from mixing with him and this particular business associate in the future.

Now, as she watched the morning's market activity around her and drank her coffee, she couldn't help wondering about that message for Zac. What was the connection between Zac and Boris? How long had Mathieu known Boris? The oft-quoted phrase about Monaco being 'a sunny place for shady people' came into her mind. What were Zac and Mathieu up to, associating with a Russian, whom, on first impressions, she personally wouldn't trust an inch?

Thoughtfully, Nanette finished her coffee, left enough euros in the saucer to cover the bill and began to make her way down to the old port. So much had changed since she lived here and yet some things were still reassuringly familiar.

From her bedroom balcony, she'd struggled to remember the lines of the old port. To her eyes, the new harbour extension, already crowded with the floating gin palaces belonging to the rich and famous, had blended in seamlessly.

Walking slowly along the quay, Nanette recognised some of the yachts, but to her relief there was no sign of *Pole Position* – the boat Zac had treated himself to after winning the US Grand Prix

in Indianapolis several years ago. Knowing that he liked to have
the yacht moored in Monaco and use it for parties both before
and after the Grand Prix, Nanette knew that once *Pole Position*
reappeared in the harbour, it wouldn't be long before Zac too, was
back in town.

Glancing up to the familiar skyline behind the Hotel de Paris
as she walked up the hill, something jarred in her memory. It was
a second or two before Nanette realised that the nineteenth-
century villa where she'd had a tiny two-room apartment had
been replaced by a large ultra-modern concrete building.

Shame; the building, one of the few old villas left, had lent a
certain charm to the skyline and had emitted a belle époque
atmosphere of the Riviera in its heyday, which she'd loved. Zac,
though, had always complained about its lack of modern conve-
niences and had rarely stayed there with her.

His own large apartment had been in one of those ultra-
modern blocks a street or two away from Casino Square. Idly,
Nanette wondered if he still lived there or whether, like Mathieu,
he had moved on to an even grander place. Whatever, she had no
intention of walking anywhere near that particular area this
morning.

Instead, she took the Avenue Monte Carlo turning and
strolled along, happily indulging in a spot of wishful window
shopping in the expensive boutiques that lined the small street.
Once, in the past, she'd happily indulged herself buying a leather
handbag in one of them. A handbag that was currently
languishing in the wardrobe in her room in Blackberry Farm.
Another time, another life.

Dodging a string of excitable Japanese tourists, Nanette
crossed the road and ran down a flight of steps into the immacu-
lately tended Casino gardens. Last night, Mathieu had mentioned

an exhibition of sculpture being shown there by a little-known Frenchwoman and she was looking forward to an hour or two wandering around the exhibits.

6

Sitting on the bed in her air-conditioned hotel bedroom, Vanessa pressed the 'save' key on Ralph's laptop which they had to share because of transport issues. Their honeymoon period was over and today their real married life together would begin. A life that for the next few months would be unlike any she had ever known. She'd promised the twins that she would take lots of photos and keep a diary for them to read when she returned. Ralph had said the deeper they went into the jungle, living with the native tribes, there was unlikely to be any hope of a regular satellite connection.

Knowing that last night's Skype connection with the twins was probably the last time she'd be able to talk to them for several weeks was hard. She could tell, though, that both of them, whilst missing her, were happy and settled in Monaco with Mathieu and Nanette. Olivia had been excited about a new friend she'd made at the International School and Pierre couldn't wait for Grand Prix weekend. Jean-Claude had figured in the conversation a lot too, Vanessa had noted. The twins were definitely growing closer to their grandfather now they were living in

Monaco which was good. She'd always got on well with Jean-Claude and after divorcing Mathieu she'd felt more than a twinge of guilt that they were missing out on a relationship with their grandfather.

With the twins hogging the computer, Vanessa had only managed a fleeting conversation with Nanette at the end. Her friend had reassured her that everything was good and she was to stop worrying about them and enjoy her adventure in the jungle. Vanessa remembered how torn she'd been when Ralph had asked her to accompany him on this trip. While she loved his enthusiasm and passion for the project and supported his decision to make a documentary about the jungle, the thought of joining him and leaving the twins for so long, scared her. And guilt had, of course, reared its head. Nanette agreeing to look after the twins with Mathieu while she was away had been the deciding factor. She'd be leaving them in the safest possible hands with two people they knew and adored. Vanessa knew it had been a big ask of Nanette to put the past behind her and return to the Principality and she'd worried about it, but hopefully it would prove to be a step forward for Nanette. It certainly seemed as though it was working out currently.

Resolutely, Vanessa pushed all thoughts of the twins and home away as she picked up the laptop and slid it into the travel bag. In a few minutes, they would be on their way to the airport and the adventure would really begin. The last week had been wonderful, but now she had to focus all her energies on spending the next few months with her new husband in one of the world's most exotic, dangerous and inaccessible places.

They would no longer be alone but part of a team. She hadn't yet met Harry and Nick, the cameramen, but Ralph had assured her they'd all get on. He'd worked with both of them before on previous documentaries.

'They're both as passionate about the environment as I am and I know they'll do all they possibly can to make sure the film shows the jungle in its current desperate state.'

When the idea of making the documentary had first surfaced, Ralph had talked to her about how the world's most important ecosystem was being destroyed. How he wanted to do something to help stop the environmental contamination.

'If the world doesn't do something about deforestation and forest degradation, sixty-five per cent of the forest is in danger of disappearing in the next fifty years. And that's before we talk about the loss of the indigenous population and their traditional way of life and the species that will die out as their habitat is destroyed.'

Vanessa knew Ralph was determined his documentary was going to record the lives of the 'real' native Amazonians they struggled to survive in a changing forest and it was one of the reasons he'd refused a sponsorship offer from a large multinational company.

'Staying independent, I can show the truth,' he'd said to Vanessa when he was outlining his plans. 'Nobody can tell me what to film or say. I can talk to whoever I want in an effort to uncover the real truth. The budget is going to be tight, but it's the only way.'

Deciding she had time for one last cool shower before Ralph returned and they left for the airport, Vanessa quickly undressed and stepped under the lukewarm water. Wrapping herself in the hotel's large bath towel afterwards, she crossed to the window and glanced out at the bustling street scene below. A burst of apprehensive excitement kicked into her thoughts. Tomorrow this room would be a memory, and the chaotic scenes outside would have been replaced by forest and vegetation inhabited by strange-sounding animals.

Their first few days in the Amazon jungle were going to be spent in the comfort of an 'eco-tourist' camp before they and the crew moved off to explore and stay in a more remote area, with the help of a native guide. Harry and Nick had flown up earlier with all their equipment and would have organised the next stage of the journey by the time she and Ralph arrived.

Vanessa turned to smile at Ralph as he closed the door behind him.

'Everything packed? Good,' Ralph said as she nodded. 'Ten minutes and we're off. Think I'll have a quick shower too. Might be sometime before we get the luxury of unlimited water again.'

Once they were both dressed, they picked up the backpacks Ralph had insisted were far more practical than suitcases in the jungle, and went to find their taxi for the trip out to the airport.

The office of the company that operated the small Cessna plane Ralph had chartered to fly them up to an outpost on the Amazon River, was situated at the edge of the airfield. Only internal flights operated from this run-down airstrip and, walking towards the shabby hut where they had to check-in, Vanessa found herself worrying about the safety of the plane she was about to board.

'They do have regular maintenance and safety checks, don't they?' she asked Ralph.

'Of course. Don't worry. José and Carlos are very proud of their planes. Carlos told me they are the best in Brazil. Ah, here's José,'

'Senhor Ralph and senhora. We are ready for you. We go and —' The shrill ring of a telephone interrupted him and he glanced towards the desk. 'Bom-dia,' he answered before immediately falling silent. When, after several moments he replaced the receiver, his eyes were bright with tears as he turned to face Ralph and Vanessa. 'That was another pilot telling me that a mutual friend has been shot down near Manaus.' José swore angrily. 'The authorities apparently mistake it for a drug-running plane. The fools! This time it is a big mistake – an American missionary and her family were on board. Now we shall have an investigation.'

Vanessa gazed at him, horror-struck. Manaus was a place on Ralph's itinerary. They were due to arrive near there in a few weeks. She moved closer to Ralph, who placed a comforting arm around her shoulders.

'Do they often shoot planes out of the sky?' she asked.

José nodded vehemently. 'It happens,' he said shortly.

Vanessa shivered. Of course, she'd known they were going into a drug-smuggling area, but she didn't do drugs, nobody she knew did drugs and she hadn't envisaged the drug trade would impinge on her life.

Images of the twins came into her mind. What if she and Ralph were... No! She couldn't, wouldn't, follow that thought. Ralph had warned her about the dangers of this trip, from mosquitoes to alligators, but the shooting down of planes had never been mentioned.

Ralph glanced at José. 'I need to have a private word with my wife. Give us a couple of minutes, will you, please?'

José nodded. 'I'll wait by the plane. We need to take off in the next quarter of an hour, so don't take too long.'

As José strolled off to prepare the plane and do the last-minute checks, Ralph took Vanessa gently in his arms.

'Are you sure you want to go through with this? I know you're thinking about the consequences for the twins if we'd been on that plane. After this flight into the jungle, I promise our exploring will be done on foot, or by water. So, after today, the next plane you get on will be the one taking us home.' He gently kissed her on the forehead. 'On the other hand, if you'd rather I continued on my own and you want to return home now, I'll understand.'

Standing in the circle of Ralph's arms, Vanessa took several deep breaths. Did he really understand how she was feeling? How torn she felt right now? Should she tell Ralph she couldn't go with him after all and instead of flying deep into the jungle with José, catch the next available flight back to England and her children. The decision was hers alone to make.

7

'Do you know what time we can expect Mathieu back from Switzerland?' Jean-Claude asked. 'If at all?'

'No,' Nanette said. 'I think he was hoping to be back before the twins went to bed tonight.'

It was Sunday morning and Jean-Claude had invited Nanette and the twins for a swim and to have lunch. Nanette and Jean-Claude were sitting on the terrace of his villa, set in the hills at the back of Monte Carlo, with a wonderful view out over the Mediterranean. Down below the terrace, the blue water of the swimming pool shimmered in the heat of the sun and the twins were happily playing with the water toys they'd found in the pool house.

'Does he say anything to you about his recent trouble?' Jean-Claude asked.

Nanette shook her head. 'Seems to have blown over. He was worried that the authorities wouldn't let him leave but...' She shrugged. 'That doesn't seem to have happened.'

'He refuses to talk to me about it at all,' Jean-Claude said, shaking his head. 'All he say is for me not to worry. Everything is under control and is being sorted out. I just wish I knew what was going on. Friends tell me he's mixing with some bad company.'

Nanette was silent, not knowing what to say. The last time Mathieu had been home, he'd been in a very upbeat mood, saying that life and business was good, but, like Jean-Claude, she was concerned about who he was doing business with. What sort of business was he dealing in anyway? She still worried too about the connection between him, Zac and this man, Boris.

'I'm a go-between,' Mathieu had said, when she'd casually asked him about his business before he left on this latest trip. 'A broker, if you like. I find what people need, who's got it and put them together. I keep most of the info in my head, so very little paperwork.'

Which is conveniently untraceable, Nanette couldn't help thinking.

Looking at Jean-Claude, Nanette asked, 'Do you know a man called Boris?'

'Only by reputation. I've never met him,' Jean-Claude said. 'Why?'

Nanette hesitated before answering. 'I think he was the business acquaintance who paid Mathieu's bail. He has some sort of connection with Zac, too.'

Before Jean-Claude could respond, his housekeeper appeared to say that lunch would be ready in fifteen minutes.

'Thank you, Anneka. We need to round up the twins,' Jean-Claude said.

They both stood up and, leaving the terrace, began making their way downstairs through the villa to the garden and the pool. As they passed the open door of Jean-Claude's office, Nanette was amazed to see piles of papers and folders littering the desk and spilling on to the floor. Nanette knew he ran a hugely successful wine export business, but Jean-Claude clearly didn't follow his son's business philosophy of keeping paperwork to a minimum.

Jean-Claude saw her looking and said, 'My PA left a few weeks ago and I haven't had a chance to find a replacement.' He hesitated. 'You wouldn't have time to help me sort out my bureau, would you? Mathieu, he say in the past that Zac was lucky to have you as his PA. You are très efficient.'

'Of course, I'll help,' Nanette said, ignoring the mention of Zac. 'I'd like to. Florence takes care of everything at the apartment and politely refuses all my offers of help. I'll come up tomorrow after I've taken the twins to school and make a start.' Work always helped to take her mind off things and now the twins were at school for most of the day, finding something to occupy herself with had proved difficult. There was a limit to how many coffees she could drink sitting at a pavement table at the Café de Paris.

'There is another favour I ask,' Jean-Claude said. 'I have to go to a business cocktail party at the Hôtel de Paris in the week and I need a partner. Perhaps I can persuade you to accompany me? It's just a couple of hours. We could go for dinner somewhere afterwards if you like.'

Nanette hesitated, not sure she wanted to get involved in the Monte Carlo social scene again. She hadn't particularly enjoyed it in the days she'd accompanied Zac to various parties organised by friends and the sponsors of F1. She'd never felt she had much in common with the high-maintenance women hanging off the arms of the wealthy men who were invariably there.

Jean-Claude was looking at her anxiously, waiting for her answer. It was only a cocktail party after all, not the Red Cross Ball, one of the major social events of the season's calendar. With still over a month to go to the Monaco GP, it was extremely unlikely that there would be anybody from the motor-racing world at the party.

She smiled at Jean-Claude. 'I'd love to come with you.'

'Très bien. Now we have lunch.'

Lunch, cooked and placed on the table by Anneka, was a delicious mixture of spicy fried chicken, ratatouille, a green salad and a bowl of crispy frites especially for the twins, although neither Jean-Claude or Nanette could resist helping themselves to some. Dessert was individual pots of raspberry mousse served with meringues.

'That was a delicious meal, thank you,' Nanette said. 'I'd forgotten how seriously home-made food is taken down here.' She'd also forgotten it was the first European Grand Prix of the season that afternoon until Pierre mentioned it as they were eating dessert.

'Papa Jean-Claude, may I watch the San Marino Grand Prix, please? Zac is on pole position.'

At the mention of Zac, Nanette's heart lurched and she inwardly chided herself. He was miles away in Italy and besides he didn't mean anything to her these days.

Olivia gave an exaggerated groan.

'Sure you can, and I'll keep you company for a while,' Jean-Claude said. 'If you want to watch the introduction and driver interviews, hurry up and finish your mousse. The programme, it starts in five minutes,' he added, looking at his watch.

'Can I go in the pool again, please?' Olivia said. 'I don't want to watch the stupid race.'

'You can't go swimming straight after lunch. You'll have to wait for a bit,' Nanette said.

'That's OK. I'll read *The Lion, The Witch and The Wardrobe* until then.'

'How about you, Nanette? Are you going to watch the race with us?' Jean-Claude asked.

Nanette shook her head. It was years since she'd watched a Grand Prix, her interest in Formula 1 having hit an all-time low when Zac had abandoned her. Silly really, when it was her love of F1 and her PA job that had brought them together in the first place.

'No thanks. I'll go for a wander around the garden if that's all right,' she said. 'Then maybe I'll join Olivia in the pool.'

Strolling around the garden, Nanette found herself thinking about the race Zac had always called his home Grand Prix. Although there were two more races before the Formula 1 circus arrived in town for the most glamorous race on the calendar, Monaco streets were already in the process of being barricaded into a race circuit. During the next few weeks, the streets would be transformed with steel safety barriers and huge tiers of seating would appear around the racetrack.

Nanette knew that day-to-day living would become increasingly difficult as everything became geared to the smooth running of the biggest money-spinning event of the year. She also knew that the chances of her avoiding people from her past were slim when she went out and about during the week leading up to and including Grand Prix weekend. Returning to the terrace, she sank down onto one of the wicker chairs and tried to banish her negative thoughts about being in town for the Grand Prix.

Moments later Jean-Claude appeared on the terrace with cups of coffee for them both. 'Thanks. How's the race going?'

'Usual procession,' Jean-Claude said. 'Need a few pit stops to start changing the order of cars and liven things up a bit.' He glanced at her. 'Nanette, I know it's none of my business, but are you going to be okay being in town for the Grand Prix next month? You know, better than most people I suspect, how invasive the whole Formula 1 thing is. It takes the Principality over completely. Escaping certain people will be difficult.'

Nanette nodded, knowing that what he was saying was true. Hordes of people descended on the place, not just the drivers and their teams, but also the TV crews, the hospitality caravans, the photographers, journalists and, of course, tens of thousands of fans. She gave Jean-Claude a grateful smile, realising that he was looking out for her. He really was a lovely man. Before she could say anything, Jean-Claude continued.

'Vanessa tells me you have the nightmares. You also still have no memory of how the accident happen. Perhaps you should not be in town for the Grand Prix. If you want to stay up here, or even go back to the UK for a few days, I can take care of the twins if Mathieu happens to be away.' Jean-Claude regarded Nanette anxiously as she took a sip of her coffee

'Thank you,' Nanette said, 'but I think I have to stay.' She was silent for a few seconds before adding quietly. 'It's the third anniversary of my accident the week after the Grand Prix. I still have no clear recollection of what exactly happened that evening. Perhaps coming back to the scene of the crime will jerk my memory into action. Like the police doing reconstruction scenes in the hope of finding new witnesses.' She hoped her words sounded optimistic and didn't betray the fear she felt inwardly at the prospect.

'Oh, I don't know, Nanette,' Jean-Claude said. 'It could do more harm than good to put yourself through something like that. All I can say is, if you ever need a... I think the English say a shoulder to cry on? Then I'm here.'

'Thank you,' she said gratefully. He really was one of the kindest men and she knew instinctively that if she was ever in trouble, he would be the first to come to her aid.

'Olivia and I may well take you up on the offer of spending the actual race day up here.'

8

Vanessa trembled as she stood in the circle of Ralph's arms, longing to whisper, '*Yes, I do want to go home right now – with you. I don't want anything to happen to either of us. I want to stay safe for the twins.*' As Ralph's calm voice assured her that it was extremely unlikely another plane would be shot out of the sky in the near future because 'lessons will have been learnt,' she prayed that he was right.

Back in the UK nothing had daunted her enthusiasm at the thought of joining the expedition, not the poisonous bites from insects or snakes, twisted or broken bones from a fall due to the uneven jungle floor, the heat, torrential rain, or fever, Ralph had mentioned. But the reality was very different and they weren't even in the jungle proper yet. She knew how important this expedition and her presence on it was to Ralph though – could she really let him down at the first hint of danger? No.

She took a deep breath and steeled herself to continue as planned on their adventure. Clutching his hand tightly, she climbed into the small plane.

To her surprise, once they were airborne, she relaxed and

began to enjoy the long flight. José flew them over volcanoes, rivers and acres and acres of jungle. Ralph, quickly realising he was extremely knowledgeable about his country, spent most of the journey quizzing him about life in the jungle.

From her vantage point in the small plane high above, the green jungle canopy below looked to Vanessa like nothing more than giant knobbly heads of broccoli that had been allowed to grow and grow.

Eventually, José landed on a dirt runway that appeared to be in the middle of a native village. As the door of the plane opened and she stepped out, the heat and the humidity enveloped Vanessa completely and a sudden wave of nausea threatened to overcome her. Horrified and embarrassed, Vanessa knew if she didn't find some shade quickly, she was in danger of being publicly sick.

Seeing her discomfort, José immediately summoned one of the native women who had clustered around to take her to the shelter of a small hut and give her a cool drink. Ten minutes later, after watching José take off safely for his return journey, Ralph joined Vanessa in the hut.

'How are you feeling now?' he asked anxiously.

Vanessa nodded. 'I think I'm fine now. It was just the heat.'

'Ready for the next part?' Ralph asked. 'The boat is waiting.'

Taking her hand, he helped her down a short flight of rickety wooden steps to a small jetty, where a large motorised wooden canoe was moored.

Once on board, a canopy almost the length of the boat shielded the passengers from the intense heat and, as the canoe began to chug through the water, Vanessa appreciated the light breeze that fanned her face. As they made their way upriver, the noise of the boat's engine mingled with the squawking of a large flock of parakeets. With the rainy season well underway, the river was high and much of the surrounding lowland was flooded.

'Look,' Ralph said, laughing, as he pointed to a log floating downstream. It took Vanessa a couple of seconds before she too, saw the family of turtles hitching a lift on the water-sodden trunk. Quickly, she held up her new satellite phone and took a picture for the twins, wondering as she did so whether the charge on her phone would last until the solar charger was set up in the next camp.

Gazing out across the wide expanse of water, Vanessa tried to see the way ahead, but the river appeared to snake its way forever through lush jungle, giving no hint of what lay beyond.

The journey took over two hours and by the time they reached the camp where they were due to spend a couple of days acclimatising themselves to their surroundings, Vanessa's clothes were damp and sticking uncomfortably to her body. The canoe was tied up alongside a small quay and suddenly native Amazonians were all around, helping them to climb out of the boat and then to negotiate a bridged wooden walkway that led to the village.

Built by the villagers using traditional materials and techniques, there were several thatched wooden structures of various sizes, all on stilts, giving the appearance of an authentic and indigenous rainforest village. It was only when she saw the western touches that had been added in the form of private bathrooms with sun-heated showers to the guest cabins that Vanessa realised the place was purpose-built for tourists. So civilised.

Exhausted, Vanessa climbed into the hut allocated to her and Ralph, determined to at least shower and change her clothes before joining the others for a meal.

Served in the communal dining-room, they met the other

guests, who were amazed to learn of Ralph's plans to take his new wife on a trek through the unchartered, inhospitable jungle.

As they tucked into a hearty local soup, followed by fish baked in vine leaves, Vanessa heard one earnest man tell Ralph quietly, 'Remember, all the money in the world won't get you and your wife out of the jungle in a hurry.'

'Well, I don't have all the money in the world, so I'd better hope I don't need to get out in a hurry,' Ralph answered.

Making their way back to their hut at the end of the evening, Vanessa asked Ralph what the man was warning him about.

'Usual stuff about drug barons and gold smugglers.' Ralph shrugged. 'He didn't seem to grasp the fact that my interest is in what remains of the ecological system, not the people who have ruined it. I have no intention of crossing swords with the local bandits.'

That first night in the eco-tourism camp, Vanessa struggled to sleep under the mosquito net in the hammock slung between two beams of the traditional native hut, reliving the last few hours over and over in her mind, And worrying about what horrors the next days and weeks would throw her way.

She smothered a sigh, what had she been thinking, wanting to join Ralph on this expedition into the jungle. At home, excursions into the tame Somerset countryside had always been taken on a daily basis, returning home every evening or to a hotel guest house. She'd never spent a night under canvas, let alone under a roof made of vegetation from the jungle.

She shifted in her hammock, trying to shut out the jungle's night-time noises of howler monkeys and raucous insects. What other animals were out there, unheard, going about their nocturnal lives close to the encampment?

She shivered apprehensively. While they were getting ready for this first night in their hammocks, Ralph had told her about his decision to bring their departure from this camp forward by a day. In twenty-four hours, she wouldn't even have the comfort of the hut in an eco-camp between her and the jungle inhabitants.

'Harry and Nick have everything organised, so no point in hanging around in this pseudo environment,' he'd said disparagingly, waving his hand around the campsite. 'I know it is helping to remedy years of destruction to the jungle, but I want to get to where the real jungle is. Join some natives living in the traditional way.'

So tomorrow they would leave the comforts of the eco-camp behind them and then, 'Our adventure really will begin,' Ralph had said excitedly, as they'd kissed each other goodnight.

Vanessa glanced across at Ralph gently snoring in his hammock. With no real idea of what the next few months might bring, she simply had to trust the man she loved enough to marry and have faith it would be an adventure she'd never forget – for all the right reasons.

9

Nanette switched off the radio alarm on her bedside table and lay in bed for a few moments, thinking and planning the day ahead. Once she'd walked the twins to school, she was going shopping for a dress to wear to the evening's cocktail party with Jean-Claude. All her posh frocks were hanging in the wardrobe in her room at Blackberry Farm. She hadn't bothered to pack any, not anticipating joining the social scene while she was here. Early that afternoon, she had an appointment at the hairdressers, so fingers crossed she'd quickly find a dress she loved, leaving her plenty of time to get back for that.

Knowing how immaculate the women who attended these parties always looked, Nanette wanted to make an effort, not just for herself, but also for Jean-Claude's sake. She didn't want to let him down with his business acquaintances. Slipping her feet into her slippers, she stood up, stretching her arms above her head as she did so, only to freeze in mid-action as she glanced out of the window.

Several yachts were about to enter the harbour and one of them looked uncomfortably familiar. Pulling her dressing gown tight, Nanette stepped out on to her balcony and watched as the boats motored in.

The crew of *Pole Position* worked quickly and efficiently and it was only a matter of minutes before the yacht was secured in her berth – directly opposite the block of apartments. Once the boat was tied up and the gangway lowered to the quay, Nanette held her breath, waiting to see if Zac would appear.

A lone crew member ran down the gangway and disappeared along the embankment in the direction of the supermarket, reappearing minutes later with several baguettes and a bag bulging with what Nanette guessed were croissants for the crew's breakfast.

She stood watching for a few moments before turning away and heading for the shower. If she didn't get a move on, the twins would be late walking to school and she'd miss the train connection to take her to Cap 3000 at Saint-Laurent-du-Var – the largest shopping centre in the area. Not only would she get more choice there, but a new dress wouldn't hurt her credit card like it would if she shopped in one of the trendy Monaco boutiques.

An hour later, she was sitting on the train as it sped westwards along the coast on the half-hour journey, debating with herself about the kind of dress she needed to buy. Too glitzy and it would only end up hanging in her wardrobe for months before she wore it again as cocktail parties really weren't on her radar these days. On the other hand, she didn't want to play too safe by opting for a boring little black dress.

She knew the moment she slipped on the royal blue dress with its three-quarter-length sleeves, round neckline and a fitted midi skirt with a fluted ruffle hem at the front that it was the one. As she looked at her reflection in the changing-room mirror, for the first time in months, years, she felt a small burst of confidence returning to both her abused body and mind. The dress was glamorous in an understated way and suited her to perfection.

At the thought of the evening ahead of her with Jean-Claude, a frisson of excitement sneaked into Nanette's mind and she realised she was looking forward to it. And to dinner afterwards, just the two of them.

But the excitement was instantly doused by worry. The cocktail party was an important business get-together for Jean-Claude and she prayed she wouldn't let him down. It was so long since she'd had to make small talk with strangers that she wasn't sure she remembered how.

* * *

Once back in Monaco, Nanette hung the dress in the wardrobe and got on with the rest of her day before nervously leaving the apartment for her afternoon hairdresser's appointment in nearby Rue Princess Caroline. She'd deliberately not booked a rendezvous in the salon near the Casino, where years ago she'd been a regular client, in case anyone remembered her. Thankfully, a quick glance around as she entered reassured her that she didn't recognise any of the stylists or customers and soon her head was being gently massaged as her hair was washed by an un-named efficient teenager.

Minutes later, as the stylist – Adam, according to the badge pinned to his pristine designer-label shirt – was carefully blow-drying her hair, Nanette stiffened. The mirror she was sat in front of not only reflected her head and shoulders and Adam working away but also the coming and goings of the busy salon behind her. Quickly, Nanette looked down at her hands in her lap and half closed her eyes, hoping to avoid catching the gaze of the woman who had just entered, Frances Scott.

The one and only time Nanette had met Frances had been the night of the accident. As the current girlfriend of one of Zac's fellow racing drivers, she'd been his 'plus-one' for Nanette's birthday dinner at the Mougins restaurant. Nanette, who normally didn't judge anyone on their appearance, had been stunned by the woman's over-the-top appearance and, later, her behaviour. She remembered whispering to Zac at some stage of the evening, 'Is she on something?' Zac had shrugged and grinned at her.

Peering at the reflection in the mirror as Frances sashayed across the salon, following one of the receptionists towards a washing unit, Nanette could see that the woman, unlike herself, hadn't changed. She still dressed in the skimpy clothes that drew attention to her surgically enhanced figure. Nanette knew that while she had no difficulty in recognising Frances after three years, Frances was unlikely to recognise her. The long hair, high-lighted with streaks of blonde on the night of the party, was no more. Brutally cut short in the aftermath of the accident, Nanette had kept it short ever since. Memories of that birthday party had been soured by the way the evening had ended. Long hair had had no place in Nanette's new life.

She released the breath she hadn't realised she'd been holding as she saw Frances submit to the ministrations of the same teenager who had washed her own hair.

Nanette knew it would be impossible for her to make even the smallest of small talk about the evening when her life had changed forever with a woman she barely knew if she was recognised. Adam was tweaking her hair now with the final touches after her blow-dry. With luck, she'd have paid and be long gone before Frances Scott was able to cast her eyes around the salon in search of any new or old acquaintances.

* * *

Early evening and a thoughtful Nanette added a generous amount of rose essence oil to the bath as the water gushed out of the taps. With his yacht back in the harbour, it could only be a matter of time now before Zac appeared in Monaco. Fleetingly, she wondered what his reaction to her being in town would be. She didn't for one moment imagine it would be unadulterated delight, which, thinking about it, would suit her fine. Letting Zac back into even the fringes of her life whilst she was here in Monaco was not in the plan. Ignoring each other's presence would be ideal.

Stepping into the tub and sinking into the hot, scented water, Nanette tried to drown out all thoughts of the past and Zac from her mind. Just because his yacht was here didn't mean he was likely to be out and about this evening.

'Mmm, you smell nice, Netty,' Olivia said, when Nanette appeared in the sitting room an hour later, where Jean-Claude was waiting. 'Your dress is cool.'

'Thank you. I hope it's the sort of thing people wear to cocktail parties. It's years since I've been to one, so I'm a bit out of touch these days,' she said, glancing anxiously at Jean-Claude for reassurance. 'You're looking extremely smart yourself.' Nanette smiled. She'd forgotten how de rigueur the wearing of a bow tie was in Monaco. In his charcoal grey suit, crisp white shirt and black leather dress shoes, he looked the picture of the successful businessman she knew he was.

'You look lovely,' Jean-Claude said. 'The taxi is waiting, so shall we go? Is Mathieu home for the twins?'

Nanette shook her head. 'No. He rang earlier to say it will be late tonight before he gets back. Florence is here. I'll just tell her we're leaving.'

Early-evening traffic was heavy and the taxi crawled up the hill towards Place du Casino.

'You're very quiet,' Jean-Claude said, glancing at her. 'Are you OK?'

'I'm fine. Just a bit nervous. I haven't done much socialising recently.' She didn't like to admit to Jean-Claude that this event tonight would be the first time in years she'd ventured into any sort of social gathering not made up of family and known, personal, friends.

'It's not a particularly big gathering tonight,' Jean-Claude said. 'And if you're worrying about *Pole Position* being back on its mooring, I happen to know Zac Ewart isn't in town this evening,' he added quietly.

Nanette looked at him, surprised.

'When I saw the yacht this morning, I knew you'd be worried, so I made enquiries. Zac is busy testing in Jerez with his team for the next two days.'

'Oh, JC, thank you for that,' Nanette said gratefully, feeling the tension drain from her body. 'Now I can relax and help you with whatever you want me to do. Do you hope to promote your business tonight? Or is it a case of other businesses wanting you to use them? What's the matter?' she asked anxiously, as Jean-Claude stared at her, a strange look on his face.

'My late wife was the only person who ever called me JC,' Jean-Claude said slowly.

'I'm sorry. I didn't mean to upset you. It slipped out, without me even thinking about it,' Nanette said, embarrassed at her first faux pas of the evening. She hadn't even realised that she'd called him JC rather than Jean-Claude. 'I'll stick to your full name in future.'

'No. It's fine. It was just the shock of hearing you say it. Please, I'd like you to call me JC, only perhaps not in front of my business associates tonight.' He smiled at her. A smile Nanette returned, happy in the knowledge she hadn't upset him, or brought back sad memories.

As the taxi drew up in front of the Hotel de Paris, the uniformed doorman opened the door and ushered them up the steps into the opulent foyer with its chandeliers, deep carpets, marble stairs and enough fresh flowers to stock a florist's. Once inside, where the head maître d' greeted Jean-Claude personally, they made their way to the Salon Berlioz, already buzzing with people.

Accepting glasses of champagne from an attentive waitress, Jean-Claude said, 'Right. Better start mixing. Let's start by talking to Robert, one of the vineyard owners I buy from. Normally I have to drive down to his chateau in the Var to meet him.'

For the next hour, Jean-Claude circulated, introducing Nanette to so many people she forgot their names instantly. There was only one person with whom she had any sort of rapport and that was Evie, personal assistant to Luc, a formidable bear-like man who, Evie assured her, despite appearances, 'is a real sweetie'.

'Been in Monte long?' Evie asked, taking a smoked-salmon blini from a passing waiter and gesturing to Nanette to do the same.

'Just a few weeks,' Nanette said non-committedly. 'You?'

'Six months. I love it. It's all so glamorous. I can't wait for the Grand Prix.'

Nanette smiled at her infectious enthusiasm, recognising and remembering similar feelings when she'd first arrived.

'Are you Jean-Claude's new assistant?'

'Sort of. Officially I'm his grandchildren's nanny.'

'Really? Gosh, he doesn't look old enough to have grandkids,' Evie said, looking across at Jean-Claude who was chatting and laughing with Luc. 'You know that old black and white photo of Princess Grace and that popular actor she made a film with – Cary Grant? That's who he reminds me of.'

Nanette followed her gaze and nodded in agreement. 'Definite resemblance. Fancy meeting up for a coffee sometime?' she said impulsively. 'I'm missing my sister and girlfriend from back home and could do with some girly chat.'

'Love to,' Evie said. 'Take my card and give me a ring next week. Better go, I think Luc wants me. Ciao.'

'Ciao,' Nanette answered, smiling.

She was still smiling when Jean-Claude joined her a couple of minutes later.

'Shall we go? I booked a table for nine o'clock at my favourite fish restaurant on Boulevard Grande-Bretagne.' He stopped suddenly and looked at her anxiously. 'You do like fish, don't you? I didn't think to ask!'

'Yes, JC, I do,' Nanette laughingly reassured him.

A crowd of paparazzi had gathered on the pavement outside the Casino and flashbulbs started to pop as they walked past. Nanette, glancing briefly across to see if she recognised the blonde celebrity posing in the Casino entrance, failed to notice a lone photographer moving backwards.

Jean-Claude's warning shout to the man, 'Hey, mind where you're going,' and his attempt to pull her out of the way were both too late. The photographer collided with her heavily and they both fell over the small hedge that separated the pavement from the parkland grass in the middle of the Place du Casino.

Dazed, Nanette sat on the ground, taking deep breaths for several moments and trying in vain to ignore the cameras that were now aimed in her direction.

'Are you all right?' asked a concerned Jean-Claude. 'Do you think you've broken anything?'

Nanette shook her head. 'I'll be fine. I'm just winded. I could do with a hand to get up though.'

Gently, Jean-Claude helped her to her feet.

'Mademoiselle, I am so sorry,' the photographer said.

'It's OK,' Nanette replied. 'I wasn't looking where I was going either.' She looked at Jean-Claude. 'Could we just get to the restaurant please? I'd like some water.'

'Hey!' the photographer said suddenly. 'I recognise you. Aren't you the woman who nearly killed Zac Ewart?'

10

The words 'Aren't you the woman who nearly killed Zac Ewart?' were destined to ring in Nanette's head for days after the accident. She'd known it was inevitable that someone from the past would recognise her, but somehow she'd expected it to happen during Grand Prix week when people she'd worked with years ago were sure to be in town. Was she destined to always be remembered by complete strangers for an event she wished had never happened?

As she'd stared at the photographer, shocked into silence by his words, Jean-Claude had stopped a passing taxi, helped her into it and taken her back to his villa. He had comforted her, telling her that it was an isolated incident.

'You might have a certain notoriety for a few days now the press have realised you're back. Especially,' he hesitated before continuing, 'when Zac Ewart arrives. I promise you it will pass.'

He'd insisted she sat on the terrace and sipped the brandy he poured her while he phoned the restaurant and cancelled the table reservation. Once that was done, he cooked them a simple supper of pasta, served with a slice of walnut and onion tart and a green salad. They ate the meal sitting out on the terrace watc the lights of Monaco twinkle below them as dusk fell. Nanette brushed aside Jean-Claude's apologies for it not being the dinner he'd planned to treat her to and promised they'd go another evening.

'Honestly, JC, I'm perfectly happy with the meal. The setting too is perfect.' She gestured out over the terrace to the view. 'And it's so peaceful – unlike the apartment.' Nanette took a sip of the water that Jean-Claude had poured her. 'Were you happy with tonight's get-together from a business point of view?' She didn't like to voice the words she really wanted to say, *I hope I didn't let you down,* in case it made her sound needy, when really she just hoped she'd played her part of 'plus-one' for the evening to his satisfaction.

Jean-Claude smiled. 'Yes. As networking events go, it was good.' He glanced at her. 'Thank you for coming with me, and I hope it wasn't too much of an ordeal?'

Nanette shook her head. 'No, I enjoyed it. I met someone new too – Evie.'

'That's good. Maybe we can do it again – only if you'd like to of course.' Jean-Claude hesitated before adding, 'These things are so much more enjoyable with a friend at my side,'

'I'd love to come with you, JC,' Nanette said. 'Next time, I may know a little more about your business as I'm intending to come up and do some tidying up of your office this week.'

'Thank you. Let me know which day and I'll ask Anneka to make lunch for two.'

Once they'd finished their impromptu supper, the two of them sat companionably chatting as darkness fell until Jean-Claude stood up.

'I think it's time I took you home,' he said.

Nanette glanced at her watch. 'I hadn't realised it was so late. I'm sorry about my silly accident. Dinner at the restaurant would have been good, I'm sure, but this has been a lovely end to the evening. Thank you.' She didn't dare put into words just how much she'd enjoyed Jean-Claude's company for the last couple of hours in case he thought she was gushing. But it was a long time since she'd felt so comfortable and at ease with a man.

Jean-Claude gave her a look she found impossible to interpret. 'I'd suggest we walk down, but I think it better if I call a taxi.'

* * *

Mathieu was in when they let themselves in to the apartment. Nanette wouldn't have mentioned her fall, but Jean-Claude quickly told him about the evening's incident before wishing Nanette. 'Goodnight. I hope you are not too bruised in the morning.'

As he left, Nanette went through the sitting room, opened the patio doors and stepped out onto the balcony. Standing there watching the lights and looking over the harbour, she was deep in thought when Mathieu joined her.

'I see *Pole Position* is back,' he said, looking down towards the yachts. There was a pause before he added, 'Zac is planning a big party on board in a couple of weeks, I understand.'

'Of course he is,' Nanette said shortly, remembering when she'd done the organising for the on-board parties. 'Knowing Zac, he won't stop at the one.'

Mathieu looked at her. 'Are you all right?' he asked gently.

Nanette nodded. 'Sorry, I didn't mean to snap. It's just that photographer tonight...' She sighed, shook her head and didn't finish the sentence.

'Don't let it worry you,' Mathieu said. 'A couple more weeks when Fi is in town, the paparazzi will be busy chasing the scoop that will make their fortune.'

'I hope you're right,' Nanette answered. She looked at him hesitantly before asking, 'Are you in touch with Zac?'

Mathieu nodded. 'He's getting some pit-lane passes for me.'

'Does he know I'm here?'

'Yes, I told him you were coming to look after the twins for me.'

'How did he react?'

Mathieu shrugged. 'He didn't say anything, so I can't tell you.'

Mathieu was the first to speak again after a short silence.

'Talking of parties. We've got the Vintage Grand Prix this year the weekend before the main one and I'm giving a lunch on the Sunday. Just friends and a few business contacts.' He glanced at her. 'I hope you'll join us?'

'Thanks. Of course, you're directly above the start line here,' Nanette said, leaning on the balcony, watching the cars moving along the Boulevard Albert 1er below. 'You'll have a great view. People will be begging to come.'

'The sound effects are always pretty awesome too,' Mathieu said. 'Even from the old cars.'

'What about the twins though?' Nanette asked. 'Pierre will be keen, but Olivia will find the whole thing terribly boring.'

Mathieu smiled. 'Maybe when she hears a certain pop star is on the guest list, she'll come round.' He paused. 'Nanette, I meant what I said the other evening about us getting to know each other better – I'm aiming to be home more in the next few weeks, so I hope we can spend some time together. I'm sorry the offer of tickets for the tennis fell through, but I hope you won't hold that against me.'

'Of course not. I've been busy with the twins anyway.' Although, in truth, she had been disappointed when Mathieu hadn't mentioned the tennis tournament again after their night out.

'I've promised the twins I'll take them out next Monday as it's a fête day. I've got some friends who have a place up in the country near Entrevaux who've invited us for the day. Olivia and Pierre love it up there. Will you come, too?'

Before Nanette could reply, his mobile rang and, with an apologetic smile, Mathieu turned from her and answered it.

Nanette closed the balcony doors, mouthed 'goodnight' to a distracted Mathieu and went to her room. As she undressed and hung her dress in the wardrobe, she heard the door of the apartment open and close, followed ten seconds later by the subdued noise of the private lift descending. Nanette finished getting ready for bed, wondering where Mathieu was off to so late in the day.

11

A dishevelled Mathieu appeared the next morning as Nanette was getting the twins ready to leave for school.

'Morning,' he said, helping himself to a cup of coffee and joining the twins as they ate their pain au chocolat at the breakfast bar in the kitchen. 'I've got to go away again this morning for a couple of days,' he said to the twins.

'What about our day out to Entrevaux?' Pierre asked sulkily. 'You promised you'd take us. We're not going to have to cancel again, are we?'

'Definitely not,' Mathieu said. 'I'll be back for that, and the good news is that Netty is coming with us.'

'Mathieu, I've been thinking about that and I need to talk to you about it,' Nanette said.

Mathieu glanced at her. 'Talk later. Right now, there are one or two papers I need to find for my trip and you two had better get a move on or you'll be late for school.' With that, Mathieu disappeared into the sitting room. Seconds later, he could be heard talking on his phone.

Nanette stifled a sigh. 'Come on, you two. Dad's right. Let's go.'

Once she'd walked the twins to school and seen them into the grounds, Nanette took her time returning home. Walking through the small park behind the apartment block, she sat down on a bench overlooking a tiny fountain where the sparrows were enjoying the water and rang Patsy.

'How are you?' she asked when her sister answered.

Patsy gave a deep sigh. 'Promise me you'll stand up for me and give evidence in court when I'm charged with Helen's murder?'

'What's she done now?'

'You know how some women become "Bridezillas" when they're getting married? Well, Helen has turned into the "Grannyzilla" from hell. She's buying every mothering, parenting, healthy-eating magazine she can lay her hands on. Keeps telling me she's worried because I'm old to be having a first baby – practically geriatric according to her. She's joined a Granny forum on Facebook and now knows the name of every designer brand of anything baby-related. She's continually giving me advice – and then contradicts it by adding she can't believe how so much has changed from her day when, of course, it was *so* much harder.' Patsy gave another deeper sigh. 'She wants to be involved in everything. And I mean *everything*!'

'She's excited for you both,' Nanette said. 'You'll be glad she's around in a few months when you're desperate for some uninterrupted sleep and she looks after junior for you.' For all her interfering ways, basically Helen meant well and Nanette hoped that Patsy would eventually come to realise and accept that.

'Well, I've told her she's not being my birthing partner as I've already lined you up for that job.'

'I bet that went down well.'

'She still insisted I name her in my notes in case you're unavoidably delayed, as she put it. Enough. How's life over there in the sun? It's raining here by the way.'

'Life here in the sun is, um, let's say interesting,' Nanette said. 'Mathieu's business seems to be going through a decidedly "dodgy" phase, Zac is in town and knows that I'm here but hasn't made contact, thank goodness. And JC took me to a do at the Hôtel de Paris, which ended in a bit of a disaster.' Nanette quickly told Patsy about the photographer recognising her. 'I've been psyching myself up to bumping into people who knew me years ago during Grand Prix time, but there's still a couple of weeks to go before then. I simply wasn't expecting it that evening.'

'Did you hurt yourself?' Patsy asked anxiously.

'Just my pride really.'

'The next week or two is going to throw up all sorts of memories and people,' Patsy said gently. 'Are you sure you can cope?'

'There's only one way to find out, isn't there?' It was Nanette who gave a deep sigh this time. 'It was my decision to come and I'm determined not to let Vanessa down. If it all gets too much, I can always take JC up on his offer of hiding away in his villa.'

'Maybe that's the answer,' Patsy said thoughtfully.

'In the meantime, Mathieu wants me to spend a day with him, the twins and friends up in the back country. If the friends are who I suspect they are, he's not going to be happy when I refuse to go.'

'Talking of the twins, how are they? Have they heard from their mum?' Patsy asked.

'Vanessa sent them an email and FaceTimed them the day they left Brazil for the jungle. There's been just one satellite phone call since, which the twins were excited about. Vanessa promised she'd try and phone once a week, but it would depend on where exactly they are in the jungle.'

'I've got to go,' Patsy said suddenly. 'She who must be obeyed has arrived. Sorry about my rant earlier. Talk soon,' and Patsy ended the call.

Nanette smiled to herself. Helen might currently be driving Patsy mad, but she only wanted what was the best for her close family.

Slipping her phone into her bag, Nanette made her way back to the apartment, hoping that Mathieu would still be there.

Florence was busy vacuuming as Nanette let herself into the apartment. Because Nanette now had the bedroom Mathieu would normally have used as his office, he'd moved his computer, desk and a two-drawer filing cabinet into a tiny windowless area at the back of the sitting room that housed a small fridge and a drinks cabinet for when he was entertaining friends on the balcony.

She walked straight through the sitting room, and found Mathieu in his office watching the printer, waiting for the last piece of paper to join a freshly printed batch, whilst mumbling into his phone. He jumped visibly at the sound of Nanette's voice as she said, 'Hi' and he hurriedly switched the phone off before turning to face her.

'Please don't sneak up on me like that in future.'

Nanette stepped back from Mathieu. Now was clearly not the best moment to bring the subject up, but she'd say it anyway.

'I'm sorry if I interrupted your phone call, but I wanted to talk to you about this day trip to Entrevaux you're planning for the twins. Is it the de Oliviers' farm you're visiting?'

'Yes.'

'In that case, I'd rather not go with you.'

'Why on earth not?'

Nanette looked at him quizzically. 'Why do you think? They were Zac's friends and we used to visit them regularly when they lived up at Eze. I'm sure they—'

'Would be very pleased to see you again,' Mathieu interrupted.

Nanette shook her head. 'I'd still rather not go.'

Mathieu looked at her before saying stonily, 'You are here to look after the twins. It's not really for you to decide whether you go or not. I could insist you accompany us or return to the UK.'

'I do look after the twins – when they are not at school, I organise their lives,' Nanette said, taking a deep breath. 'I've actually seen more of them than you have in the last few weeks – you're always dashing off somewhere or other for "business". You certainly weren't around for Pierre's after-school football match, or Olivia's music exam,' she added crossly. 'Olivia has already told me how much they are both looking forward to having you to themselves on Monday.' She paused, before adding slowly, 'Mathieu, if you don't think I'm doing enough for the twins, you can always take over the job yourself. I'd be quite happy to go home – I came for Vanessa and the twins' sake, not yours. Personally, I had no intention of ever returning to Monaco.' Nanette looked him straight in the eyes before concluding, 'I'm not sure how Vanessa would react to you sending me home though.' And then she turned and left him standing there.

12

'You sure you won't change your mind and come with us?'
Mathieu asked, before he and the twins left for their day out in
the country. 'It will be quiet here on your own all day.'

The outing hadn't been mentioned since their argument a few
days before and Nanette was relieved that Mathieu had allowed
the subject to drop. This morning, he seemed to have forgotten
his earlier accusations and was happy to be going with the twins
on his own after all.

Nanette shook her head. 'Quite sure, thanks. Besides, I won't
be on my own all day – I'm meeting Jean-Claude later. Enjoy
yourselves.'

She was just closing the door behind them when Mathieu
called out, 'Nanette, there's a package for you in my office. I'm
sorry I forgot to tell you yesterday when it came. It's on my desk.'

Nanette recognised Patsy's handwriting on the large envelope.
Taking a paperknife out of the desk tidy, she carefully slit open
the envelope.

Replacing the paperknife, a crumpled piece of paper beside

the wastepaper basket caught her attention. Picking it up, she saw it was a detailed map of the Amazon, clearly torn out of an atlas.

The twins were hoping to follow Vanessa and Ralph's progress, so there was nothing unusual in Mathieu having a map of the trip – in fact, there was a large-scale one pinned to the wall – but this one had some of the place names circled in red and haphazardly linked with numbers written against them.

Puzzled, Nanette tried to work out what they could possibly represent, before deciding that it was probably a piece of scrap paper that Mathieu had been doodling on and thrown at the wastepaper basket, where he'd obviously intended it to go.

Going to her own room, Nanette carefully pulled out the contents of the envelope. A short note from Patsy was sellotaped around a sealed brown official envelope. Pensively, Nanette placed both in the drawer of her dressing table. Even without opening it, she knew exactly what the official envelope contained. Pushing the drawer closed, she went through to the kitchen to make a cup of coffee.

Because it was a fête day, Florence had the day off and for the first time since she'd arrived, Nanette was completely alone in the apartment. Coffee cup in hand, she wandered around, enjoying the solitude.

Pausing outside Mathieu's closed bedroom door, she realised she'd only ever had glimpses of that particular room – the door was always closed. Curiously, and smothering her guilty feelings, Nanette turned the handle, only to find the door was locked.

Nanette mused, as she sipped her coffee, was Mathieu just keen on privacy, or simply wanted to keep the twins from messing up his room? Or did he have something to hide in there?

Deep in thought, she returned to Mathieu's temporary office. The computer was switched off. The desk, apart from the desk tidy, was empty. Not even a diary. The filing cabinet was locked.

The only discordant thing in the room was the crumpled atlas page in the wastepaper basket. She retrieved it and, smoothing it out, wandered back into the sitting room. Maybe it was only a piece of waste paper, but somehow she had a feeling it was more than that. Perhaps she'd show it to Jean-Claude later and see if he had any ideas.

Standing by the sitting-room window, she glanced out at the harbour and froze as she saw a figure sitting at a table on the stern deck of *Pole Position*. Even from her viewpoint nine floors up, she had no difficulty in recognising Zac – or the man he was now standing up to welcome on board – the Russian, Boris.

Hoping she was shielded from view by the tall lemon tree in its pot on the balcony, Nanette watched as the two men were served coffee by a stewardess, before Boris handed Zac what looked like a large packet.

Ten minutes later, both men stood up, shook hands and Boris took his leave of Zac, making his way slowly along the gangway back to a large black car waiting for him on the harbour road.

On board *Pole Position*, Nanette could see Zac punching a number into his mobile phone before holding it up to his ear, and moving his head so that it was obvious he was looking directly up at the apartment.

Nanette stepped slowly away from the window. Had he seen her after all? Realised she'd been watching him and Boris?

The shrill buzz of the apartment doorbell made her jump and she hurried to open it.

'Bonjour, Nanette. Happy May Day.' Jean-Claude lightly kissed her on both cheeks before handing her a pot of lilies of the valley.

'Thank you, JC,' Nanette said, surprised. She'd forgotten all about the tradition of giving the highly scented flowers on the first of May as a sign of friendship – and love.

'You look a little flustered,' Jean-Claude said, looking at her anxiously. 'Nothing wrong, is there?'

'Zac is in town. I've just been watching him and his friend, Boris, meeting on *Pole Position*,' she explained.

'Is this Boris still there? I would be interested in seeing what he looks like,' Jean-Claude said, walking out quickly on to the balcony.

'No. He left a few minutes ago. Zac is still on board.'

Joining him out on the balcony, Nanette could see Zac now in the cockpit, gesticulating at one of his crew. As they watched, Zac turned and glanced upwards, raising his hand in greeting as he saw Jean-Claude and Nanette standing on the balcony.

Rather than acknowledge him, Nanette turned and went back into the sitting room.

'I thought we'd have lunch at the Automobile Club,' Jean-Claude said, following her. 'Or anywhere you like,' he added quickly, seeing the look on her face.

'It's just that with Zac in town,' Nanette apologised, 'I know it's his favourite place for lunch and I'm not quite ready to meet him socially yet. Could we go somewhere else, please?'

'Why don't we walk up to Saint Nicholas Square?' Jean-Claude said, unfazed at her request. 'It's a bit touristy, but, on the plus side, I doubt that Zac will venture up that way on a fête day.'

Nanette looked at him gratefully. 'I'll just get my bag.'

To Nanette's relief, and by mutual unspoken agreement, they left the apartment block by the quieter exit on to a back street so she didn't have to set foot on the quay with the possibility of bumping into Zac.

The weather for the May Day holiday was perfect – blue sky, a gentle breeze and warm sunshine. Joining the throngs of tourists, they began making their way up towards the Palace.

Saint Nicholas Square was in the labyrinth of busy narrow

streets that clustered around the cathedral in the old town. Choosing an outside table at one of the restaurants, they sat down under a gaily striped umbrella. Snatched conversations in French, English, Italian, Japanese and Chinese floated in the air around them.

An attentive waiter handed them a menu and took their aperitif order. A glass of cool rosé for both of them.

'Avez-vous décidéz... Ah, pardon, Nanette. I forget. I will speak English,' Jean-Claude said. 'Have you decided what you'd like to eat?'

'JC, please speak in French,' Nanette answered. 'Not using it for three years, mine's a bit rusty, but I do still understand. I need to start speaking it again too.' She glanced at the menu. 'I think I'll have the plat du jour, s'il vous plait.'

Sipping her glass of ice-cold rosé, Nanette looked at Jean-Claude.

'Something else I haven't used for three years arrived today,' she said quietly.

Jean-Claude gave her a puzzled look.

Nanette pictured the envelope in the drawer before saying quietly, 'My driving licence has been returned. My driving ban is finished.'

'That is good, isn't it?' Jean-Claude said. 'Now you can truly put the past behind you and start driving again.'

'I'm not sure that I have the confidence to get behind the wheel of a car again.' Nanette fiddled with her wine glass.

'If you are nervous, I come with you for the first few times,' Jean-Claude offered.

'I don't know that it's that simple, JC.' Nanette hesitated. 'What if—'

Jean-Claude stopped her in mid-sentence. 'Non. No what ifs, Nanette. You've been punished for the accident. Now you put it behind you and get on with your life. I forbid you to let it blight the future.'

In spite of herself, Nanette smiled at the stern look on Jean-Claude's face. 'I know you're right, but I don't have a car at the moment anyway, so...' she shrugged. 'I shall avoid the issue for at least a few more weeks. Maybe when I go home.'

After an exasperated 'Tch', Jean-Claude changed the subject. 'I hope Mathieu has invited you to the lunch he's hosting on Vintage Grand Prix weekend?'

'I'm looking forward to it. Will you be there?'

'Yes, and no. I've been persuaded to get my Lotus out of mothballs and give it an outing, so I shall be spending most of the weekend in the pit lane with the mechanics before the race on Sunday. Be interesting to drive in a race again after so long. Especially here in Monaco, my home circuit.'

'I didn't know you'd been a racing driver,' Nanette said, surprised. 'You kept that very quiet.' Although there was a lot she didn't know about Jean-Claude, she realised.

'Only very briefly. It was at the time the sport was changing rapidly into big business with the manufacturers taking over. It simply became too expensive without a sponsor; I found myself priced out of the market.' He shrugged. 'If I'm honest, I lacked the competitive edge that all successful F1 drivers need. But I kept the car, which has been under wraps for a good few years. I've got the next few days or so to finish checking it over mechanically and prepare it. Of course, I don't expect to be placed, but I admit I look forward to driving in a race again.'

'Who have you got supporting you on the day?' Nanette asked. 'You'll need someone in the pits to help.'

'Not a problem. There are always young lads wanting to get involved and I've got a mechanic called David coming over from Le Cannet to help. He used to work the circuit, so he knows the ropes.' He glanced at her. 'Zac, he also offer me the expertise of one of his mechanics if I need it. The Formula 1 circus will be arriving in town by then, with only a week to go to the Grand Prix proper. Looks as though it might be Zac's year,' he added casually. 'I see he's leading the championship and is favourite to win next week in Germany.'

Nanette nodded. Despite herself, she'd been keeping an eye on the results since early in the season when the drivers had arrived back in Europe after the first few races.

'My offer still stands by the way,' Jean-Claude said. 'You're more than welcome to use the villa as a hideaway anytime – not just on race day. After the Spanish race, Zac is certain to be in town in the run-up to the Grand Prix.'

'I know,' Nanette said diffidently, remembering previous years when Zac had used the run-up to the Monaco Grand Prix to do a lot of socialising. She sighed inwardly. The inevitable meeting was getting closer.

'You will have to meet him face to face one day, Nanette. What will you do then?' Jean-Claude asked gently.

Nanette shook her head before looking at him and saying slowly, 'I honestly have no idea, JC.'

'Perhaps it would be better for you to make the arrangement to meet him first,' Jean-Claude said. 'That way it will be easier, I think, for you to cope.'

Nanette bit her lip as she looked at him. Maybe Jean-Claude was right, but the mere thought of having to contact Zac to arrange a meeting made her feel ill.

13

Vanessa stumbled over some exposed roots of an immense tree that towered above her as she followed their machete-wielding guide along the muddy track, taking them deeper and deeper into the forest with its dense undergrowth. After that one night in the eco-camp they'd left the relative comforts it offered behind and set off for the remote village in the jungle that was to be the focal point of Ralph's documentary.

All day, they had hacked their way into the depths of the steamy, lush forest. Now their destination, a native village, was only an hour away. Trudging in single file behind Ralph and the others, Vanessa felt both tired and exhilarated.

The clean, oxygen-filled air, heavy with moisture, had initially somehow bestowed a feeling of euphoria and excitement on her, but now her clothes were beginning to smell and feel damp from all the humidity. Her skin was itching where unknown insects had feasted on her. Her head was sweaty from the wide-brimmed hat she was wearing to deflect the sun and to stop the legions of creepy-crawlies above her in the rainforest's canopy from falling into her hair. She longed for the day to end.

Their trek had taken them between columns of trees so tall their tops disappeared from view, with long liana vines hanging down and wrapping themselves around the trunks. Vast spider-webs had spanned the green vegetation, where some leaves were as huge as the parasol Vanessa dreamily imagined sitting under and relaxing.

At ground level, everything appeared to be in a state of flux. Strange smells wafted up from where plants were growing, decaying, dying, surrounded by bugs, snakes and other things that Vanessa just knew were waiting to take a bite out of her.

As the day wore on, the sounds of the jungle had become familiar. Sloths shaking the treetops looking for a resting spot, the echoing cries of the howler monkeys as they swung through the trees and the ever-present noise of the cicadas mingling with birdsong became background noises to the group as they hacked their way through the rainforest.

The village clearing appeared unexpectedly. One minute, the guide was leading them along a muddy track beneath the jungle canopy, the next, they came to an abrupt standstill as their way was barred by a group of native Amazonians holding their hunting spears at arm's-length.

For one heart-stopping moment, Vanessa thought they were about to be attacked, but it was simply the welcoming party come to escort them into the village.

The primitive palm-thatched huts on their stilts stood around the edge of the clearing, where the village animals, including a fat pig and several roosters, were roaming freely, scouring the ground for scraps.

Walking to the centre of the encampment with curious villagers eyeing them from a distance, Vanessa noticed a small child standing close to her mother watching the strangers with wide brown eyes.

Vanessa smiled at her and the little girl rewarded her with a
shy smile in return as she turned to run after a piglet, before
settling down in the dust to stroke and play with it. A memory
came to Vanessa of Olivia at a similar age on a visit to a small
animals farm, where she'd fallen in love with a baby goat and
begged and begged for one. Looking at the child now in front of
her, naked and beautifully brown, with her bare feet planted
firmly on the earth, the phrase 'being at one with nature' came
into Vanessa's mind. This little girl was definitely in harmony
with the natural world that she lived in.

Briefly, Vanessa envied her the simplicity of her childhood –
and her life to come. A sudden longing to throw her arms around
Pierre and Olivia and hold them tight engulfed her and she had
to take several deep breaths to steady herself. Hugging her children close again wouldn't happen for nearly five months. Hopefully, once they were settled in this village, the solar charger for
the satellite phone would work and she'd be able to phone and at
least hear their voices.

The chief shaman came forward to welcome them and
showed them to the hut reserved for visitors. They'd barely had
time to sling their hammocks between the beams and change
their damp clothes before a young woman appeared, inviting
them to come and eat the special meal the villagers had prepared
in their honour.

There were bowls of yucca soup, rice, fish, fruit and, to Vanessa's horror, large white live grubs and what was clearly organ
meat from various animals, all laid out before them. She looked
at Ralph in dismay.

'I don't want to upset anyone, but I can't eat those things,' she
whispered, pointing to the wriggling white grubs and the meat.

'Stick to the rice and fish,' Ralph advised quietly. 'Have some
fruit.'

As Vanessa began to peel a banana, a small monkey, who had been wandering around scratching the earth, suddenly ran up, snatching the banana from her, before jumping on to her lap and settling down to eat it. The little girl she'd seen earlier giggled as Vanessa looked at the monkey in amazement. She must remember to tell the twins about this.

Listening to fragments of the conversation around her as she watched the monkey, Vanessa realised the village was struggling to survive. Angela, the mother of the little girl, was shaking her head sadly as she spoke to Ralph in fragmented Spanish.

'It is terrible with the forest – so much destruction. People need to find a way of surviving, of helping the jungle to grow back. Much is being done, but the bandits, they still spoil things.' She shrugged her shoulders. 'The drugs and the gold smuggling is taking over our culture even here in this tiny village. We have a school now, but the children – what future do they have? The government want our people to report anyone who abuses the forest, but we're not going to risk our lives, are we?' Angela looked at Ralph in distress. 'How will my daughter, Maya, survive if I end up with a rifle barrel in my mouth?'

Vanessa almost choked on the exclamation of horror that she tried desperately to stop escaping. Suddenly she was glad her own children were thousands of miles away. How could any mother live with the knowledge that not only was her own life in danger but that of her children as well?

14

Half a world away, Monaco continued to gear itself up for the busiest, noisiest and most extravagant event of its year. The needs of the vintage Grand Prix held the weekend before the main event complicated things, as everything had to be ready a week early, which added a manic frenzy to the normal annual busy preparations.

Walking to school every day, Nanette and the twins got used to dodging around obstacles on the pavement, lorries parked unloading yet more essential street furniture and the inevitable crowds of tourists being disembarked into the Principality for the day from the cruise ships moored in the harbour.

Every street had an army of workmen busy hammering and fixing things into place. Terraces of stands had taken over the hillside and the harbour, large television screens had appeared in strategic places and the barriers were in place around the length of the circuit. Fresh white paint detailed the starting grid on the road below Nanette's balcony.

The main players in the Formula 1 circus, the teams and their large motorhomes, had yet to arrive, but the supporting sideshow of trucks, traders and hangers-on were already making their presence felt. The harbour was jam-packed with luxury yachts whose owners were all determined to be a part of the glamorous scene.

Nanette had so far managed to avoid walking directly past *Pole Position*, but this morning, returning from taking the twins to school, she had no choice but to walk along that side of the embankment, as the other side had been blocked. Looking straight ahead, she walked quickly, not looking at the boats until she was certain she had left *Pole Position* well behind.

Mathieu had asked her to pick up some croissants for his breakfast on her way back. 'Florence won't be in this morning – dentist or something,' Mathieu had said.

With a deep breath of relief, Nanette found a gap in the barriers being erected and quickly crossed the road to make her way into the small supermarket. Resisting the urge to buy herself a pomme de tart for her own breakfast, she paid and left holding the still warm croissants carefully.

Once back at the apartment, she switched on the coffee machine before laying a tray with cups and plates and the croissants.

'Hi Mathieu. I'm back,' she called. 'Do you want your croissants and coffee on the balcony?' The words died in her throat as a familiar figure appeared in the kitchen doorway.

'The balcony sounds fine. Hello, Nanette.'

Nanette, frozen into a shocked stillness, stared as her former fiancé, Zac Ewart, walked purposefully into the kitchen and back into her life, as if he'd never left.

Dressed in his favoured black jeans and polo shirt, a suede jacket slung casually over his shoulders, sunglasses perched on top of his head, Zac regarded Nanette contemplatively, his eyes taking in everything about her appearance.

Seconds passed before Nanette managed a strangled, 'Hello, Zac.'

'That's not much of a greeting for an old friend,' and Zac moved forward to kiss her cheek.

'Don't you dare,' Nanette said, between clenched teeth.

Zac stepped back, his hands in the air. 'Sorry.'

'How did you get in here anyway?'

'Mathieu let me in – and then remembered he had an urgent appointment in Fontvieille.' Zac gazed at her serenely. 'So, we have the place to ourselves. We can catch up with all our news over breakfast.' He picked up the breakfast tray. 'I think we agreed on the balcony?'

Nanette, knowing there was no urgent appointment for Mathieu and determined to have words with him later, reluctantly followed Zac slowly out to the balcony. Every instinct told her this was a mistake and that she should either order him to leave or leave herself. But maybe she could finally get some answers to the questions she desperately wanted to ask him.

'How are you?' Zac asked, as he placed the tray on the table.

'How am I? Why the hell do you care now? It's been three years – three years, Zac – since the accident, without a word from you. Why the sudden interest?' There was a fraction of a seconds pause before Zac answered her.

'I was glad to hear you were back. I care about you – I've missed you.'

Nanette gazed at him in disbelief. 'If you missed me that much, why didn't you get in touch? Visit me in England?' Nanette took a deep breath. 'I thought you more than cared for me – I thought you loved me. We were engaged. Disappearing out of my life without even officially breaking off our engagement was cruel, Zac.'

Zac regarded her steadily. 'I'm sorry, Nanette. It seemed the right thing to do at the time.'

'Right for whom?'

'Me. Selfish, I know, but there it is,' and he shrugged his shoulders apologetically.

Nanette turned away and leant on the balcony rail, her senses in disarray. She'd spent so much time with this man, had thought she was going to spend the rest of her life with him, but their three years apart had turned him into a stranger, and she didn't know what to say to him.

'Coffee?' Zac handed her a cup. 'Has Mathieu told you about my party next week? The Monday after the Vintage Grand Prix. I hope you're coming.'

Nanette shook her head, but before she could say anything, Zac continued.

'I'd at least feel you were starting to forgive and forget the past, and my running out on you, if you'd come.'

'I don't know that I do forgive you,' Nanette said sharply. 'As for forgetting, well, my memory is still hazy about the actual accident, but I doubt that I'll ever forget its consequences, or the hell of the last three years.'

Zac, Nanette noted, had the grace to look upset at her outburst.

'You still don't remember any details of the accident then?' he asked, stirring his coffee, not looking at her.

'No. Other than it was only the second time I'd driven the car,' Nanette said.

She didn't tell him she remembered vividly all the details of the afternoon when Zac had presented her with the racy convertible – an early birthday present.

She'd loved it and had immediately jumped into it and driven Zac around Monaco, showing the car off to all their friends. Nine hours later, the car was a mangled wreck on the autoroute and she was in intensive care in the Princess Grace Hospital, fighting for her life.

She pulled her thoughts back to the present and stared at Zac as he placed his spoon on the tray.

'Nobody has ever explained why I was flown back to the UK within forty-eight hours of coming out of intensive care. Why wasn't I just allowed to stay here and recover?'

'Everyone thought you'd be better off recovering at home,' Zac said evasively, finally glancing at her, an unfathomable look in his eyes.

'This was my home at that time. Who's this everyone?' Nanette demanded.

There was a brief silence as Zac pulled his croissant apart before turning to face her. 'It was my decision,' he said quietly. 'I made all the arrangements.'

Nanette nodded slowly. 'I thought as much. Didn't want the responsibility of caring for me, is that it? Scared I was going to be permanently scarred or disabled?'

Zac shook his head. 'I just thought you'd be better off where Patsy could administer some tender loving care. Nurse you back to health. Come on, Nanette, you know what my racing schedule is like from March to November, I'm never in town for more than two or three days at a time. There was no way I could play doctors and patient all summer.'

'Nobody would have expected you to drop everything to look after me. But why didn't you at least keep in touch?'

Zac held up his hands. 'Stop. Enough questions. All I can say is, I'm sorry I hurt you, but as far as I'm concerned, it's history. I'm glad you're back in Monaco looking so well and I hope we can be friends.' As he said this, he looked at her quizzically before adding, 'Or, at the very least, be civil to each other when we meet.'

When she didn't answer, he sighed before reaching into the

inside pocket of his jacket and taking out a brown envelope.

'Pit-lane passes for Mathieu and the twins for the Grand Prix. If I don't see you before, maybe I'll see you over Vintage Grand Prix weekend – and please think about coming to my party next Monday. *Pole Position* has been refurbished recently – she's looking really smart, I'd like you to see the changes. Right, thanks for breakfast. Stay there. I'll see myself out. Ciao.'

As the apartment door slammed behind him, Nanette sank down trembling on to a chair, relief that Zac had left flooding through her body. The meeting she'd been dreading was over and she could only be grateful that it had taken place privately, not in public. At least now that it had happened she wouldn't have to skulk around Monaco worrying she was about to bump into him and wondering what his reaction would be. He was right, of course, they were bound to meet up from time to time and it would be far better all round if they were civil to each other.

Not that she felt very civil towards him right now, after that casual remark about forgiving and forgetting the past. As if it was that easy. He still hadn't explained why he had not been in touch once he'd shipped her back to Patsy.

Sitting there, trying to analyse her true feelings about Zac Ewart, Nanette frowned. There were still questions about the accident to which she wanted answers and until her memory returned fully, Zac Ewart was the only person who could give them, which clearly he had no intention of doing. She needed to know too, why he'd abandoned her so cruelly when surely he must have known how much she needed him. Blaming his absence on the summer racing schedule was too convenient. There had to be another reason.

Sighing, she returned the breakfast tray to the kitchen. Her fingers were shaking as she picked up her phone from the kitchen table. She needed to talk to Patsy.

'Zac ambushed me in the apartment this morning,' she burst out as soon as Patsy answered. 'It was awful.'

'What d'you mean "ambushed"?' Patsy's voice was full of concern.

'He made sure that I was alone – even Mathieu had agreed to leave – so that no-one could overhear his little "let's be friends" speech. He seemed to think as the whole episode was three years ago...' Nanette took a gulp of air. 'That we should kiss and make up.'

'Well, that clearly didn't happen,' Patsy said. 'So what happens now?'

Nanette shrugged in answer, before realising Patsy couldn't see her. 'No idea. How about I just shut myself away in the apartment until the Grand Prix is over?'

'No,' Patsy said. 'You have the twins to look after. You can't just stay indoors.'

Nanette smothered a sigh. 'I know. Okay. The last thing I want is to get caught up in a public scene, so if I bump into him anywhere, I'll... I'll just walk on by.'

'That sounds very civilised.' Patsy said. 'What are you up to today?'

'Working in JC's office sorting it out,' Nanette answered. 'I'd better get going, he'll be wondering where I am. Thank goodness I know the back streets! Patsy?'

'Yes?'

'Thanks for listening.'

For some reason, as she ended the call, Nanette saw Zac's face again as he failed to meet her eyes when he'd asked about her non-returning memory. Almost as if he felt guilty asking her the question. Could he possibly be blaming himself for the accident because if he'd never given her the car in the first place, they'd still be together, maybe even married by now?

15

Life in the jungle settled into a pattern for Vanessa as she and Ralph became absorbed into the routine of village life. Ralph, busy helping and recording the building of a small dam on a river near the village, disappeared early every morning with the men, leaving Vanessa to spend her days with Angela and the other women.

Vanessa had known life in the jungle would be a whole new experience, something to take her out of her comfort zone, and she'd looked forward to it. Ralph had talked to her, shown her films, given her books to read, but now she was here the reality of day-to-day life was hard to take in. Looking after a family in the jungle was exhausting for the village women – her own life back in England, even with all its stresses and first-world problems, was nothing compared to what these women endured. Several times as she helped cook the evening meal and stirred something indescribable bubbling in the pot swinging on its tripod over an open fire, she thought of her high-tech kitchen at home. What would Angela and her friends make of her gleaming Aga and all the labour-saving gadgets her house contained?

The lack of available communication with the outside world bothered Vanessa too. They might have satellite phones, but getting them charged via the solar panels wasn't an exact science due to the dense nature of the forest. She'd also learnt that bad weather hundreds of miles away could affect the efficiency of the satellite. Ralph took the charging panel and the phone with him every morning, hoping to recharge the phone in a small space open to the skies near the river, but would inevitably return shaking his head in the evening. Vanessa longed to have a proper conversation with Pierre and Olivia rather than the one or two sentences they managed before the connection died. She wouldn't, couldn't, of course, admit to Ralph or even talk to Angela about how difficult she was finding it to adapt to her current lifestyle.

She and Ralph spent their evenings in the large communal hut, where, as honoured guests, they were feted with the best the villagers could provide and entertained with traditional songs and music. Afterwards, in the small hut allocated to them, Vanessa wrote about the day's experiences in her diary.

In their hammocks at night before they settled down to sleep, Ralph talked to Vanessa about his worries for the village.

That night, he said, 'They seem to think this dam we're building to help with the gold panning is going to be their path to untold riches. Now some sleaze from Rio has appeared on the scene telling them his boss will help to fund enlarging the mine and sell the gold on for them – all for a big fat rake-off, of course.' He shook his head. 'They know the mercury he's going to provide for separating the gold is poisonous and so bad for the forest, but they hear of other villages prospering and they want to do the same. The fact that they'll probably end up polluting their water supply, poisoning the fish and eroding the forest even more doesn't seem to be an issue for them.'

'Can't you persuade them to stick to just panning for gold without the mercury?' Vanessa asked.

'I've tried, but they're desperate and see this as the only way to survive. I wish I could think of some other way they could make the money to buy the essentials like stock and seeds so they can carry on farming in the traditional way.'

'Eco-tourism like the first village we stayed in?' Vanessa suggested.

'The villagers aren't that keen on the idea of too many strangers in the village. Besides, they're so poor they don't have the money to even improve their own basic living conditions. Being so deep in the jungle here too, it wouldn't be easy to organise. I know, I had a few problems getting us here. Most of those eco-camps are within two hours of the Amazon River. Nowhere as deep in the jungle as we are.' Ralph sighed. 'The trouble is we're here for such a short time, there's not a lot we can do. The dam should be finished tomorrow, maybe I'll get a chance to talk to the head shaman then.' He leant across and gave Vanessa a kiss. 'Nearly forget to tell you: Luigi, the guide, has offered to take us to see the young dolphins in a couple of days. It's a long trek to get to where they're being born, but should be well worth it.' Ralph smiled happily at his wife.

'That's good of Luigi,' Vanessa said, smiling at Ralph. 'Something to look forward to.'

The next morning, Ralph left as usual and Vanessa joined Angela and the other women for the daily chores. Today, besides the normal cooking and husbandry of the small animals that roamed around the village, they were planning to plant seedlings.

As ever, the humidity in the jungle was high and Vanessa struggled to keep pace with Angela and the others as they went to collect the seedlings from the large government-controlled farm where they'd been grown. It proved to be a long, hard day as they planted the small trees on cleared forestland previously grazed by cattle. From time to time, thunderstorms rolled across the sky and torrential rain forced them to stop work and seek shelter. During one of these breaks, Vanessa noticed that a couple of the women were muttering unhappily together.

'They have nothing,' Angela explained. 'Life is getting harder and all they hear is how we must take care of the forest. Who is going to take care of us? We have to survive too.' She shook her head. 'We have a school now, but what work is there going to be for the children? What kind of future do Maya and the other children face?'

Vanessa was silent. How could she possibly answer that question?

'Will a bigger gold mine help?' she said finally. 'Ralph says it's not the answer, but what do you think?'

Angela bit her bottom lip before replying, 'If it was a legal gold mine it would help more, but, as usual, the wrong people will benefit from it.'

Vanessa gazed at her, horrified. Did Ralph know he was building a dam to help an illegal gold mine operate?

Before she could ask any more, the rain stopped and the women began to move back out on to the wetland.

'If we are to survive living off the land, we need more legitimate help,' Angela added quietly, as she handed over a trowel and another box of seedlings.

Thoughtfully, Vanessa began the rhythmic business of planting the tiny trees – dig hole, drop seedling in, cover and press, on to the next – while trying to work out how Ralph would respond to the news about the mine.

It was late afternoon when Vanessa removed her hat and pushed her damp hair back from her face. Her clothes were wet and sticking to her body and she remembered longingly the delights of a cool shower. At least it would soon be time to return to the village and help prepare the evening meal in the shade of the trees surrounding the encampment.

As the women were gathering their things, one of the young native boys returning from the day's work on the dam, ran up to Angela and said something to her urgently. Vanessa felt a tremor of fear pass through her body as Angela glanced across at her, a look of concern on her face, before walking towards her.

'What's happened? Something has happened to Ralph, hasn't it?' Fear made her voice sound shrill even to her own ears.

'Ralph has been taken ill,' Angela said quietly. 'The men are bringing him back to the village.'

'I must go to him,' Vanessa said, panic-stricken, and went to run towards the huddle of men approaching the village.

Angela placed a restraining hand on her. 'Wait here,' she said gently. 'Let the men deal with it.'

Vanessa's heart was in her mouth as she watched the group approaching. She forced herself to stay still as two of the village men carried an unconscious Ralph on a makeshift stretcher into the compound before carefully placing him in the medicine man's hut.

16

Early Sunday morning on Vintage Grand Prix weekend, Mathieu handed the pit-lane passes that Jean-Claude had obtained to Nanette and suggested she took the twins out of the way.

Mathieu had practically pushed them all out of the apartment, despite Olivia protesting she'd rather stay in her room. 'Papa Jean-Claude's down there getting ready. Go and wish him good luck. He'd love to see you all. Florence and I need to get the apartment ready for the lunch party.'

With the pit-lane passes hanging around their necks on ribbons, Nanette and the twins crossed the Boulevard Albert 1er at a designated crossing place between the barriers, and made their way down the pit lane to the garage, where Jean-Claude was fine-tuning his Lotus before the race.

Along the pit lane, the cars with their curiously old-fashioned looks were the star attractions. Pierre was fascinated to see a car that had raced in the very first Monaco Grand Prix over sixty years ago on display at the end of the pit-lane enclosure. Even Olivia was impressed when Jean-Claude told them how well his qualifying laps had gone.

'Can't believe the old girl went so well. Fourth on the grid. Just have to hope she keeps going now.' Jean-Claude patted the dark green bonnet of the car gently. 'Imagine – I'm alongside Damon Hill on the second row,' he said, looking at Nanette.

Nanette smiled at his boyish enthusiasm. 'Good luck,' she said. 'We'll be cheering you on from the balcony.' And the three of them left Jean-Claude and his mechanic to finish their last-minute adjustments to the car.

Strolling along the pit lane with the twins, Nanette remembered the countless times she'd been involved in preparations for Grand Prix races with Zac all over the world, but there was something different about this pit lane. It took her several minutes to realise exactly what it was.

There were crowds of people milling around and there was the usual frenzy of mechanics preparing cars for racing, but it was all rather subdued and, like the cars, old-fashioned. The razzamatazz atmosphere of a modern Formula 1 grand prix was missing.

Next week, Monaco would be in the grip of twenty-first-century racing-car fever as the modern Formula 1 roadshow took over and Monaco turned itself into the most glamorous race-track in the world, but this Sunday morning, it was all about nostalgia.

Knowing that once the racing started they wouldn't be able to leave the pit lane, Nanette ushered the twins across the road and they made their way slowly home.

Back in the apartment, Pierre grabbed Mathieu's binoculars and took up his position on the balcony, where he had a good view of both the starting grid and the pit-lane exit. Guests were starting to arrive. Olivia took one look at one of them, a tall, lanky teenager, and gasped.

'Dad didn't say he was coming,' she said.

Nanette laughed at the expression on her face. 'Who is he?' she asked.

Olivia looked at her in disbelief. 'You must recognise him. It's Foxey. He's the lead singer with a really, really cool band. Les Grenouilles.'

'Oh,' Nanette said, watching as Olivia ran to her room to change into her 'best' jeans – the ones with the tear in the knee – and to fetch her autograph book.

'Be really cool if he'd sign it for me,' she said. 'Do you think he will?'

'I don't see why not,' Nanette said. 'Go and ask him nicely before anyone else arrives.'

She watched as Olivia shyly approached the young singer, held out her autograph book and politely asked in perfect French. 'Would you please sign it for me?'

Nanette held her breath in case the boy refused, but she needn't have worried, He smiled at Olivia as he asked her name before writing in her treasured book.

Nanette was less than thrilled to see the next person who arrived – Boris. Accompanied by a group of six men and the blonde woman Nanette had seen with him in the restaurant, he walked confidently into the apartment. After a cursory glance in her direction and a polite 'Bonjour,' he went through to join Foxey and the other guests on the balcony.

Nanette stood undecided. She didn't fancy going out there and being ignored by Boris and his cronies. She'd wait until all the guests had arrived.

When the doorbell rang, she quickly called out to Florence, 'Don't worry, I'll get it,' and opened the door to find Evie and her boss, Luc, standing there.

'Evie. What a lovely surprise to see you again,' Nanette said as

Luc went through to join Boris on the balcony, leaving Evie with Nanette.

Together they went into the sitting room, where Mathieu was now supervising pre-lunch nibbles and drinks with Florence. Accepting a glass and taking a plate of hors d'oeuvres, Nanette and Evie edged their way outside towards Pierre and Olivia on the balcony.

Several of the cars were already on the grid, having driven round the circuit to get to their starting positions, and their mechanics were thronging around, giving them final checks in the last twenty minutes before the formation lap.

'It's Papa Jean-Claude's race next,' Pierre said. 'Look, here he comes out of the pits,' and he trained the binoculars down on the pit-lane exit.

'Gosh, from up here they look like the Dinky toys my kid brother used to play with,' Evie said, leaning over to get a better look.

Huge TV screens had been positioned around the circuit, including one at the tight first corner, Sainte-Dévote, where the cars would still be jostling for position after the start.

Nanette watched as Jean-Claude began his drive round the circuit to get to his place on the starting grid ready for the formation lap. For some reason, her stomach was a mass of knots, much like it had been whenever she watched Zac race. Knowing how much the opportunity to race his Lotus again meant to him, she so wanted Jean-Claude to have a good, safe, race.

By the time he emerged from the tunnel and was negotiating the bends by the swimming pool in front of them, all of Mathieu's guests had arrived and the balcony was buzzing.

Nanette, looking out across the harbour, saw Zac on the deck of *Pole Position*. Thankfully, he was obviously not planning to join them for lunch. Since the morning of his surprise appearance in the apartment, talking about forgiving and forgetting and expressing the desire that they should be civil to each in public, Nanette had been wondering where and when their next encounter would be.

Evie saw her looking at the yachts. 'Is that *Pole Position*? I've been invited to a party on board tomorrow. Do you know Zac Ewart?'

Nanette smiled. Evie was exactly the kind of girl Zac liked to surround himself with. She nodded. 'I've known Zac for years.'

She glanced at Evie as she said this. Evie clearly had no idea of her past relationship with Zac.

Nanette, knowing the way the Monaco grapevine worked, knew it wouldn't be long before someone told Evie all the gory details. She hesitated, perhaps she should get in first with her version – the details she could remember, anyway.

'Oh great, you'll be going to the party then,' Evie said, and the opportunity was gone.

'Not sure,' Nanette said evasively.

A party on board the boat on which she had organised many a party in the past, full of people who hadn't given her a single thought after the accident, wasn't a scenario she fancied. Could she really face it? Did she want to put herself through what would undoubtedly be an ordeal? Even if there was an outside chance that it could help to revive her memory and fill in the blanks for her.

'The race is about to start,' Pierre said excitedly. 'The lights are on.'

Watching the old cars take off, Nanette hoped Jean-Claude would do well – or at least finish the race and not break down. She held her breath every time the Lotus passed below them on the way to the first corner of the next lap, willing him on with every vibe. In the event, he held on to his grid position right to the end and came in fourth. As he took the chequered flag, Nanette joined the twins in cheering loudly, relieved that he'd finished without any problems but sad that he'd just missed out on a podium position.

It was mid-afternoon before a happy Jean-Claude joined them up in the apartment, going straight to the kitchen, where Nanette had retreated to give Florence a hand.

'Congratulations, JC,' Nanette said, turning to him with a smile on her face, before surprising both herself and Jean-Claude when she kissed him on the cheek before pouring and handing him a glass of champagne.

'Merci.'

Nanette smiled at him again, not sure whether he was thanking her for the champagne or the kiss.

'Any food left? I'm starving,' he asked.

'Of course. Why don't you join the others on the balcony while I plate you up some?'

Jean-Claude shook his head. 'Not in the mood for meeting Boris and company. I stay here with you.'

As Nanette quickly made up a plate of food for him, Mathieu appeared in the doorway.

'Congratulations, Papa. You had a good race there,' before he turned to Nanette. 'Are you still planning to spend next Sunday up at the villa rather than stay here in the apartment? Now that you and Zac have kissed and made up, I thought you might watch the race from the back of his garage in the pit lane?'

Nanette looked at him, shocked. 'Mathieu, I don't know what Zac has told you, but we certainly haven't kissed and made up. I've still got a lot of questions I'd like him to answer before that happens – if it ever does,' Nanette said sharply. 'Does it matter where I spend next Sunday?'

'I've just agreed that Boris can use the apartment to watch the race,' Mathieu said. 'Apparently the apartment he was hoping to use is no longer available. I've told him Pierre and I will be here and possibly you and Olivia, which isn't a problem for him.'

'Pierre definitely wants to watch the race and Olivia would prefer not to,' Nanette said. 'So, I'll take her up to the villa for the day and leave Pierre here with you, if that's OK with you, JC?'

'Fine by me,' Jean-Claude assured her. He glanced at Mathieu. 'Are you going to Zac's party tomorrow night?'

'Of course, and I'm hoping Nanette is coming as my partner,' Mathieu answered, looking at her.

Nanette looked at him, surprised. He hadn't mentioned that possibility to her. 'Thanks, Mathieu, Zac invited me, but I've decided not to go.'

Mathieu looked disappointed but merely said. 'That's a shame, but if you change your mind, I'll be leaving here about nine thirty. You'll remember how Zac's parties never take off until late.'

17

The night she spent sitting in the shaman's hut beside a delirious Ralph was one of the longest of Vanessa's life. For two hours after the native bearers had placed him in the hut, Vanessa had paced up and down outside. Refused admittance by the chief shaman, she could do nothing but pray for her husband and wonder what was going on in there.

Nick and Harry, the cameramen, gave her a brief account of what had happened out by the mine.

'Ralph didn't feel well all morning, said his stomach was hurting. He ate very little lunch before he was sick.'

'Why on earth didn't he return to camp?' Vanessa said.

'Thought he'd be better working through it,' Harry answered. 'Said he must have eaten a grub or some other local delicacy last night that didn't agree with him. Once he'd been sick, he did seem a bit brighter. We managed to persuade him to have a short snooze before work started again and he seemed better for it.'

Vanessa listened, horrified, as Nick then told her about the large boulder that had slipped as the men had tried to manoeuvre it into position for the dam. Breaking the wooden stakes they were using to guide it into position, it had fallen, giving Ralph's head a glancing blow and knocking him unconscious into the stream.

Listening to Nick's matter-of-fact account of what had happened, Vanessa remembered the words of the tourist in the eco-camp. 'All the money in the world won't get you out of the jungle in a hurry.'

What if Ralph didn't respond to whatever mumbo jumbo they were saying and administering to him in there? How was she going to get him to a proper hospital?

As if reading her thoughts, Harry said, 'If he hasn't regained consciousness by tomorrow, we'll get him carried down to the tributary and hire a canoe to take him to the Amazon River itself. Then hopefully we can get him to a hospital in one of the large towns.'

Vanessa looked at him in despair. 'That will take days.'

There was a second or two's pause, before Nick said quietly, 'Let's pray it won't be necessary. I'm told some of these natural medicines the natives use are amazingly effective.'

Both Nick and Harry stayed with her until Angela appeared with some food for Vanessa and insisted she ate it. 'It is going to be a long night,' she said quietly. 'You will need all your strength.'

Angela was still with her when the head shaman came out and said Vanessa could finally see Ralph. Fearful of how Ralph would look, Vanessa clutched Angela's hand and walked slowly into the hut.

'You stay with him tonight?' the shaman asked. 'I show you what to do.'

Looking at Ralph's injured face and his battered body, daubed with what Vanessa took to be some sort of native ointment and protected in places with primitive dressings, she forced herself to concentrate on what she had to do for Ralph.

'The next few hours are critical,' Angela said.

The medicine man and Angela showed her how to gently bathe Ralph's cuts and bruises with a sticky substance that Angela explained was a sap taken from trees in the forest.

'Sango de Grado – it is good,' Angela assured Vanessa. 'You see, tomorrow, Ralph will look better. He will be better.' She hesitated before continuing.

'I think I have to tell you, the word in the village is that this was no accident. Somebody wants Ralph gone – one way or the other.'

Vanessa could only stare at Angela, horrified.

That night she did a lot of praying as she tended to Ralph. Applying cooling compresses to a large bump on his temple and gently stroking his hand, she willed him to regain consciousness.

It was around two o'clock when he began to mumble and restlessly move his head from side to side. Quickly, Vanessa changed the compress for a cooler, fresh one. As she gently held it in place, she scrutinised his face for any further glimmer of life, but he'd lapsed back into unconsciousness and the long night continued.

At regular intervals, one of the native men would appear in the doorway of the hut and stand there looking at Ralph for several seconds, before vanishing back into the darkness. The first time it happened, it spooked Vanessa, but as the hours went on, she welcomed the fleeting visits.

Dawn was beginning to filter through the canopy of trees surrounding the hut when Ralph finally opened his eyes and smiled at her. Vanessa felt a huge wave of relief sweep through her body and she gave him a gentle kiss.

'Hi, welcome back.'

'Sorry about the dolphins.'

For a moment Vanessa thought Ralph was still delirious

before remembering tomorrow was the day they were to have trekked to the breeding grounds to see the young dolphins.

She shook her head. 'It doesn't matter. You're more important. How do you feel?'

'Groggy – and thirsty.'

Carefully, Vanessa held a cup of water to his lips as Ralph took several sips.

'Do you remember what happened to you?'

'I was in the way of the boulder when it broke the wooden runners and fell. We were so close to finishing the dam too. Still, hopefully today the boys will be able to sort it.'

'Just so long as you're not thinking of joining them,' Vanessa said.

Ralph shook his head and then groaned with the pain it generated.

Vanessa waited a couple of seconds before saying quietly, 'I'm not sure you're well enough to hear this, but you need to know.'

Ralph glanced at her, puzzled, as she took a breath before continuing.

'Angela was here earlier, talking to me. She doesn't think any of this was an accident.'

Ralph sighed and reached out for her hand. 'I know. Neither do I. The head shaman warned me to be careful a couple of days ago.'

'Why didn't you tell me? The villagers seemed happy to have us around when we arrived,' Vanessa said. 'What's changed?'

'Since this guy from Rio has become involved, some of the men have become wary of me filming the village activities. Particularly the dam,' Ralph explained quietly.

'Is that because of the mercury they're going to be using? Will the profits from the gold still go to the village?' Vanessa asked.

Ralph's fingers squeezed hers before saying slowly, 'Not as much as the villagers hope.'

Vanessa was silent, remembering how worried Angela was about the future of the village and its people, how they desperately needed to find a reliable way of sustaining their way of life.

'There must be another way,' Vanessa said thoughtfully. 'Something legal they can do to survive.'

'If we could think of another option, I'd be only too happy to help them set it up,' Ralph said quietly, 'but as far as I can see, there is nothing we can do. There's something else... They want us to leave. They're afraid our presence here will upset this guy from Rio.'

Vanessa's heart skipped a beat. After what had happened to Ralph she personally couldn't wait to leave the jungle. 'Are we going to?'

But her heart sank at Ralph's reply.

'Not immediately, no. I've still got a couple of things I'd like to film. I've promised to stay away from the dam – which suits me. The less I know about it, the better.'

Vanessa sighed and stroked his forehead gently.

'How much longer do you think we'll be here?' she asked quietly.

'A couple of weeks, maybe a bit less – depends on how quickly I get better from this little incident,' Ralph said. 'Could I have another drink please?'

As she held the water to Ralph's lips, Vanessa thought about Ralph's 'little incident'. It was typical of him to play down the seriousness of the accident, but Vanessa knew it could have turned out so differently. She could have been a widow before they'd been married even six months. She smothered a sigh. A few more weeks to go and then they could trek out of the jungle and back to civilisation and proper doctors.

Ralph was regarding her anxiously. 'If you want to leave and wait for me in the eco-camp, I'm sure Angela could arrange for a guide.'

'I'm not leaving you,' Vanessa said fiercely. 'We came together and we'll leave together. OK?'

Ralph nodded weakly and closed his eyes. 'Love you,' he whispered as he drifted, exhausted, back into sleep.

Vanessa sat at his side, still holding his hand and wishing they were already in the comparative safety of the eco-camp.

18

The night of Zac's party, Monaco Old Port was a mass of twinkling lights from the yachts and the restaurants that lined the
harbour. Grand Prix fever was definitely in the air as Monaco
slipped into party mode for the biggest week of its year.

Nanette had spent an hour or two during the day up at Jean-
Claude's villa finishing the sorting out of his office and making
sure his diary was up to date. She'd found several invitations to
various summer events along the Riviera, including one to the
famous Red Cross Ball and another for the Monte Carlo Gala for
the Global Ocean at the end of the summer season. When she
asked about them, Jean-Claude had immediately told her to
RSVP declining the Red Cross invitation but to put the date of the
other one in the diary, while he responded and accepted the
invitation.

'I alternate between them,' he'd explained. 'This year I go to
the Global Ocean event.'

When Nanette saw the size of the cheque he'd written to
accompany his response and to reserve a table at the charity
money raising event, she remembered how expensive it was to

have a social life amongst the VIP residents of Monaco. Supporting a charity in Monte Carlo required deep pockets.

Now, a few hours later, standing on the balcony surveying the evening scene below her, Nanette took in the atmosphere. Whereas it had once been commonplace in her life, she was now so detached from the social scene that watching it had something of a surreal quality for her.

After the laid-back nostalgic atmosphere of the weekend, it was clear the big boys were now gathering in town ready to play. Music from several parties already in full swing on various boats floated up on the sultry air. Couples strolled nonchalantly past the luxury yachts, stopping occasionally to gaze on board, in the hope of seeing a famous face or two amongst all the glamorous people.

Nanette picked up her mobile and took a short video of the harbour down below: *Pole Position* lit from stem to stern, the music and the buzz of laughter drifting up on the air. She sent it to Patsy with the cryptic comment: 'Guess who's having an on-board party tonight?'

Her phone rang five seconds later.

'Are you all right? Is it bringing back memories? Please don't let them upset you,' Patsy said.

'I'm not,' Nanette answered. 'It's surreal really, watching it going on from a distance, knowing the kind of thing that is happening on board. I definitely don't miss it,' she assured her sister, surprising herself with the truth. 'How are things with you and the bump?'

'Good. The sickness has gone, thank goodness. Putting on too much weight, according to Helen, but the midwife assures me I'm in the normal range for this trimester, so I'm listening to her and not Grannyzilla.'

'Have you called her that to her face yet?' Nanette laughed.

'No, thankfully. It's not funny,' Patsy protested. 'I've asked Bryan to have a word with her this Sunday when they do their weekly afternoon walk together. I've told him he *has* to make her listen, otherwise I'm going to book myself into a B&B down on the coast and get completely away. I need some space,' she added quietly. 'I wish Mum and Dad were still alive. I could do with one of Mum's hugs at the moment.'

'Oh, Patsy love,' Nanette said, realising her unflappable big sister was close to tears. 'I wish I wasn't so far away right now. I promise you I'll come and give you lots of hugs when I get back. And I'll keep Helen off your back. Hang on in there.'

'Talking to you has helped,' Patsy said. 'I'm going to bed to read now for a bit. Night.'

'Night,' Nanette echoed.

Scrolling through her contacts on the phone, she found the florist she always used and ordered a big bunch of flowers to be delivered to Patsy the next day. Hopefully that would cheer her up.

Mathieu appeared as she closed her phone and turned her attention back to the scenes on the quay in front.

'I'm off. Sure you won't change your mind and come to the party?' Mathieu asked.

Nanette shook her head. 'Enjoy yourself. You look very smart, by the way, in your tuxedo.'

'Thanks.' Mathieu hesitated for a second, as though about to say something else, changed his mind and left.

Nanette heard him open the door and was surprised to hear Jean-Claude's voice saying hello.

'What are you doing here, Papa?' Mathieu asked. 'Aren't you coming to Zac's party either?'

'I keep Nanette company first,' Jean-Claude said. 'Enjoy the party. I'll catch you later,' and he closed the door behind Mathieu, cutting off any more questions from his son.

Joining Nanette on the balcony, Jean-Claude smiled at her. 'Great atmosphere down there.'

Nanette nodded. 'Mmm. Can I get you a drink or anything?'

'Maybe in a minute, but first I would like to talk to you.' Jean-Claude glanced at her before continuing quietly. 'I think you go and make an appearance at Zac's party tonight. If only for five minutes.'

'Oh, JC,' Nanette sighed.

'I know you tell me how upsetting and difficult you found seeing Zac recently,' Jean-Claude said, 'but going tonight would be another step to getting the past behind you. Zac, he has expressed a desire to be friends, and his guests are unlikely to create a scene or be rude to you in front of him.'

There was silence as Nanette gazed out unseeingly over the harbour. Knowing that Jean-Claude was right didn't help and she shrugged helplessly as she turned to face him.

'Why don't you go and put on a party dress and we go together?' Jean-Claude said gently. 'We don't have to stay long and I promise not to leave your side.' As Nanette bit her lip and looked at him, he added, 'It will be fine. Go and change. I'll have a word with Florence to keep an ear out for the twins, but I'm sure they'll be fast asleep by now anyway.'

Nanette hesitated. Deep down she knew Jean-Claude was right. Going to the party and being civil to Zac would be a major step forward and meeting him with Jean-Claude at her side would make things so much easier. She gave him a tremulous smile before saying, 'Okay.'

In her room, Nanette stood uncertainly in front of her wardrobe wondering which dress to wear. She rejected the one she'd worn to accompany Jean-Claude to the Hôtel de Paris as being too dressy and chose instead a summery white one with a lace bolero jacket over the shoulders.

'Do I look OK?' she asked Jean-Claude anxiously as she rejoined him in the sitting room.

'Nanette, you always look lovely to me whatever you're wearing,' Jean-Claude said quietly.

Struck by the sincere intensity in his voice, Nanette looked at him in surprise before smiling at him shyly and leading the way out of the apartment. Now the decision to go to the party had been taken, she was determined to be strong and face things, people, head on.

Together they walked past yacht after yacht, each one positively humming with revellers. Everywhere, there was noise, laughter, music and glamorous women. As they approached *Pole Position*, dressed overall with lights from stern to bow, and moored between two boats busy with their own parties, Nanette felt her heart quicken and apprehension pushed all her new found determination aside. What had she been thinking?

The sudden strident noise of police sirens as several police cars streaked their way along the Boulevard Albert 1er frightened Nanette and she looked around quickly.

'Probably heading for the autoroute,' Jean-Claude said. 'Hope it's nothing too serious.' He gestured to her to go ahead of him as a crew member waited at the head of the gangway to welcome them aboard.

Slipping her shoes off and placing them in the woven wicker basket provided, before stepping on to the teak deck of *Pole Position*, Nanette's nerves almost got the better of her and she would have run back down to the embankment, if Jean-Claude hadn't unexpectedly taken her hand at that moment, making escape impossible. It was as if he sensed her wanting to run as he squeezed her hand in a comforting, reassuring way, letting her know he was there for her.

The main cabin of the boat was bursting with people and, as they squeezed their way through the throng, Nanette saw several people she knew. She returned a quiet 'hello' to the ones who acknowledged her and did her best not to mind the ones who deliberately turned their backs.

Jean-Claude took two glasses of champagne from the steward at the small bar and handed her one.

Nanette looked around curiously as she sipped her drink. Over three years since she'd stepped foot on the yacht that had been her and Zac's private bolt hole. In those days the interior had been a mixture of off-white furniture with Zac's growing collection of original art on the wall spaces between the windows and a cream carpet on the floor. This evening she saw that while the fitted furniture was the same, the carpet had been replaced by wooden parquet flooring, several of the paintings had disappeared and a large Lalique glass panel depicting a F1 racing car had taken their place. Vaguely, Nanette wondered what had happened to the paintings.

'What do you think of the makeover Zac had done earlier this year?' Jean-Claude asked.

'Umm, not sure,' Nanette replied evasively. 'I liked it the way it was. Wonder where Zac is?' The sooner he realised she was on board and they could get over any awkwardness in their greeting and move on, the better.

'Probably out on deck. Shall we go look?'

When Nanette nodded, Jean-Claude took her by the hand again and they made their way through one of the open doors out on to the side deck.

Outside, they could see Zac and Mathieu up in the bow talking to Boris. By mutual unspoken consent, Nanette and Jean-

Claude stayed where they were. Neither of them wanted to have to make small talk with Boris.

As they stood sipping their drinks and watching the other party guests, Nanette slowly relaxed. Just as they were about to return to the main cabin, Evie joined them.

'Hi. I thought it was you. Isn't it a great party? I've been talking to one of the racing drivers, but now he's looking for Zac. He's got a message for him from his technical support team. Apparently, the police have stopped the Formula 1 car transporters up on the autoroute for a random search.'

'Nothing unusual in that,' Nanette said. 'It happens quite a lot. Never found anything yet.'

'Oh, but this time they reckon they've had a tip-off and they're searching them all from top to bottom. They seem certain of finding something.' Evie said. 'My friend is telling Zac the news now.'

Nanette glanced across in time to catch the concerned look Zac exchanged with Boris and Mathieu. Mathieu moved away from the others and began to push his way towards the stern and the gangway.

Nanette felt a sudden knot of apprehension tighten in her stomach and she moved closer to Jean-Claude. Gently, she felt for his hand and together they watched Mathieu jump off *Pole Position* before being swallowed up by the crowds still thronging the harbourside and disappearing from view.

Standing on the deck in silence watching Mathieu running away into the night, Nanette felt Jean-Claude's tension as she held his hand and hoped against hope that his worry was groundless.

Nanette glanced around. The party seemed to have come to a premature end with the news of the police raid on the Formula 1 transporters. The deck was still vibrating from the disco music playing in the main cabin, but people were leaving, including Boris and his entourage.

'Shall we go?' Nanette asked Jean-Claude quietly.

He nodded in answer and they turned to make their way back to the gangway Nanette, hoping that they would be able to leave unnoticed, was disconcerted to see Zac standing in the stern, saying goodnight to people.

'Nanette, Jean-Claude, I'm sorry you're leaving. Can't you both stay longer? I haven't even had a chance to dance with you yet, Nanette. Another glass of champagne perhaps?'

Nanette glanced at him sharply. The last thing she wanted was to dance with Zac.

'Non,' Jean-Claude said brusquely. 'I need to find Mathieu. Perhaps you tell me where he's gone?' Jean-Claude glared at Zac.

'How would I know?' Zac said.

'Because I believe you've involved my son in one of your suspect business enterprises,' Jean-Claude said angrily.

Zac looked at him steadily. 'Mathieu is a businessman – he makes his own decisions as to the deals he gets involved in. Nobody twists his arm.'

'So, he is mixed up with you and the Russian in something then?' Jean-Claude demanded.

Zac sighed. 'Jean-Claude, if Mathieu has chosen not to confide in you about his business, I can't help you. Now, are you sure I can't persuade you to stay?' and he looked at Nanette hopefully.

She shook her head and moved away to retrieve her high-heeled sandals from the jumble of footwear now in the basket at the head of the gangway.

Slipping them on, she saw Jean-Claude move closer to Zac and place a hand on his shoulder before leaning towards him and saying something that was clearly intended for his ears alone.

Zac's face darkened and he vehemently shrugged Jean-Claude's hand off his shoulder before turning away and making for the bar in the main cabin.

Both Nanette and Jean-Claude were silent as they made their way along the embankment to the apartment, each lost in their own thoughts.

Jean-Claude took her arm as they prepared to cross the road. 'Join me for a coffee, please, before I see you home,' he said.

The pavement café at the bottom of Rue Princess Caroline was noisy with late-night revellers as they sat at a small table and ordered their cafés noisettes.

'Try not to worry too much about Mathieu,' Nanette said gently. 'Didn't he tell you that things were under control and everything would be sorted soon?'

Jean-Claude nodded.

'So try to trust him for a bit longer. Difficult, I know.'

As Nanette looked at him sympathetically, he reached out and squeezed her hand.

'I know you're right,' he said, shaking his head as he looked at her. 'I just wish I didn't have fear in the pit of my stomach.'

19

Mathieu wasn't home when Nanette took the twins to school the next morning. Strolling back to the apartment, Nanette wondered where he was. When her mobile rang, she answered it quickly, half expecting it to be him, but it was Jean-Claude.

'Have you seen Mathieu?'

'No. According to Florence his bed hadn't been slept in,' Nanette said. 'Have you heard anything more about the raid?'

'Apparently the police did find something, but nobody knows what exactly – although rumour has it as a case full of money.'

'Did they arrest anyone?'

'A couple of the truck drivers have been spoken to, but the motorhomes and transporters were all allowed to park up without any problems. The Formula 1 circus keeps to a very tight schedule, as you know, and nothing must interfere with race week. The police are still up on site searching some of them.' There was a short pause before Jean-Claude continued. 'Will you let me know when Mathieu returns?'

'Yes, of course.'

Replacing the phone in her bag, Nanette wandered slowly

along a side street filled with various stalls selling Formula 1 racing paraphernalia and fast food. Even at this early hour there were fans strolling around, mixing with the locals trying to go about their normal lives despite the inconvenience of barriers and streets filled with seating stands. Tomorrow – a practice day – the road around town and along the harbour would be closed to traffic as the drivers began to get to grips with driving around the narrow winding street circuit at a crazy speed.

Although it was several years since Nanette had been in Monaco for the Grand Prix, it was still all so familiar. Walking past the souvenir stands and the touts already up and about trying to sell tickets for lunch on practice day at restaurants with views of the circuit, she even recognised one or two people and smiled briefly in their direction.

Ferrari red was the dominant colour of the bunting hanging from balconies and the smell of socca cooking on a mobile catering stall on the corner, competing with the usual breakfast smell of fresh croissants from the boulangerie, was hard to resist.

Nanette pushed open the glass door of the foyer to the apartment building and pressed the lift button. The two concierges behind the reception desk stopped in mid-conversation as she entered, but not before Nanette heard the words 'Monsieur Mathieu'.

As she walked into the sitting room, Florence appeared and pointed to Mathieu's bedroom.

'Mathieu has returned. He is sleeping and asked not to be disturbed,' she said quietly.

Quickly, Nanette rang Jean-Claude to tell him the news.

'I'm on my way down,' he said.

Nanette and Jean-Claude spent the morning drinking coffee and waiting for Mathieu to surface. A couple of times, when a frustrated Jean-Claude threatened to go and wake him, Nanette managed to persuade him it wasn't a good idea.

At one o'clock, the two of them ate the salad lunch that Florence had prepared for them, sitting out on the balcony. Jean-Claude, Nanette could see, had a hard time eating anything.

It was another hour before Mathieu appeared and Jean-Claude was immediately firing questions at him about the raid. Nanette felt increasingly uncomfortable witnessing the mounting row between father and son and wondered if perhaps she should leave them to it. But if it did turn out that Mathieu was involved with something dodgy she needed to know the facts so that she could protect the twins.

'So, they found a suitcase of money? It's not a crime to keep your money in cash,' Mathieu said, going to the fridge and pouring a glass of milk.

'Depends on where the money came from – and where it's going,' Jean-Claude replied.

'One of the mechanics in one of the smaller teams apparently had a lucky bet on the Spanish Grand Prix. He simply hadn't had time to bank his winnings,' Mathieu said.

'OK. We'll accept that story – for now. Just tell us why you ran from Zac's party when you heard about the police raid.'

Jean-Claude's face was impassive as he watched Mathieu, waiting for his reply.

'I didn't run anywhere.'

'Let's say you left Zac's party in a hurry then. We were there and saw you.'

'Coincidence. I was about to leave anyway. I'd arranged to meet someone at the Automobile Club and I was late.' Mathieu simply shrugged as Jean-Claude stared disbelievingly at him. 'Interrogation finished? I need a shower and then I promised

Pierre I'd meet him from school, take him down to the pits and Zac would introduce him to a couple of the drivers.'

'Non. It is not finished,' Jean-Claude shouted at his son. 'Not until you tell me the truth about what is going on.'

Mathieu shook his head as he looked at his father. 'I can't tell you anything, but if it's the family reputation you're worrying about, don't.'

'It's you I'm worried about, not the family name. Scandals can be lived through, but the repercussions can never be underestimated.'

Nanette gnawed on her bottom lip as she silently watched the two of them. Neither of them seemed prepared to back down, with Mathieu unprepared to tell his father anything, or even to apologise for the worry he was clearly causing.

'Oh, believe me,' Mathieu said grimly, 'the repercussions in this case will be catastrophic for certain people in Monaco.' With that cryptic remark, he disappeared back into his room to get ready to go out.

Jean-Claude looked at Nanette, worry lines etched on his face. 'At least he's finally admitted to being involved in something,' he sighed. 'Did you believe him – about the money and the Automobile Club?'

'The mechanic's gambling winnings? It's possible. It's always a mad dash to pack things up and move on to the next race. As for Mathieu having an appointment...' Nanette shook her head. 'I don't know.'

'I've got an appointment of my own tomorrow,' Jean-Claude said quietly, glancing at Mathieu's closed bedroom door. 'I'm meeting a private detective to have Mathieu followed for a couple of weeks. I need to know what is going on.'

'Oh, JC – please be careful. If Mathieu discovers what you are up to, he'll be furious.' Nanette reached out and touched his arm.

Jean-Claude took hold of her hand and held it tight. 'I have to risk it. I'm not convinced he's not in real trouble. I just want some reassurance that he's not getting out of his depth with the wrong crowd. I also want to be prepared in case of...' Jean-Claude left the sentence unfinished, as he shrugged his shoulders and shook his head in despair.

Nanette looked at Jean-Claude in silence, not knowing what to say or do that could possibly help. Like him, she too was starting to feel that whatever Mathieu was involved with was a serious matter. All she could do was to somehow let Jean-Claude know she was there for him and she squeezed his hand hard in sympathy.

20

'That stuff tastes vile,' Ralph said, as Vanessa handed him some diluted Sangre de Grado to swallow. 'Do I have to?'

Vanessa nodded. 'Yes, you do. I need to rub some of the ointment on to the last of your bruises, too.'

Nearly a week after his accident and, to Vanessa's relief, Ralph was a lot better. Whether it was the smelly concoctions that the head shaman had given her to administer on a regular basis or whether he hadn't been as badly injured as it was first feared, Vanessa didn't know. She was just relieved he was alive.

'I don't know what's in this stuff,' Vanessa said, as she rubbed the reddish sticky ointment into Ralph's body, 'but it's certainly worked.'

'Seems to take the pain away, too,' Ralph said. 'Can't believe that something so primitive has such great healing properties.'

'Don't forget the TLC I've given you will have made a difference as well,' Vanessa teased.

Ralph caught hold of her hand. 'I know,' he said seriously. 'I'm sorry things haven't worked out as we planned. Nick and Harry were in here earlier saying that as they can't do any filming near the dam, they've persuaded Luigi to take them to film the young pink dolphins. I know it's a long trek, but why don't you go too?'

Vanessa shook her head. 'I'd rather be here with you. Besides, I've promised Angela I'll help her and the other women this afternoon.'

'If you're sure. With a bit of luck, we might see some dolphins on our own trek northwards when we finally leave here anyway. Ah, here comes Matron and the consultant doing their rounds,' he added *sotto voce* as Angela and the head shaman appeared at the entrance to the hut.

After the medicine man had pronounced himself happy with Ralph's progress, he said something urgently to Angela before leaving.

'He says you can get up today,' Angela said. 'There will be a feast in the village soon to celebrate your recovery.'

Early that afternoon, Vanessa left Ralph writing in his journal and reviewing the plans for the next part of their adventure. Making her way towards the hut where the women were working at the far end of the village compound, she listened to the, now familiar, exotic chorus of birdsong from high in the surrounding trees.

She stopped to watch a crowd of yellow crowned Amazon parrots squawking and bickering over some spilt seeds whilst the village pig rooted in some undergrowth just metres away. The small monkey who'd taken her banana the very first day they'd arrived in the village ran towards her, chattering excitedly, weaving in and out of her legs as she approached the hut.

Angela was busy sorting through a haphazard pile of muddy boots and dangerous-looking machetes and smiled her welcome at Vanessa. Standing in the entrance of the hut, Vanessa watched as several of the village women began sorting through the remains of the Brazil nut harvest. She was surprised by how few nuts there were.

'We have to sell most of the harvest,' Angela explained. 'This year was not very productive. I hope next year will be better, but then the *aviamento* will have changed too.' She shrugged. 'We know already we will be paying a higher price before the next harvest.'

Vanessa looked at her questioningly. '*Aviamento*?'

'It's the system that provides these,' Angela said, gesticulating towards the boots and machetes. 'We get the stuff necessary to do the harvesting on the understanding that this go-between will buy the nuts from us at a low price. He will sell them on and take any profit we should have had.'

'That's terrible.' Vanessa looked at Angela, shocked. 'Can't you sell the nuts direct?'

'No. We need the equipment to gather them and don't have the money to buy it.'

'The government farm where you got the seedlings from – can't they help?'

Angela shook her head. 'In the past they talked about helping us to change the system, but nothing happened. Now this foreign guy's man from Rio has muscled in on the dam as well as the nuts. Apparently, he "helped" a village over to the west dam their river last year and wants to do the same for us.' She glanced up. 'Luigi thinks we'll end up being forced to leave. We don't need much money to survive here, but we do need land and food. Brazil nuts give us both our flour and oil.'

'Is there enough there for the villagers until the next harvest?' Vanessa asked.

Angela shrugged. 'Depends on how well they keep. It's difficult to stop them going mouldy in this humidity as we don't have proper storage.'

There was a short silence as both women looked around, each lost in their own thoughts. It was Vanessa who broke the silence.

'Do you want a hand cleaning those machetes then? Or is there something else you want me to do?'

'Be careful how you handle them,' was all Angela said, as she handed her a piece of rag.

As she carefully cleaned the lethal tools, Vanessa couldn't stop thinking about the problems the villagers faced. There had to be an answer.

Ambling back through the compound after the work was finished, deep in thought, Vanessa found Ralph waiting for her outside the large communal hut. Pleased to see him outside on his feet she gave him an absent smile.

'Don't overdo things,' she cautioned. 'You still have to take things easy for a bit.'

'I will, I promise. You don't look very happy,' Ralph said, taking her hand as they walked towards their own hut.

Vanessa sighed. 'I just feel so sad for this place. Everyone knows the rainforest is dying because of the way agriculture is taking over and clearing the land, but the people are dying too – if not physically, by being forced to move out of their villages, give up their traditional way of life. Even Angela is talking of leaving.'

Ralph was silent as a frustrated Vanessa aimlessly scuffed up some earth with her foot.

'I'm hoping my film will make people sit up and take notice. Do something about the problems,' he said quietly.

'I know you came to film the true story of the Amazonians,' she said, squeezing his hand. 'I just hope it isn't too late and it just serves as archive material for the way it all was.' There was a short pause before Vanessa deliberately changed the subject. 'How are you feeling? It's lovely to have you up and about again, but you mustn't overdo it. I must ask Angela to show me how to make that ointment before we leave and take some home with us. The twins are always falling over, getting bruises and...' She stopped in her tracks and pulled Ralph round to face her. 'That's it,' she said excitedly.

'What?' Ralph asked, confused.

'I've thought of something we *can* do to help the villagers and preserve their way of life – if they'll let us. We could help them form a cooperative to sell their natural remedies and their produce, including the Brazil nuts. With a cooperative, at least the villagers would be in control themselves and not some sleazy middleman.'

21

Sunday morning of Grand Prix weekend and Monaco was buzzing in anticipation of race day. Yesterday had seen thousands of spectators descend on the Principality to watch the qualifying rounds for this morning's all-important grid positions. As well as in the stands around the harbour, people had gathered early on the steep wooded slope between the port and the Grimaldi palace on the headland, ready to picnic and enjoy the day's racing against the clock.

Actual race day would be no different. Thousands of spectators were already in town and more were arriving by the minute. Like yesterday, the slope below the palace was filling with eager racegoers and people were finding their seats in the stands. Celebrities taking time off from the Cannes Film Festival were out in force, nonchalantly strolling along the pit lane, there to be seen as much as to watch the race, eager too, for photo opportunities with the drivers.

Mid-morning and Nanette stood for a few moments on the sitting-room balcony, watching the crowds of people making their way to their highly prized seats in the harbourside grandstands.

She'd been away for so long, she'd almost forgotten the frenzied excitement Monaco generated on race weekend, both on the track and off, as the jet set indulged themselves with a combination of high-octane living and fast cars. The sound of highly tuned engines being revved was beginning to fill the air – a sign of the frenzied activity that Nanette knew would already be taking place out of sight in the garages at the back of the pit lane.

Looking out across the starting grid, Nanette could see cameramen and journalists milling around with the crowds in the pit lane, eager to get an exclusive early interview with anyone willing to express an opinion on the way they thought the day's race would go. Who was tipped to win today on the dangerous circuit that was a favourite with the drivers? The one they all wanted the honour of winning.

Down in the harbour, yacht crews on the luxury boats, moored so close to each other their fenders were barely able to keep the gleaming hulls apart, were busy serving strong coffee and croissants to guests who had partied the night away on board.

Nanette, glancing towards *Pole Position*, knew that Zac would have been up early to prepare for the day and wasn't surprised to see just the crew moving around the boat's foredeck. It had always been one of Zac's unwritten rules – no guests on board the Saturday night before the Grand Prix – even if, like last night, he would have been celebrating pole position on the grid. Maybe the F1 experts and pundits were right and this year would see Zac crowned world champion. She knew, though, that his thoughts this morning would be focused on today's race. He'd certainly have the crowd behind him this afternoon, if the cheers that had greeted his pole position yesterday were anything to go by.

She turned as she heard the apartment door open and close. Mathieu.

'That's Olivia sorted for the day,' he said, joining Nanette on the balcony. 'A day at the Aqua Splash Park with friends is much more to her liking than watching a boring car race.'

He leant on the balcony rail and surveyed the crowds and the activity down below him.

'Make you nostalgic for your old life?' he asked, glancing at her. 'All those VIP parties and events you and Zac used to go to.'

'No, not really,' Nanette answered. 'It seems a lifetime away, so much has happened. It was fun at the time, but things change – I've changed.'

'Things certainly do change,' Mathieu said, so quietly that Nanette barely heard him. He was silent for a few moments, simply staring down into the pits area.

'Mathieu, is everything all right?' Nanette eventually dared to asked. 'Is there anything I can help with?' She realised the answer was likely to be no, but having spent the last couple of days since he and Jean-Claude had rowed worrying about what was going on, she wanted Mathieu to know that if she could help, she would.

'Thanks,' Mathieu said. 'Things are a bit difficult at the moment, but everything is under control.' He smiled at her before changing the subject, effectively stopping her from asking any questions. 'Should be a good race today. Zac did well, qualifying for pole yesterday – let's hope he can stay out in front for the race. Monaco is one circuit he hasn't won.'

'A win today would be put him well in the lead for the championship too,' Nanette said. 'We all know he's desperate to be world champion,' she added drily. She hesitated before continuing. 'Mathieu, I have to ask, are you sure it's okay with Boris that I stay today?'

Mathieu looked at her, surprised. 'Why on earth wouldn't it be?'

Nanette shrugged. 'It's just that I thought Boris wanted the place for him and his cronies. The plan originally was for Olivia and me to go to Jean-Claude's, if you remember.'

'It's fine for both you and Pierre to be here. Papa is coming down too,' Mathieu said. 'So relax and enjoy the day.'

Nanette thought it best not to tell Mathieu that it was Jean-Claude who had decided to change their plans, wanting to keep an eye on his son and try to suss out how involved he was with Boris.

The apartment bell rang at that moment and Mathieu turned to greet the first of his guests.

Boris acknowledged Nanette with a 'Bonjour, mademoiselle' and a tilt of his head before roughly ruffling Pierre's hair – an action that had the boy dodging out of his way. Within minutes, the rest of Boris's party had arrived and Nanette and Pierre were ignored for the next hour.

To Nanette's relief, Jean-Claude arrived just as lunch was being served and together they sat at one of the small round tables that Florence had set up at the far end of the long balcony. Pierre, more interested in watching the scenes below than eating his lunch, had the binoculars trained on the pit lane.

The atmosphere on the balcony appeared to be one of genial conviviality. Florence was handing food around and Mathieu was busy organising drinks for everyone.

'Mathieu seems in good spirits today,' Jean-Claude said, glancing across at him.

'Yes,' Nanette agreed. 'Although something is definitely worrying him, he's very stressed.'

Jean-Claude raised his eyebrows questioningly.

'I don't know what, JC, but his repeated "everything is under control" earlier this morning seemed to be a mantra he was repeating to reassure himself as much as anything,' Nanette said quietly, with an anxious glance at Pierre.

'Any news from Vanessa and Ralph?' Jean-Claude asked, taking the hint and deftly changing the subject.

'We had a letter from Mum yesterday,' Pierre said, without removing his gaze from the cars lining up on the grid. 'She'd given it to someone in the first eco-camp they stayed in to post when they went back to civilisation. It's taken *ages* to get here. Wish we could email her, but the village they are in doesn't have electricity and the solar charger for the satellite phone doesn't work that well in the jungle.'

'Did she say how things were going?' Jean-Claude asked.

'Just that she was seeing some amazing things and would write again and phone when possible.'

The cars took off for their formation lap at that moment and Pierre pulled the official ear-protectors Zac had given him over his ears. By the time the warm-up lap was completed and the cars were back on the grid ready for the off, Boris and his guests were crowded on the balcony, waiting for the start. Nanette, a FI fan long before she'd worked for Zac, felt the first stirrings of a rush of excitement that she'd always experienced at the beginning of a race. Not watching any races since her accident, she'd forgotten how exciting it always was watching the cars speed away.

Everyone gazed as, one by one, the red starting lights went out and then the ear-shattering sound of high-performance cars making for the Sainte-Dévote bend at high speed before disappearing up the hill towards the Casino blasted through the apartment.

A loud cheer went up as Zac, making a perfect start, kept his lead, and within seconds had disappeared from view, leaving the cars behind him to juggle for better positions as best they could.

Now everyone's attention switched to the large TV screen set up by the Sainte-Dévote corner. As Nanette watched the screen, Zac flew past the Hôtel de Paris on his way towards the Horse-shoe Bend for the first time.

Nanette hoped that the race would be trouble-free. Monaco Grand Prix might be a firm favourite with the drivers because of the challenges the street circuit gave them, but Nanette knew that simple fact alone made it one of the most dangerous racetracks in the world. There was simply nowhere to go if something went wrong – a puncture or driver error here could have serious conse-quences and these modern cars were so fast.

Racing out of the tunnel and coming back down towards the harbour, Zac was continuing to pull away from the cars behind him and had already put five seconds between himself and the rest of the field when he roared past the apartment again starting his second lap.

Boris and two of his guests moved back into the sitting room soon after the start and began talking quietly amongst them-selves, occasionally glancing at the race on the small television on the sideboard. Nanette, fetching a bottle of water from the kitchen, strained to hear what they were saying as she walked past but caught only the words 'money' and 'yacht'.

Zac stayed comfortably ahead for the race, his team providing him with two perfect pit stops to keep him in the lead. Nanette, watching him climb the hill past the Hérmitage Hotel on his sixty-ninth lap, knew that with just nine laps left, he was finally on target to win the Monaco Grand Prix with a nineteen-second lead over the car in second place.

It was lap seventy-two when disaster struck. The driver in fourth position misjudged La Rascasse corner and drove into the wall. The uninjured, but frustrated driver, climbed out of his car, shaking his head sadly at the crowds. Yellow flags were waved and the safety car was soon out on the track and the drivers were forced to slow down to stay behind it. Under racing rules, all cars were forced to keep to their current positions – overtaking was not allowed whilst the safety car was on the race track.

By the time the track was cleared of the crashed car and its debris, there were only two laps of the race left, all the remaining cars had bunched up behind each other - and Zac's unbeatable nineteen-second lead had disappeared. As the safety car left the track, everyone watching held their breath, willing Zac to stay out of danger – and out front, knowing that he would now have a real fight on his hands to win the race that before the crash he'd led from the start.

As he negotiated the chicane before the swimming pool complex for the final time, the second and third cars were just seconds behind him, but it was Zac who rounded La Rascasse and roared across the finishing line first to take the chequered flag.

Nanette joined in the spontaneous cheering that erupted along the balcony. Despite all that had happened between them, she couldn't help but be pleased for him.

'Can I go down and watch the presentation?' Pierre asked, excitedly.

'We'll come with you,' Jean-Claude answered, knowing Nanette wouldn't let Pierre go alone and Mathieu wouldn't leave his guests.

Downstairs, the mechanics and other team members were crowding around the barriers, watching Prince Albert, Princess Charlene and the rest of the royal family who had appeared, ready to present the trophies.

Nanette, Jean-Claude and Pierre managed to squeeze into a small space alongside the presentation stand. Standing there watching the ceremony as a jubilant Zac received his trophy from Prince Albert and held it aloft, Nanette felt a certain sense of déjà vu washing over her. How many times had she watched similar ceremonies and then been at Zac's side as he'd partied through the night? Now, as the champagne was shaken and sprayed everywhere, she joined in with the general noise of the victory celebrations, but her feelings were somehow detached from what was going on around her.

Running across the track to give the champagne bottle to his mechanics, Zac waved to Pierre and saw Nanette and Jean-Claude standing alongside him. Immediately, he changed course and came over to them.

'Congratulations, Zac,' Nanette and Jean-Claude said together.

'Thanks.' Zac looked at Nanette. 'Dinner, tomorrow night. I'll pick you up at eight o'clock. No excuses. I need to talk to you urgently.'

And he was gone back to his mechanics, leaving Nanette no time to refuse – and angry with his assumption that, of course, she would accept his invitation. An invitation that had sounded more like an order she had to comply with.

'That man is bloody impossible,' she muttered under her breath.

'I agree,' Jean-Claude said. 'I tell him no for you if you like? And you come to the villa with me tomorrow evening? In case he...' Jean-Claude left the rest of the sentence hanging in the air as he looked at Nanette seriously.

'Thank you, JC. Maybe,' Nanette answered gratefully. 'I need to think about how to handle this.'

22

A loud bang on the road outside the apartment block woke Nanette with a jolt early on Monday morning. Startled, it took her a second or two to realise it was the workmen starting the long process of dismantling barriers and stands and returning Monaco to its normal state for the next ten months.

Lying in bed for a few more moments, Nanette thought about Zac and his dinner 'invitation'. She had talked more about it to Jean-Claude last night before he returned to his villa.

'I still have questions I'd like Zac to answer,' she'd said. 'Maybe this is my opportunity. Perhaps he's decided to talk to me – answer any questions I have about...' her voice had trailed away. 'Maybe he just wants to take me out to dinner and knew I wouldn't willingly consider it, so he didn't give me a chance to refuse. Although I can always phone him and tell him no way.'

'I think he is a man who does not like the word no, and in my experience, Zac Ewart never does anything without a reason,' Jean-Claude had said quietly.

'True,' Nanette had agreed thoughtfully. 'But I think I'll go and try to take advantage of the situation. Once, whatever it is that Zac wants to talk to me about urgently is over, I'll ask him a few questions of my own. Insist he gives me the answers I need.'

Jean-Claude had sighed as he'd taken her hands in his. 'I don't trust him, Nanette. Make sure you take your mobile. If you need me, call me. Promise?'

Nanette had smiled at him. 'I promise.' It was a long time since a man had worried about her, wanted to protect her. But, in all honesty, it was just dinner in a Monaco restaurant with an ex-fiancé and she could always walk away.

For several seconds, Jean-Claude had held her gaze before letting go of her hands and saying goodnight.

All day, as she went about her normal routine, Nanette thought about Zac and the evening ahead of her. She knew that Zac, master of the unexpected daredevil manoeuvre on the race track, was a lot less spontaneous in real life. When she'd first worked for him, she'd realised he was a man ruled by his head rather than his heart. Later, when they were romantically involved, she'd got to know the softer side of Zac that very few people ever saw. But even then, when they were really close, she accepted that he wasn't the easiest or the most romantic man on the planet. Oh, there were presents on her birthday and at Christmas, some expensive, some not, but unexpected gifts of flowers or chocolates for no reason or just because he wanted to treat her were rare.

By 8 p.m., when Zac rang the apartment bell, she'd almost convinced herself that their shared past was the reason, the only reason, Zac wanted to take her out for dinner. There was no ulterior motive. A nostalgic talk about places they'd been, things they'd done together. Clearly, he was hoping that he could persuade Nanette to forget the past and be friends again. Nothing more sinister than that. Convincing him that he was wasting his time, as being civil to him in public was all she was prepared to agree to, was going to be difficult.

'Where are we going?' Nanette asked, as the lift took them down to the ground floor.

'We're eating on board *Pole Position*,' Zac said. 'I've got a brilliant chef this year and he's promised me a meal to remember.'

Nanette, having forgotten Zac's tendency to like privacy when he didn't have to show a public persona for the sponsors, realised she should have anticipated that dinner would be an on-board meal.

As Zac ushered her up the gangway and she stepped onto the deck, the yacht's crew sprang into well-rehearsed action, ensuring everything went smoothly.

Sipping her champagne and nibbling canapés, Nanette looked around the main saloon as Zac pressed a couple of hidden buttons on the wall. Simultaneously, the side windows opened, letting in a gentle sea breeze, while romantic piano music filtered in through the sound system.

Nanette glanced at Zac. What exactly was he playing at tonight? Candles in elaborate candelabra casting shadows, seductive music playing in the background, the moon shining on the Mediterranean. It was a perfect setting for a romantic evening.

'Dance with me for old times' sake,' Zac said quietly.

Before she realised what was happening, Zac had taken her glass away and Nanette was in his arms and the two of them were swaying to 'Lady in Red' – a favourite of theirs from the past.

As Zac held her close, it was as if the last three years apart had never happened. He appeared to have conveniently forgotten the trauma, the hurt, the broken body, as well as the broken heart he'd left her with. Nanette, though, hadn't and even if old emotions that she'd thought were dead and buried forever were rising to the surface, she had no intention of giving in to them.

When Zac began placing gentle kisses on her head, a tremor of anger flooded through her body. She had to put a stop to this.

'No, Zac, stop it now, otherwise I'm leaving.' Nanette pushed him away.

Zac dropped his arms and shrugged. 'I just thought maybe you'd like to forget the past – put it behind us.'

Nanette glared at him. 'Something you've clearly already done. Whereas I...' she paused. 'I'll never forget the worst three years of my life.'

Zac closed his eyes briefly and shook his head at her. 'Let's try and enjoy this evening, at least,' he said. 'We're having lobster. I bought it in especially for you. I know it always used to be your favourite.'

Throughout the meal, Zac, clearly still on a high from his win the day before, seemed determined to wine and dine himself back into Nanette's favour. As he helped her to a generous portion of her favourite dish, Nanette's thoughts drifted back three years, to a time when evenings like this with Zac had been normal. Almost commonplace, but so much had changed since then.

When she tried to ask him something about the accident, he placed a gentle finger against her lips.

'Not this evening, Nanette. Tonight is a new beginning.' He clicked his wine glass against hers. 'Santé.'

Nanette looked at him, exasperated. 'You said you wanted to talk to me urgently and I still have questions I want answered.'

'Are you doing anything special for your birthday this year?' Zac asked, ignoring her words.

Nanette shook her head. 'No, nothing planned.' She didn't add she hadn't celebrated her birthday properly in the years since the accident. The two anniversaries were too close together.

'I remember we always used to celebrate it early as I was

racing. This year I'll be in Canada, so I'll miss it again. You'll have to think of this as an early birthday treat,' Zac said.

'So long as you don't plan to present me with a car later,' Nanette said shortly. 'Because...' She stopped in mid-sentence and stared at him.

'Because what?' Zac glanced at her curiously.

'Because I'd have to decline of course,' Nanette said. She placed her hand over her wine glass as Zac went to top it up. 'No more wine for me, thanks.' Carefully, she placed her napkin on the table. 'I've had a lovely meal, but if you're not going to talk to me or answer any of my questions, then it's time for me to go,' and Nanette stood up determinedly, throwing Zac a defiant look, daring him to stop her.

Zac regarded her for several seconds, a strange look in his eyes, before he too stood up. 'I did invite you here tonight for a reason, other than for the simple pleasure of your company. I have a proposal for you. One to which I hope very much you will say yes.'

'Whatever your "proposal" is, I'm not interested.' Nanette's voice was cold. She knew that no matter what the proposal was, it wouldn't be the explanation or the apology she'd been hoping for. It was a big mistake on her part to have even come this evening in the hope of extracting either from Zac.

Zac followed Nanette as she began to make her way out on deck. More upset by the whole fiasco than she cared to admit, the only thing she wanted to do was get off the yacht.

'Come back and have another glass of champagne,' Zac had urged. 'I really do want to talk to you.'

'Then you should have spoken at the beginning of the evening, not wasted your time trying to turn the clock back.'

She'd thought she was over Zac and yet here he was, proving he still had the power to upset her. She was about to step on the gangway when he called her name. Swallowing hard, she turned her head to look at him, her hand gripping the gangway rope tightly for support as Zac spoke. She was unbelievably angry with him over his actions – both past and present. Holding her breath, Nanette waited for him to speak and was determined not to let him see how shaken she was.

'I want you to come back and work for me, Nanette. We were a good team in the past.'

His unexpected request fell into a lengthening silence as Nanette stared at him. All this wining and dining and faux romancing was because he wanted her to work for him?

'What?' She looked at him in disbelief. 'That's what you wanted to talk about urgently?'

'I'm starting a new holiday business and I need someone I can trust totally,' Zac said.

'I've got a job – looking after the twins. When Vanessa and Ralph return from their Amazon adventure, I shall go back to the UK with them.'

'Come on, Nanette – you're capable of much more than playing nursemaid to a couple of kids. You were the best PA I ever had.'

'If I was that good, why no word, no job offer from you before – when I needed all the help I could get?' Nanette asked angrily.

'I cut back on my business activities when I realised you weren't going to be around for a long time,' Zac said, shrugging. 'I was too busy racing and simply didn't have the time to find a new PA.'

Nanette nodded her head slowly as she looked at him. She wasn't going to let him see how much those words hurt her. She'd been his fiancée as well as his PA but that didn't appear to count. She swallowed hard before asking.

'Now you've got time for a new venture?'

'This time I'm trying to invest in a business that I can work at when I give up racing.'

'You're giving up racing?' Nanette asked, shocked. That wasn't something she'd anticipated hearing.

'Not immediately, but I don't fancy being the oldest driver on the circuit fighting for a drive. Realistically, I suppose I've got another two or three years, but if I don't win the championship this year' – Zac grimaced – 'who knows? I might just walk away from it all at the end of the season.' He paused and smiled at her. 'I also thought it would be an ideal opportunity to try to make up for the hurt that I've caused you in the past. We could both go places with this new business.'

Zac looked at her expectantly, waiting for her response.

Nanette sighed. Zac could sound so plausible when he turned on the charm. She'd seen it work in the past, when he'd wanted his own way over something. Not this time, not with her.

'Except that I'm not looking for another job – I'm happy caring for the twins – working for you again is not something I've ever thought about.'

'Will you think about it now?' Zac persisted. 'The twins are growing up, they won't need you forever.'

'You don't need me either, Zac.' The words, 'And I definitely don't need you in my life again', remained unspoken in her head.

'Oh, but, Nanette, I do,' Zac said, again reaching out to take hold of her hands and squeeze them tightly. 'I leave for Canada tomorrow and then I'm back here afterwards, for maybe a day, before the French Grand Prix. Please think about it while I'm away. We'll have supper when I return and you can give me your decision then.'

'I don't need time to think, Zac. I don't—'

'Shh.' Zac effectively stopped her by placing his fingers firmly against her lips. 'Next week.'

'Goodnight, Zac.' Once again, she turned away from him, stepping back on to the gangway to leave.

'Just give me two minutes while I fetch something from the saloon.'

Feeling the need to put some firm ground underneath her feet, Nanette jumped off the yacht's gangway and stood waiting on the quay. Standing there, watching the evening activity of the harbour, Nanette felt curiously light-headed. The events of the past couple of hours had been totally unexpected, but she was pleased she'd kept her cool and been able to be so resolute in facing up to Zac, despite her hammering heart. A heart that was hammering, she realised, from sheer nerves and anger, not because she still felt anything for him.

'Here you are – some bedtime reading,' Zac said, reappearing with a large envelope marked 'Vacances au Soleil' and bulging with papers.

'What part of no do you not understand?' Nanette demanded. 'Watch my lips. I. Am. Not. Interested.'

'At least have a look at it while I'm away,' Zac said when Nanette tried to refuse to take it. 'I'd like your opinion on it anyway. You were always pretty savvy over my previous investments. You never know, reading about it might change your mind.'

Realising the only way she was going to get him off the subject was to take the envelope, Nanette reluctantly accepted it, inwardly vowing to hand it back to him next week, unopened and unread. As she took it, Zac leaned in and kissed her cheek before turning and walking away, leaving Nanette furious at his presumption.

It was too late to phone her sister when she got back to the apartment, but early the next morning, after a restless night, Nanette picked up her mobile to talk to Patsy from the comfort of her bed. Patsy, being a farmer's wife, was always up early to have breakfast with Bryan before he started his day of chores on the farm.

After the usual, 'how are you keeping' questions had been exchanged, Patsy said, 'Okay. What's up to warrant this early chat?'

Nanette took a deep breath and told her about her evening with Zac. 'Can you believe Zac wants me to work for him again?'

'I hope you told him where he could put his job?'

'Not in so many words, but I did say no. The only problem is he wasn't listening.' Nanette sighed. 'I think I may have to ask JC to help me get the message across.'

'I'll do it,' Patsy said. 'Give me his phone number. There is nothing I'd enjoy more than telling Zac Ewart where to go.'

Nanette laughed at the eager tone to her sister's voice. 'Thanks, but I think he'll listen to JC telling him to leave me alone more than you.'

'Well, I've got your back and I'm on standby,' Patsy said.

They chatted for a few more moments before Nanette ended the call and got up. Time to shower and get organised for the day.

As she dressed, her gaze fell on the envelope on the dressing table where she'd thrown it last night, intending to ignore it until she handed it back to Zac. She had to admit to being a tiny bit curious about the business Zac planned to build his life around after he retired from racing. There was no way she intended to become involved with him again, but remembering Zac saying he'd like her opinion on it anyway, Nanette reached out a hand and picked up the envelope. Carefully, she opened the envelope and withdrew all the papers and started to read.

23

'How did your dinner date with Zac go?' Mathieu asked. 'Are you two finally friends again now?'

Mathieu posed his questions as he, Nanette and the twins walked around the headland towards the open-air cinema. The twins, excited at the prospect of seeing the latest *Star Wars* blockbuster, had rushed ahead.

'Not really,' Nanette replied slowly. 'Nothing's really changed. Zac certainly hasn't.' Inwardly, she was still in turmoil from the evening she'd spent with him despite being determined that Zac had no place in her life any more. 'Besides, it wasn't a date on my part.' Nanette glanced at Mathieu. 'Did you know Zac is starting up a new business for when he retires from racing?'

'I'd heard a rumour. Some sort of holiday business.'

'Can you believe he's asked me to help him run it,' Nanette said, exasperated.

'How does Zac want you to be involved? Behind the scenes, organising the business, I presume?'

Nanette nodded. 'He gave me an envelope last night with details of what he has planned. Initially, the office would be on board *Pole Position*. According to the job description he'd thought-fully included, he would also want me to travel to inspect the places and make sure they're exclusive enough. Starting next month.'

'Could be fun,' Mathieu said. 'Does it have a name, this business?'

Nanette hesitated. Mathieu might be Zac's best friend, but would he want her talking about his business? He hadn't told her not to, and Mathieu seemed to know a bit about it anyway. Years ago, discretion and loyalty had been key words in her life with Zac Ewart. Not any more. She didn't feel she owed him a single ounce of loyalty. Not since he'd so cruelly walked away from her after the accident.

'Vacances au Soleil, an exclusive holiday club, which will, for a large amount of money, naturally, arrange dream holidays for their members, anywhere in the world. Dubai, St Tropez, Rio, Sun City and, of course, Monaco.' And Nanette told Mathieu what she'd learned from the papers in the envelope. 'I admit it's the kind of job I'd be interested in if I was looking for something different – and if it were for anyone else other than Zac. He's conveniently brushed aside the events of the last three years – and the fact that I look after the twins.' She paused. 'Besides, it's only a few weeks before the long summer break begins. Even if I was tempted, which I'm not and I've told him that, there is no way I could possibly let Vanessa and Ralph – or you – down in that way.'

Mathieu was silent for a moment before glancing at her.

'Do you have any plans for the future? The twins are growing up – they won't need a nanny for much longer. Maybe Zac would keep the job open for you? Or you could start with just an hour or so a day while the twins are at school.'

Nanette gazed at him, exasperated. 'Mathieu, what part of

this don't you understand? I don't ever want to work for Zac Ewart again. I don't belong in his world any more. I don't think I even like him any more. I certainly don't trust him.' She breathed a sigh of relief as they reached the entrance to the open-air cinema. Hopefully, Mathieu would have to let the conversation end now.

Mathieu paid for their tickets and sent the twins off to buy a snack from the refreshment cabin before turning to her, a serious look on his face.

'I can't tell you the details, but this "thing" I'm involved with is getting more complicated,' he said quietly. 'I could do with some inside help.' He glanced at her. 'You working for Zac, having access to papers and his associates, might be very useful to me.'

'Are you saying Zac too, is involved in this "thing"?' Nanette demanded, shocked.

Mathieu didn't answer directly, simply giving a slight shrug of his shoulders.

'Is Jean-Claude right, too, in thinking you've become embroiled in something illicit?' Nanette asked worriedly.

Mathieu sighed. 'It's not as simple as being illicit or illegal, and now, to complicate matters even more, I think I'm being followed.'

The twins arrived back at that moment, clutching crisps and popcorn and clamouring to go and find their seats.

'Come on, Dad, the film starts in five minutes,' Pierre said.

Mathieu gave Nanette an apologetic glance. 'We'll talk later – let's go watch space adventures!'

Sitting under a cloudless sky as dusk fell over the Mediter-ranean, Nanette tried to concentrate on the film, but not even the special effects of the imagined futuristic world she was watching could take her mind off her own problems and the problems of the man sitting next to her. Mathieu was clearly involved in something dodgy and Jean-Claude was right to be worried, but where did Zac fit into things?

She smothered a sigh. No way did she want to get embroiled in something that sounded seedy, to say the least, to her, plus there was Mathieu's reluctance to label what he was up to as illegal or illicit.

As for his 'I think I'm being followed' statement – how could she possibly tell him that was the least of his troubles as the person behind that particular problem was his own father?

24

In the hours and days following Vanessa's idea of forming a cooperative to sell the village produce, she and Ralph endlessly
discussed the kind of things they could do – things that they
thought would make a real difference.

List after list littered the floor of their hut. Ralph wrote down
the names of possible sponsors – people who owed him favours
and would be happy to participate. Vanessa wrote down every
product she could think of that could be sold and then both she
and Ralph tried to look at the logistics of the whole thing. From
producing, to harvesting, to storing, to marketing and – a major
stumbling block in itself – getting the stuff out of the jungle.

'We need to organise a meeting with the villagers,' Ralph said,
'before we get too carried away. Find out exactly how they would
like things to work – if in fact they think it's a good idea.'

'You do think they'll go for it, don't you?' Vanessa asked
anxiously. 'It's for their future, not ours.'

Ralph was silent for a moment. 'I'm not sure. Remember the
warning I was given before my accident not to interfere? Not all
the villagers like us – me – being here. This Rio guy seems to have

the villagers agreeing to his boss's every move. You need to convince the head shaman that the villagers will benefit. It's all a matter of trust,' he added. 'They like you so hopefully they will trust you enough to work with you.' He glanced at her. 'You know what they call you, don't you?'

Vanessa shook her head.

'*Pacchumama* – roughly translated it means Earth Mother. They love the way you are with the animals and the children.'

Vanessa smiled. 'Do they really? Maybe at the celebration tonight we can put our ideas to them and see if they've got any of their own,' Vanessa said. 'You're right – we do need to get them involved from the very beginning – if only to prove to them we don't have any ulterior motives.'

'You do realise just how much it is going to take to get this project off the ground and to keep it running?' Ralph said. 'I'm not just talking about money here – it's going to take a huge amount of time.'

'I know, but we've got to try,' Vanessa replied.

'I'll give you all the help I can, but I'm already committed to other projects when we get back. I won't be around full-time – most of the organising will fall on you.'

'Organising is something I'm good at. And Nanette will want to get involved too, I know. It's the kind of work she always used to excel at,' Vanessa said. 'Right, I'll talk to Angela and the others, and tonight at the celebration party for your recovery we can talk to the villagers about our idea.'

Angela was openly enthusiastic, but some of the other women were hostile to the idea and Vanessa found herself having to explain time and time again how a cooperative would work to their advantage. And, no, she repeatedly assured them, she wouldn't personally benefit from it.

By the time she was sitting on the floor next to the head

shaman that evening and outlining the way the villagers could protect their own futures, it was clear that opinion was divided.

'We have an agreement with the outsider,' said the head shaman, resplendent in his native dress and war paint. 'He is already helping with the gold mine and next year he has promised to help with equipment for the nut harvest. His man is due here soon to pay us for the gold we have mined, so we shall have money for necessary supplies.'

At his words, Vanessa felt her heart sink. 'You don't think our idea will work and be better for the village?'

He held his hand up to stop her. 'We are people of our word. So, I thank you for your concerns, but we are already committed.'

Beside her, Angela said something quickly and the shaman answered with an emphatic shake of his head before he stood up and moved away.

'Is that it, then?' Vanessa said, turning to Angela.

Angela nodded. 'The men are sure this man will do more to help us – besides, they are also aware of the dangers of upsetting him,' she added quietly.

'What about the women? They could do something themselves,' Vanessa said, trying to hide her disappointment.

Angela shook her head. 'The men would forbid it.'

Later that night when Vanessa and Ralph had returned to their hut and were preparing to climb into their hammocks, she said sadly, 'I was really looking forward to organising the co-op. I even had a name ready, Fruits of the Forest.'

'Maybe it's for the best,' Ralph said, trying to comfort her. 'We'll be home in a few weeks. You'll have to put your organisational skills to work on marketing my film. Bring the plight of the jungle and its inhabitants to the world's attention that way.'

'Of course, I'll do everything possible to publicise your film,' Vanessa said, 'but I wanted to do something, try to make a difference, myself. I still can't believe that they've turned the idea of a cooperative down because of some sleazy guy the head shaman has given his word to.' She paused. 'This outsider, as the shaman calls him, clearly thinks he's on to something sending his henchman from Rio all this way into the forest.'

'I wonder who he is?' Ralph added thoughtfully.

Vanessa shrugged and shook her head. 'We'll never know. I just wish the villagers could see that the cooperative would have given them so much more control over their own future – and that of the jungle,' she added.

* * *

For the next couple of weeks, Ralph concentrated on recovering from his accident and getting as much filming done as possible, before they began their long trek back to civilisation and then home. With their day of departure still some time away, Vanessa found herself thinking increasingly about the twins.

Keeping in touch had proved as impossible as she'd known it would from so deep in the jungle and she was looking forward to reaching Manaus on the Amazon in a week or two and being able to telephone them. She'd missed them so much and couldn't wait to hug them both tight to her.

She didn't mention the cooperative idea to anyone again and was surprised when late one afternoon, Angela brought the subject up as they prepared bowls of vegetables for the evening meal together.

'Do you really believe your idea of a cooperative would work for the village?'

'Of course,' Vanessa said. 'It would take a few months to organise and find outlets, but it's the kind of thing I'm good at doing. The village would be totally self-supporting – nobody could muscle their way in and take the profits like they do now.'

Angela placed a bowl of vine leaves on the table before looking at Vanessa. 'The villagers are angry with you and Ralph. The man from Rio has failed to come to buy our gold.' Angela paused. 'Some of the men think you have put the evil eye on it.'

Vanessa looked at her, horrified.

'The shaman is insisting that you and Ralph attend a village council meeting this evening. He wants to hear what you have to say before deciding what to do about you.'

25

Sunday morning and Jean-Claude and Nanette were on their way to Antibes for lunch, when Jean-Claude took an unexpected detour before pulling to a stop in a deserted supermarket car park.

'You need to drive again,' he said gently. 'And this place is perfect for a trial run.'

Nanette looked at him. She'd been looking forward to today from the moment Mathieu had said he was taking the twins out for the day.

'I'll be away for most of next week,' he'd said. 'So I thought I'd treat them to a day's sailing in Italy.'

Jean-Claude, who was in the apartment at the time, had immediately asked Nanette to spend the day with him, an invitation she was happy to accept.

Apart from the fact that she loved spending time with him, it would also be an ideal opportunity for them to talk. For Nanette to tell him how Mathieu had suggested she took up Zac's job offer. But now, as Jean-Claude got out of the car and walked round to open the passenger car door for her, she froze.

She shook her head. 'I can't do it.'

'Like a horse – you fall off, you get back on,' Jean-Claude insisted. 'Otherwise the fear takes over. That, I think, is what happened with you. Come on, just try for me.' He held out his hand to help her out of the car. Nanette could feel her legs trembling as she stood and walked round to the driver's side of the car.

Nanette had to force herself to get into the driver's seat of the immaculate Jaguar F-type sports car and fastened the seat belt with trembling fingers.

Jean-Claude pointed to the push button start and waited patiently as Nanette steadied her nerves.

Nanette took a deep breath, gripped the steering wheel tightly, and gently pressed the accelerator pedal. As the car began to move forward, she found herself hardly daring to breathe.

'Relax,' Jean-Claude said. 'Nothing is going to happen. Just drive around. Get the feel of driving again.'

Nanette steered the car around the large car park usually filled to bursting with people and cars, but with the supermarket closed on Sundays, it was just a wide, open space.

By the time she'd driven round half a dozen or so times, changing gear, accelerating, braking, she had relaxed and, to her surprise, the enjoyment she'd always taken in driving had returned. She pulled into a parking space and pulled on the handbrake before glancing across at Jean-Claude.

'I enjoyed that, thank you, JC. It feels good to be behind the wheel again. Thank you for insisting it was time.'

'Fancy driving along the coast road then?' Jean-Claude asked quietly.

Nanette hesitated for all of two seconds before saying. 'Why not?'

'If you turn left out of the exit and then take the next right, we'll be back on the Bord de Mer.'

It was a mere couple of hundred metres to the busy main road and Nanette was surprised at how quickly she found herself back in the mindset of automatically judging the speed of the traffic. Quickly slipping into a gap between cars, she found herself enjoying driving along the coast road for the first time in three years.

Five minutes later, a noisy scooter, swerving in and out of the traffic, unnerved her and when the driver clipped her passenger-door wing mirror as he passed too close on the wrong side of the road, she abruptly pulled over and parked in the first roadside space she could find.

She was shaking as she pulled on the handbrake and stopped the engine before turning to Jean-Claude. 'It's the third anniversary of my accident next week. That scooter just reminded me how quickly accidents can happen and change things.'

'That wasn't your fault,' he said. 'You must remember how irresponsible the young scooter drivers down here are – they cut everyone up from all angles.'

'I'd forgotten. I was really enjoying myself until then, so thanks, JC, for insisting I faced the fear,' Nanette said, undoing her seat belt and opening her door. 'I've had enough for today though. You drive the rest of the way please.'

Twenty minutes later, the car was parked and they were strolling along the ancient Antibes ramparts on their way to one of Jean-Claude's favourite restaurants. As they settled themselves at a window table, Nanette gave him a happy smile.

The restaurant, popular with both locals and tourists, was busy, but the staff were attentive and within minutes Nanette and Jean-Claude had aperitifs and the bread basket in front of them and the waiter had disappeared to fetch the glass of wine Jean-Claude had chosen to accompany Nanette's main course, while he stuck with water.

'I need to talk to you about something,' Nanette said quietly. 'You know I told you about Zac wanting me to work for him and his new business venture?'

Jean-Claude nodded.

'When I told Patsy, she virtually had a heart attack at the thought of me even considering working for Zac. Wanted me to let her tell him what he could do with his job,' Nanette said, hesitating. 'Mathieu, on the other hand, would like me to take the job. He thinks I could help him,' she added quietly.

Jean-Claude was instantly alert. 'How?'

Natalie shrugged. 'I'm not sure. He simply said me working for Zac, having access to papers and the names of his associates, might be very useful for him.' She took a sip of her wine. 'I didn't say yes, but I didn't say no either. I know you're worried about Mathieu, would it help you too, if I did some work for Zac, because it does look as if they are both embroiled in something?'

Jean-Claude reached out for her hand and held it tightly. 'Nanette, listen to me. I can't forbid you to work for Zac, but please don't. I don't care what Mathieu says about it helping him – he is so wrong to try to involve you.' He looked at her intently. 'Promise me you won't even think about it. I don't want you in any sort of danger. I'd never forgive myself.'

Shocked by the intensity of his words, and the look in his eyes, Nanette could only say quietly, 'I promise, JC.' She paused. 'Mathieu knows he's being followed, you know,' Nanette said. 'He doesn't know who's arranged it, though,' she added quickly.

The waiter appeared with their food at that moment and Jean-Claude released her hand.

'Has the private detective discovered anything?' Nanette asked once they were alone again and eating their meals.

'Non. Nothing new anyway. Mathieu has had dinner several times at the Automobile Club. Boris was there on one occasion.

Zac on another. My detective wasn't the only one surveying things. He recognised an ex-gendarmerie colleague who now runs an agency in Nice.'

'Was he watching Mathieu as well?'

'Apparently not. He followed Boris when he left. Which makes me wonder, who was paying him to do that?'

'Your man can't ask his ex-colleague?'

'He can ask, but he can't tell me. Client confidentiality and all that,' Jean-Claude said, shaking his head.

Jean-Claude was silent for a few seconds, thoughtfully fingering the stem of his wine glass.

'What a mess,' he sighed. 'If only he'd tell me what was going on, I could help. I'm not without connections. I know people in the right places, as they say.' He shrugged and looked at Nanette helplessly.

'I know it's hard not to worry, but the only thing you can do really is to let things take their course and be there to step in with help whenever you can.' Nanette said, impulsively reaching out for his hand and squeezing it.

'I am sorry, Nanette, today I want to be a happy memory for us, not one full of worry. Tell me more about your sister, Patsy.'

The rest of lunch passed in a flash as they talked and laughed together and Nanette realised it was a long time since she'd felt as comfortable with a man as she did with Jean-Claude. They spent the afternoon wandering around the old town of Antibes and it was gone five before they reluctantly began to make their way back to Monaco.

The news of Zac's victory in the Canadian Grand Prix came over the car radio as they drove through Cap-d'Ail.

'I think he make champion this year,' Jean-Claude said thoughtfully. 'He's driving really well.'

Nanette nodded. 'He'll be on a real high when he gets back

next week,' she said. 'Making him accept no for an answer to his proposal will be difficult.'

'Would you like me to tell him for you?' Jean-Claude asked.

Nanette smiled at him gratefully. 'Thanks for the offer, but I think it's something I must do myself.'

As Jean-Claude stopped the car outside the apartment, Nanette impulsively leant across and kissed him gently on the cheek.

'I've really enjoyed today, JC. Thank you.'

Jean-Claude looked at her steadily before unexpectedly placing his arm around her shoulders and pulling her towards him. His kiss was gentle and undemanding and a surprised Nanette was totally unprepared for the emotions it unleashed within her. As they drew apart, she stared at him.

'I'll see you tomorrow,' Jean-Claude said, eventually releasing her.

Wordlessly, Nanette got out and closed the car door. Jean-Claude gave her an enigmatic smile before turning the steering wheel and driving away.

Nanette, her thoughts reeling, watched as the car disappeared. Had that kiss meant the same to him as it had to her? Could she be overreacting to a gesture that was maybe just a sign of loving friendship from a man she was already very fond of?

26

The following morning, Mathieu left on his business trip and Nanette's day slipped into its normal routine imposed by the twin's school timetable.

With the memory of Jean-Claude's kiss fresh in her mind, Nanette felt strangely shy when she took the twins up to his villa for an after-school swim. She needn't have worried. Jean-Claude, as always, the perfect gentlemen, greeted her and the twins in his normal manner. It was only when they were alone for a few minutes, as the twins dried and dressed themselves, that he took her in his arms and gently kissed her.

'How are you today, *ma chérie*?' he asked.

Nanette smiled at him shyly, as her heart skipped a beat at his use of the endearment. She hadn't imagined it; the kiss had meant something to him as well.

'Do you have any plans for tomorrow evening?' he asked. 'I thought maybe you'd like some company after the twins are in bed,' he added.

Realising that Jean-Claude had remembered that tomorrow

was the third anniversary of her accident, Nanette nodded. 'Please.'

'I have a business meeting early evening, but I should be with you by about nine o'clock,' Jean-Claude said.

'The twins have a school play rehearsal. I have to collect them at eight thirty, so by the time we've walked back, that would be perfect.'

'Good. I think we have things to talk about, *ma chérie*,' Jean-Claude said softly.

* * *

The following evening, the streets were quiet as Nanette walked slowly through Monaco to collect the twins. It would be another half-hour before the rush of people out to enjoy themselves for the evening began to make their way to the restaurants and nightclubs.

The hall where the twins were rehearsing was part of the modern apartment block where Zac had lived years ago and Nanette found her footsteps dragging the nearer she got to the building.

Having deliberately avoided this particular area of Monte Carlo since her return, Nanette couldn't help thinking how ironic it was that it should be this evening of all evenings that she was again having to come to this particular building.

Nanette tried to push thoughts of the past out of her mind and concentrate on present-day aspects of her life – the twins, Jean-Claude, particularly Jean-Claude – but as she crossed the road towards the apartment block, images from her past began to merge with the present-day ones.

The lights were on in various apartments, including No.5 where she and Zac had spent so much time together. As Nanette glanced up, a glamorous woman came onto the small balcony to look out over the street, before going back inside and closing the French doors, shutting Nanette and the world out.

Standing in the middle of the small service road that led to an underground garage, Nanette stared up at the window. Three years ago, she and Zac were in that apartment getting ready to go out and celebrate her birthday before he left for the next Grand Prix.

She remembered how happy she'd been as they left the apartment. Stepping, hand in hand with Zac, into the lift to go down to the garage. Walking across to her new car and driving slowly up out of the underground exit, making for the autoroute and their dinner reservation in Mougins. The start of what had been a perfect evening with the man she loved – and whom she'd thought had loved her.

An unexpected shiver racked her body and Nanette took several deep breaths, trying to regain her composure. Images from later on that fateful evening were beginning to crowd into her brain.

Things she'd forgotten until now. The champagne she'd drunk, the friends they'd met up with, the heavy rain that had begun to fall as they were in the restaurant. Zac's insistence...

Nanette jumped as a car horn blared out behind her.

'Hey, lady, that's not the best place to stand – unless you want to be run down.' The man in the expensive sports car leant out of his window and rebuked her.

Nanette smiled weakly and mouthed the word 'sorry' in his direction, before moving back on to the narrow pavement, and allowing the man and his car to disappear down the ramp into the depths of the underground garage.

Shaking, she leant against the wall. It was several minutes

before she felt strong enough to walk the few remaining metres to the rehearsal-hall entrance.

It seemed only a matter of minutes before the twins ran out to join her.

'Hi, Netty,' Olivia said, taking hold of her hand as they began to walk, while Pierre ambled along in front.

'I didn't forget a single line tonight,' Pierre said proudly.

'Well done, you,' Nanette said, struggling to talk normally. 'And you, Olivia? How did you get on?'

'OK,' Olivia said, turning to look at her. 'I've only got three or four lines to say anyway. Are you all right, Netty? You don't look very well.'

'I've got a bit of a headache,' was the only thing Nanette could think of saying. 'Come on, let's go home. Shall we have some hot chocolate when we get back?'

Once Nanette had seen the twins into bed, she went through to the balcony and looked down at the boats bobbing around on their moorings. Lights were shining out from the main cabin on *Pole Position*, and as Nanette watched, a crew member came out on deck to check the positioning of the fenders. Even though Zac wasn't on board, the crew knew to keep everything in tiptop shape. Zac had been known to arrive unexpectedly even when on a tight schedule between races.

She stared down at the yacht, wondering why her memory had suddenly started to throw pictures of the past at her. Zac's proposition? Or maybe driving on Sunday had been the trigger? Whatever the catalyst, there appeared to be no stopping the flood of painful reminiscences that were unexpectedly crowding into her mind.

Large droplets of rain blew in unexpectedly under the shelter of the balcony and Nanette grimaced to herself. She gripped the balcony rail tightly as another vignette of that dreadful evening three years ago flooded into her consciousness...

It was raining heavily as they left the restaurant. By the time they were on the autoroute and heading for the first tunnel, it was torrential and Nanette expected Zac to decree leaving at the next exit. Instead, he simply pressed the play button on the radio and the nostalgic words of 'Yesterday' struggled to be heard against the noise of the storm and the rhythmic sweep, sweep of windscreen wipers rendered useless by the force of the rain.

It was calmer in the tunnel, but a few metres after they'd they exited it, Nanette saw the huge sheet of water that lay in front of them a split second before the car rose up, aquaplaning out of control across this unexpected lake before narrowly missing another car and hitting the central reservation with a bang and coming to rest in a tangled wreck.

Drifting in and out of consciousness, Nanette had been dimly aware of the nauseous smell of petrol and of Zac dragging her out and away from the wreckage.

'I've phoned for help. Shouldn't be too long,' Zac assured her as she lay on the verge.

The paramedics were kind and gently placed her on a stretcher. As they lifted her into the ambulance, Zac leant over her and whispered something.

Now, three years later, Nanette finally remembered what those words had been.

'Nanette, I'm so sorry. Please forgive me.'

27

Nanette jumped as Jean-Claude appeared unexpectedly on the balcony. Lost in her memories, she hadn't heard the apartment door opening.

'Is everything all right? You look very pale,' Jean-Claude said, holding her tight as he gave her a greeting kiss on the cheeks.

'I'm fine, thank you. I was trying to work out what I'm going to say to Zac when he returns.'

'How about a straightforward, No, thank you. I don't want the job with Vacances au Soleil.'

'It's no longer as simple as that, JC,' Nanette said quietly. 'I also need to talk to him about...' she took a deep breath before continuing, 'about the things I've started to remember.'

'Your memory of the accident it is returning?'

Nanette nodded. 'Something triggered it off tonight as I walked past Zac's old apartment,' she said, beginning to shiver. 'Then when I came out here...' Her voice trailed away as she gestured towards *Pole Position*.

Jean-Claude pulled her back into his arms protectively. 'These memories have clearly upset you. Do you wish to tell me?'

Standing in the safe circle of his arms, looking up at his concerned face, Nanette wished she could confide in him. Ask his advice about how to approach things with Zac, but slowly she shook her head. 'I think I must talk to Zac first – see if my memory is true or whether it's playing tricks on me.'

Jean-Claude kissed her gently. '*D'accord*. You tell me when you're ready to talk about the past. Tonight, we'll talk about us and perhaps the future.'

Nanette smiled at him gratefully as he took her hand and together they left the balcony. She moved away from him to close the balcony doors and draw the heavy curtains across, but was startled by a loud ring on the apartment doorbell.

'Ah, supper,' Jean-Claude said. 'I'll get it. I missed dinner this evening because of my business appointment,' he explained, returning with several steaming containers, which he placed on the dining table. 'I hope you like Chinese?'

Nanette organised the table, while Jean-Claude deftly turned out the lights, lit candles, switched on the CD player and opened a bottle of wine. A few simple actions, but Nanette realised that Jean-Claude had somehow introduced an atmosphere of intimacy into the room. Suddenly she felt shy and self-conscious, wondering what was behind his actions.

As the voice of Charles Aznavour singing a string of romantic melodies floated through the apartment, Jean-Claude turned to her.

'*Voila*! Let's eat,' and gallantly he pulled a chair out for her.

The sweet and sour pork was delicious and Nanette was surprised to find how hungry she was.

It wasn't until Jean-Claude was pouring some wine that he glanced over and asked, 'Has Mathieu ever said anything to you about me and his mother?'

Startled, Nanette shook her head. 'No.'

'Before we talk about the future, I think I need to tell you a little about my past,' he said, replacing the bottle in the terracotta wine cooler. 'Amelia and I were childhood sweethearts – our birthdays were just two days apart. I was the youngest – a fact which always amused her. Neither of our families thought we were good enough for each other.' Jean-Claude grinned ruefully. 'However, when she became pregnant, they became united in demanding we get married. Mathieu was born on Amelia's seventeenth birthday – thirty years ago this year.'

'Gosh, you were both really young to become parents,' Nanette said, mentally adding up the two figures and realising Jean-Claude was forty-seven.

Jean-Claude nodded ruefully before taking a sip of his wine. 'At first, everything was fine, but when, a few years later, Amelia's family decided to move to Paris, she thought we should go with them. I was busy setting up my own business here and didn't want to move. In the end, she decided she wanted to go – with or without me – but taking Mathieu.'

'That must have been hard for you to deal with,' Nanette said quietly.

'*Oui*. I don't think Mathieu has ever forgiven me. Looking back, I think maybe I should have gone to Paris with them, that things could have been different.' Jean-Claude shook his head. 'One makes mistakes in life – particularly when one is so young.

'I visited as often as I could and we had some good times together, but our lives were soon going in different directions.' He sighed. 'How could they do anything else? My business was expanding rapidly. I went to Paris and begged Amelia to return now I could afford the lifestyle she wanted here. But Amelia, well, let's just say Amelia was enjoying her life in Paris. Her mother helped look after Mathieu – Amelia could go out and about and pretend she was single again. She had many admirers.'

There was a short silence as he swirled the wine in his glass.

'Mathieu was thirteen when Amelia and the current man in her life were killed in a helicopter crash and he came to live with me down here. He was not a happy boy at that time. He missed his mother a lot. But slowly things settled down and we grew close again. Until all this blew up, I thought I'd made a good job of raising a good human being. A law-abiding citizen at least. We had a small problem with a car and some credit when he was a teenager, but once he was in his twenties he seemed to grow up. Meeting and marrying Vanessa, having his own family, seemed to be the making of him. He'd become a well-adjusted, caring individual and I was proud of him. We had a good relationship. I was sad for him when his marriage broke up – not that I blame Vanessa,' Jean-Claude said, looking at Nanette. 'Sometimes these things happen, they, too, were young when they married. And now, now I just don't understand him at all.' Jean-Claude shook his head.

'JC, I'm sure things will work out for Mathieu. Like you, I don't think he is inherently bad – he's just got caught up in something that's spiralled out of control.' Nanette hesitated before asking, 'Is there any news from your detective yet?'

'Only the fact that Boris appears to be the one pulling all the strings. Apparently, the police, both here and Interpol, are quietly keeping tabs on him. Unofficially, the rumours are flying. There's talk of money-laundering, a business cartel and drugs being involved.'

'Mathieu wouldn't do drugs,' Nanette said instantly. 'It has to be something else. What about Zac? Has the detective figured out where he fits into all this?'

'*Non*. Other than that, he seems to be pulling some strings of his own, independent of Boris. Who, incidentally, is apparently in South America overseeing some business deal.'

'I wonder if that's where Mathieu is, too, this week. He didn't say where he was going. Just said it was a business trip,' Nanette said.

Jean-Claude shrugged. 'Mathieu caught a flight to London, but he could have picked up a connection to literally anywhere in the world from there. He hasn't rung to speak to the twins?'

'He emails them most days, but only phones occasionally when he's away. I know he's promised to be back in time for their school play next week.'

'Good. Somehow I feel easier when he's in town – if anything happens to him here in the Principality, at least I'll be around to help to sort it out.' Jean-Claude gazed at Nanette thoughtfully. 'Anyway, I wanted to tell you about Amelia, for you to know the truth about my past. Although it all went wrong, I did love Amelia in the beginning. And...' he reached across and took her hand in his. 'Until now, I've never even come close to loving anyone else.'

There was silence as Jean-Claude gently stroked Nanette's hand before looking up and asking quietly, 'Do you think you could ever look on me as more than a friend?'

Nanette's smile was warm as she smiled at him. 'Oh, JC, you're more than just a friend already.' Before she could say any more, her mobile rang. 'I'm sorry. I'd better answer this.'

As she went to do so, Jean-Claude sighed and began to clear the table. Nanette was still talking on the phone when he finished and he took the rest of his wine out on to the balcony to wait for her.

Nanette was smiling when she joined him a few minutes later.

'JC, I'm so sorry about that. That was Patsy and she was so excited I couldn't stop her talking. Bryan has treated her to a flight out here – she's coming for my birthday next week! You're going to meet her. Isn't that great? She wanted to know if I could meet her at Nice airport. I said yes, of course, but I don't have a car. Could you possibly take me?'

'Of course.' He placed an arm around her shoulders. 'Nanette, I need to finish our earlier conversation. I meant what I said about not loving anyone since Amelia. I know Zac hurt you very badly and I don't want to rush you into a relationship before you're sure, but do you think we could have any sort of future together? I realise I'm several years older than you but...' he looked at her anxiously.

Nanette turned towards him and kissed him gently. 'JC, I'm already very fond of you, but for the moment I can't promise anything. Can we carry on as we are? Take things slowly, get to know each other properly – see what happens? Now my memory seems to be returning, there are a few things I'd like to sort out. I need to finally close the Zac Ewart part of my life. Once I've done that, I can move on.'

She didn't add the words, 'before I can love anyone again', but as he kissed her again, she hoped Jean-Claude understood.

28

The following morning, once she'd taken the twins to school, Nanette walked slowly along the embankment towards the Old Port. The envelope containing the Vacances au Soleil papers was in her bag, ready to hand back to Zac. She was determined, too, that this time he would accept the fact that she didn't want the job he was offering her.

The crew on board *Pole Position* were busy with routine morning chores, but there was no sign of Zac. As Nanette hesitated on the quay, the yacht's captain came down the gangway.

Recognising her, he said, 'Zac's been delayed – something to do with the wrong tyres being supplied for testing. There's a chance he'll not make it back here until just before the French race.'

'I was hoping to talk to him before then,' Nanette said.

'I can give you his mobile number if that helps,' the captain offered.

About to refuse the offer, Nanette changed her mind, saying instead, 'Thanks. That could be useful.' Although it still meant she couldn't hand back the Vacances au Soleil papers.

Handing her a card with Zac's mobile number on it, the skipper said, 'I'm surprised you don't already have this – particularly as you're coming back to work for Zac.'

'Who told you that?'

'Zac did before he left for Canada.'

Inwardly furious but not wanting to discuss it with the yacht skipper, Nanette said simply, 'Oh, I see. Thanks for the number. See you around.'

Stopping at the first pavement café she reached, Nanette ordered a cappuccino. Her hand was shaking as she spooned the cream off the top and she took several deep breaths, trying to steady her nerves.

Zac was unbelievable. Back to his old tricks of assuming he could browbeat her into doing what he wanted. How dare he tell his captain that she would be working for him again, especially as she'd already told him she wasn't interested?

Opening her bag, she took out the envelope and slipped the card inside with the other papers before replacing the envelope in her bag. Tempting though it was to ring him, Nanette was determined to confront him face to face, even if she had to wait a week or two to do it.

A shadow fell across the table and Nanette looked up in surprise.

'Bonjour, Nanette.' Mathieu sat down beside her. 'Join me for another coffee?'

Nanette shook her head. 'No thanks. What are you doing here? We weren't expecting you back until at least the weekend.'

He shrugged. 'A couple of my business appointments were cancelled, so I decided to come home early. How are the twins? Still practising for their concert?'

'Of course. They'll be pleased to see you.'

'I'll meet them from school this afternoon if you like,' Mathieu offered.

'Thanks. Patsy is coming for a visit soon. Is it all right if she stays in the apartment?'

'Of course. Ask Florence to make sure the guest bedroom is ready. How long is she staying for?'

'About a week. It's just a short break for her before she gets taken over by motherhood.'

Mathieu nodded and took a sip of his coffee before asking, 'Spoken to Zac recently?'

Nanette shook her head. 'I was hoping to see him today, to sort some things out, but he's not here.'

'I know,' Mathieu said quietly. 'I was supposed to be meeting up with him, but he's been delayed.' He glanced at her. 'Do you still have the papers he gave you about Vacances au Soleil?'

'They're in my bag right now.'

'Could I have a look at them please?'

'Oh, Mathieu, I don't know,' Nanette protested. 'They're Zac's private property and his personal business.'

'Are they marked private and confidential? Did Zac ask you to keep them to yourself?' Mathieu pressed her.

'No to both questions.'

'There may just be something in them that would help me,' Mathieu said quietly.

'Help you do what? It's only papers outlining Zac's business and what I would be expected to do.' Nanette paused. 'I know I offered to help you if I could a few weeks ago but this makes me feel very uncomfortable.'

Mathieu was silent for a few seconds. 'I need a certain piece of information and there's a possibility it will be in those papers. Please, Nanette. I promise you Zac will never know I've seen them.'

Nanette closed her eyes as she took a deep breath. Opening them, she looked at Mathieu.

'Okay. I'm not happy doing this, but I will give them to you to read.' She stood up.

'Only not here. Back at the apartment.'

29

As promised, Jean-Claude drove Nanette to Nice airport to collect Patsy off the afternoon flight. Standing in the arrivals hall waiting for her sister to come through after the plane had landed, Nanette realised she was feeling, not exactly nervous, but definitely anxious. Patsy and Jean-Claude had never met before and she prayed they would like each other and get on. After the fiasco of her relationship with Zac – he and Patsy had never really taken to each other and wound each other up every time they met – she'd determined that in future it would be a case of 'if you're friends with me, you're friends with my sister'. Patsy was the only family she had left now and no friendship, or passing boyfriend, was worth the risk of falling out and being alienated from her. Although the reality was that Jean-Claude was the first man since Zac that Nanette had wanted to introduce to Patsy.

Nanette stood in front of the glass wall separating the baggage collection area from the arrivals hall, hoping for an early glimpse of her sister. Jean-Claude had stopped at the newsagents in the foyer to buy an English magazine that he claimed he could only get at the airport and still hadn't returned when passengers started to appear down the corridor leading to the baggage area. Patsy was one of the last passengers to appear and waved happily when she saw Nanette, before moving across to the conveyor belt to wait for her suitcase to turn up.

By the time Patsy had claimed her case and passed through customs and come out through the double doors into the arrivals hall dragging it behind her, Jean-Claude was standing at Nanette's side by the barrier and immediately relieved Patsy of it.

After hugging her sister, Nanette quickly made the introductions and the three of them made their way out onto the main concourse of the airport and the car park.

'Good flight?' Nanette asked.

Patsy nodded. 'Oh, it's good to see you and be back down here.' She sniffed. 'Smell that eucalyptus. I'm sure Nice airport is the only one in the world that smells so delicious.'

As Jean-Claude walked ahead to the car, Nanette glanced at her sister. 'You're looking good. Big but good!'

'I'm beginning to resemble an elephant,' Patsy grumbled. 'To think I've got another nine weeks to go.'

They were lucky with the traffic and the journey back to Monaco was a quick one. Jean-Claude left the car in the underground garage and took the suitcase up to the apartment for them before leaving.

'You sure you won't stay for something to eat?' Nanette said, as Patsy wandered out onto the balcony to gaze at the boats.

'Not today – I'll leave the two of you to catch up. Bring Patsy up to the villa for a swim and lunch whenever you like,' Jean-Claude said. 'I'll ring you later,' and he leant in to kiss her goodbye.

'Thanks for playing chauffeur this afternoon, I really appreciate it.' Nanette said, returning the kiss.

Florence had left a tea tray ready in the kitchen and Nanette made a pot of tea and carried everything out to the balcony, where Patsy was still leaning on the guard rail gazing out at the view in wonder.

'Mathieu's gone up in the world with this place, hasn't he?' she said, pulling a chair out and sitting down.

Nanette nodded and poured Patsy a cup of tea.

'It was good of Bryan to treat you to this holiday,' Nanette said. 'Shame he couldn't come with you.'

'He wanted to, he was worried about me travelling alone, but it's totally the wrong time of year for a farmer to take a holiday,' Patsy said ruefully. 'What with silage and haymaking, not to mention organising AI visits to get the cows into calf ready for calving early next year.' She glanced at Nanette. 'Actually, I'm rather ashamed to be here. I told you I asked Bryan to have a word with Helen? He did and it was fine for a week or two. But then, last Sunday, I lost it when she made some remark that I can't even remember now. I did the unthinkable – called her Grannyzilla to her face and threw the roast potatoes on the floor.' Patsy gave Nanette a half-smile. 'It did feel quite good, though, at the time.'

Nanette stared at her, realising just how uptight her unflappable sister must have been to act like that. 'Oh, Patsy, I'm sorry you were so stressed. I wish I'd been able to help more.'

'Helen cleared the mess up, muttering all the time about it being my hormones, Bryan, thankfully, realised it wasn't just that, I really did need some space. So, here I am.' Patsy smiled happily at her sister.

'Leaving your husband to the tender mercies of his mother,' Nanette teased. 'She'll probably have moved back into the farmhouse by the time you get home.'

Patsy groaned. 'Don't even joke about that. She's already suggested she moves into the spare room to be closer for the big event. I know she's Bryan's mother, I know she's excited at becoming a grandmother and I know she means well, but she does have this tendency to try to take over.' She glanced at Nanette. 'You will still be able to come back and be with me when "the bump" makes its appearance? You are still down as my birthing partner. I'll understand if you can't, though.'

'I'm going to do my best,' Nanette answered. 'It all depends. I may end up bringing the twins with me.'

Patsy gave her sister a quizzical look.

'We think – no, we know, Mathieu and Zac are both embroiled in something illegal,' Nanette said. 'Whether it's the same unlawful scheme or two different ones, we haven't yet been able to work out. As for Zac. Can you believe he's told the crew on *Pole Position* that I'm going to be working for him again?'

'I thought you were going to tell him no a second time and make sure he got the message! Honestly, Nanette, anyone would think you were considering it.'

Nanette sighed. 'I couldn't have been more definite when I said no to him, but he doesn't listen to me – or doesn't want to hear what I'm saying. Now Mathieu says it would help him if I did agree to do some work for Zac.' Nanette shrugged helplessly. 'I really, really don't want anything to do with Zac, but I know how worried JC is about Mathieu, so I was thinking...' she glanced at her sister cautiously. 'It might help if I did agree to do some – temporarily of course.' Her gut instinct was still screaming at her not to trust Zac one iota but if working for him for a few hours was the only way to find out what was going on, then maybe she should do it.

'Don't you dare,' Patsy said.

'JC is against it too, even to help Mathieu.'

'Listen to the two of us then. Does Vanessa know about your worries over Mathieu?'

Nanette shook her head. 'No. She's too far away to do anything and I don't want to worry her unless I have to. Hopefully things will have sorted themselves out by the time she and Ralph return.'

'Even if they haven't, you are not to get involved,' Patsy said firmly.

Nanette, remembering Patsy's condition, decided it would be prudent not to tell her just how involved she already was because of Jean-Claude. She glanced across at her sister. 'There's another thing. I'm starting to remember things that happened before the accident.'

'That's good,' Patsy said. 'Isn't it?'

'Yes, it's good that my memory is beginning to function again, but some of the things I'm remembering contradict the truth. Or things that I believed to be true.'

Patsy looked at her anxiously. 'You're not having nightmares again?'

'No.' Nanette shook her head. 'But what if these memories are false? Not returning memories at all. What if subconsciously I'm biased and trying to make myself believe a lie?' She fell silent for a moment before looking at Patsy and saying quietly. 'What if...' She paused, biting her lip before saying, 'What if I was not the cause of the accident?'

30

Vanessa wiped her sleeve across her face in the forlorn hope of mopping up some of the perspiration that was making her skin itch. Her hair under the hat was wet and sweat was beginning to drip down her neck. It was three hours now since they'd said goodbye to the villagers and Luigi, their guide, had led them into the jungle to begin their long trek back to civilisation.

The last forty-eight hours had been hard. Not only was their stay in the village coming to an end with Ralph unable to complete his film the way he wanted, it had seemed the friendships they'd forged with the villagers were about to be torn apart by some superstition.

Summoned to the village council, they'd apprehensively followed Angela to the main hut the evening of what should have been their last night in the village. As far as Vanessa could see, every villager, from the smallest newborn baby to the oldest native, was waiting for them, grim-faced. The hunters had returned early from a food foraging expedition and were grouped around the head shaman, still clutching their spears, staring intently at Vanessa and Ralph.

Vanessa had shivered. Did they really believe she and Ralph had put the 'evil eye' on their gold? Memories of a terrifying visit as a young girl to an exhibition of cannibalism and shrunken heads in the British Museum in London suddenly sprang unbidden into her mind. Did these natives know that those practices had been outlawed? Did they practise other, even more macabre, rituals?

Swallowing hard to stop the bile in her throat rising, Vanessa had looked fearfully at the natives she'd treated as friends for several weeks. There was a stranger, his skin glistening with sweat, his spears and machete strapped in place on his back, talking and gesturing with the head shaman. Vanessa had glanced at him curiously.

'He's one of the native runners who keep all the villages in touch. Apparently, he's brought some urgent news,' Ralph had told her, after a quick consultation with Angela.

Luigi, who with Nick the cameraman, was acting as interpreter, had moved forward and listened intently to what the man was saying. Vanessa clutched at Ralph's hand nervously as silence descended in the hut and the head shaman turned and beckoned them forward.

'We have news that our *aviamento*, Takyanov the outsider, has been detained. His word has been broken. It is not you who have cast the evil eye.' He had paused. 'We are free to trade with you.'

Vanessa had felt her whole body shudder in relief. Then the phrase 'free to trade with you' had registered in her brain and she looked at Nick and Luigi in horror. The villagers had clearly misunderstood what she was offering to do.

'Nick, Luigi, before this goes any further, you must make them understand the Fruits of the Forest cooperative would be their responsibility. I'm not buying their produce, only helping them to get organised to make and to sell it.'

Once she was convinced that the villagers, and the head shaman in particular, understood exactly what she was proposing, Vanessa had felt the tension leave her and she quickly began to outline again all the things the villagers would need to do to get the cooperative up and running.

'I just wish we weren't leaving tomorrow,' she had said. 'There's so much to explain and put into action.'

'We can stay one more day if you like,' Ralph had offered. 'No longer though, Nick and Harry have work commitments to get back for.'

Vanessa and Ralph had worked into the small hours trying to sort out a basic businesslike plan of campaign to get the cooperative off the ground. In the morning, they had held their own village council meeting to tell the head shaman and the villagers the things they needed to do.

The extra day had been a busy one with so many things to organise, not least packing up some samples of the native medicines, including several pots of the *Sangre de Grado* ointment that had helped Ralph's injuries to heal so well.

'If only we'd thought of this when we first arrived,' Vanessa had said. 'I could have done so much more before having to leave them to get on with it.' She'd sighed and looked at Ralph. 'There is one thing that still worries me, though. What happens if this Takyanov comes back and tries to muscle in on the cooperative? Angela did say the men knew there were dangers in upsetting him.'

'Don't worry. Once we get back to civilisation, we can alert the authorities to what we – you, are doing. Once you've organised some funds, you can appoint a trustworthy overseer to come out here to supervise things in your absence. Make sure there are no disruptions, no outsiders muscling in. You'll be amazed at the progress on your next visit, you'll see,' Ralph had said confidently.

Hugging Angela goodbye the following morning, Vanessa was surprised to find herself fighting back the tears. From longing to leave the jungle, she found herself strangely sad saying goodbye to Angela, her friend.

'Goodbye, *Pacchumama*. May the spirits be with you on your journey,' Angela had said, hugging her.

'I'm going to miss you, but once I've set up the cooperative for the village I'll be back to see you again.' Vanessa had bent down and given little Maya a cuddle and hugged her tight, before turning and leaving.

Now, as she tiredly followed Luigi and the porters along the muddy track, Vanessa's mind was still racing, trying to sort out the logistics of the cooperative and wondering who she'd be able to find willing to sponsor Fruits of the Forest for at least its first year in business.

Darkness had descended as they reached the camp where they were to spend their last night in the jungle proper. Wearily, Vanessa stumbled into their sleeping hut. Tomorrow they would travel by small canoe up the feeder river to the Amazon itself and then, a day, or possibly two days later, a larger boat would take them to the town of Manaus.

Their journey home had begun. Part of her was sad that their adventure in the Amazon jungle would soon be over, but inside she was buzzing with the thought of seeing Pierre and Olivia again. Giving them tight hugs. Tucking them into their safe beds. Telling them about little Maya and her so, so different life. Hoping that she would be able to help provide a proper future for her and the other children of the village. She desperately wanted Fruits of the Forest to succeed.

31

With Patsy staying, the days settled down into a different routine as Nanette made sure her sister didn't overdo things. She insisted that Patsy stayed in bed every morning while she dealt with the twins' morning routine and returned from the school run with a bag of warm croissants from the boulangerie.

Because Patsy had visited Monaco several times in the past and Nanette had shown her the touristy sights then, there was no urgent need for them to go out exploring. So, for the first couple of days, they just took gentle strolls around the harbour, stopping for a coffee at their favourite café, before returning to the apartment to sit around relaxing, which was just what Patsy needed. Evenings were spent with the twins, playing board games and competing against each other on the video games Pierre and Olivia loved playing at every opportunity. Nanette was pleased to see that Patsy looked much better and happier with every day that passed and they began to venture further afield.

They took Jean-Claude up on his invitation for a swim and had lunch with him up at the villa one day. Another day, they went to view an art exhibition at the Grimaldi Forum, followed by a takeaway pizza back at the apartment. Sitting out on the balcony afterwards flicking through a celebrity magazine, Patsy looked across at her sister.

'Is Mathieu avoiding me? He's barely been home since I've been here.'

Nanette shook her head. 'It's the way it is at the moment. Whatever it is he's caught up in seems to take up a lot of time. The twins, too, are beginning to notice he's rarely here.'

'I thought I'd offer to take everyone out for a pizza one evening as a way of saying thank you to him for letting me stay here but,' Patsy shrugged, 'it doesn't look like that idea is going to work.'

'I shouldn't worry too much,' Nanette said. 'He's told the twins he'll be around for my birthday dinner, so you'll see him then and can thank him. You can always buy him a bottle of champagne or something.'

* * *

It was late in the afternoon of Nanette's birthday and she and Patsy were out on the balcony of Mathieu's apartment arranging a magnificent bouquet of flowers from Jean-Claude.

The two of them had spent the day mooching around Monaco old town and entertaining the twins after school. Mathieu arrived after lunch and had spent the afternoon working on his computer before taking Olivia and Pierre off somewhere unspecified, leaving the sisters alone.

'I never thanked you properly for those lovely flowers you sent me,' Patsy said, carefully placing a yellow rose into the arrangement. 'I really appreciated them, in more ways than one. Just knowing that you were out there on my side was a real boost.'

'I'm glad they helped. I was trying to stop feeling guilty for not being there when you needed me,' Nanette said quietly.

'Please don't feel guilty. I know in a real emergency you would drop everything to be with me. These are beautiful flowers too,' Patsy said, smelling one of the lilies. 'Jean-Claude seems to be really fond of you. He's very attractive,' she added, with a sideways look at her sister. 'You would tell me if there was romance in the air, wouldn't you? I couldn't help but notice a certain frisson whenever you two are together.'

Nanette, not surprised that Patsy had picked up on her feelings for Jean-Claude, concentrated on carefully pushing the last orchid-like flower into the arrangement, before giving Patsy an enigmatic smile, knowing she couldn't and wouldn't deny her feelings to her sister.

'JC is a lovely man and I'm fond of him, too,' she said. 'But we're taking it slowly. All this business with Mathieu is worrying him and I still need to sort out things with Zac.'

'Shame he hasn't been around while I've been here,' Patsy said. 'I'd have enjoyed "sorting things out" with him.'

'Probably just as well then,' Nanette replied. 'I don't think Monaco is ready to hear you giving one of their favourite residents a telling-off.'

Patsy shrugged. 'I can wait.'

Florence appeared just then with another large bunch of flowers.

'The concierge just sent these up, with this card,' she said, handing an envelope to Nanette.

Even before she tore open the envelope, Nanette guessed who these particular flowers were from. She read the brief message out loud to Patsy.

'Happy Birthday. Will ring you this evening. Hope you've had a great day. Zac.'

Exasperated, Nanette said, 'They're lovely flowers, but I wish he hadn't sent them. I'm going to have to say thank you and the last thing I want to do at the moment is thank Zac Ewart for anything. Why is he going to ring me this evening?'

'We won't be here anyway, will we?' Patsy said. 'Aren't we going out to dinner in' – she looked at her watch – 'about an hour and a half, with Jean-Claude and Mathieu to celebrate your birthday in style?'

'Heavens, is it that late already? We'd better think about getting ready.'

Nanette took Zac's flowers out to the kitchen and asked Florence if she'd kindly find a vase for them.

Mathieu, arriving back with the twins just then, handed Nanette a small package. 'Olivia and Pierre thought you'd like this. Happy Birthday from us all.'

'This' turned out to be a beautiful silk scarf from one of the designer boutiques on Avenue de Monte Carlo.

'Thank you,' Nanette said, hugging the twins and gently fingering the luxurious material. 'It's lovely. I shall wear it this evening.'

* * *

The Italian restaurant where Jean-Claude had booked a table was only a short walk away and Mathieu escorted them there. Nanette acknowledged her heart's missed beat with a smile as she saw Jean-Claude standing there waiting for them.

'Happy birthday,' he said, and kissed her cheeks. The words *ma chérie* were added so quietly that only Nanette heard them and she smiled at him gratefully.

Gallantly taking her hand in his, Jean-Claude escorted her to their table, where an attentive waiter was waiting to pour the champagne before taking their orders. A pianist was playing a medley of Italian songs and several couples were making use of the small dance floor around which the tables were grouped.

'Will you excuse us while the birthday girl and I have this dance?' Jean-Claude asked, looking at Mathieu and Patsy.

'Go ahead,' Mathieu said, looking at Patsy. 'Would you like to?'

'I'll sit this one out, thanks,' Patsy answered. 'I think the bump would rather get in the way.'

Nanette, moving slowly around the dance floor, Jean-Claude's arms holding her close, breathed a sigh of happiness. A feeling that this birthday was going to herald in a year of changes to her life flooded through her body, and surely this time, they would be good changes.

'Thank you for my beautiful flowers, JC,' Nanette murmured.

'My pleasure. I have other presents for you, too, but you will have to come to the villa to collect them. Maybe when Patsy has returned home? Now, we'd better return to our table, I can see the waiters arriving with our food.'

The meal was delicious. Conversation and laughter flowed between the four of them. It was only when the waiter brought the sweet trolley for them to choose from that she realised Patsy had gone quiet.

Concerned, she looked at her. 'Patsy are you all right? You look awfully pale.'

'I'm fine – just feel a bit queasy. Probably too much rich food. I think I'll skip dessert.'

'Do you want to go back to the apartment?' Nanette asked.

'Certainly not, but if you could just point me in the direction of the ladies'?'

'I'll come with you,' Nanette said, giving her an anxious look.

'You stay here,' Patsy said, standing up. 'I'm pregnant – not incapacitated. I see they've got your favourite dessert,' she added, glancing at the trolley. 'So enjoy.'

Nanette could hardly swallow a spoonful of her tiramisu, delicious as it was. When, after ten minutes, Patsy hadn't returned, she stood up.

'I'll just go check on Patsy,' she said.

Nanette found her sister, sitting in a wicker chair, sipping a glass of water given to her by the concerned restroom attendant.

'What's going on?'

'The doctor should be here any minute,' the attendant answered. 'I've told the lady not to move.'

'Why do you need a doctor?' Nanette demanded. 'Is it the baby?'

Patsy bit her lip. 'I've started to bleed. Not a lot,' she added quickly, seeing Nanette's face. 'Just enough for me to need some medical advice.'

The restroom door swung open and a man entered.

'I'm the emergency doctor. I gather we have a problem with a pregnant lady? Perhaps I could ask everyone to wait outside for a while?'

'Doctor, my sister doesn't speak French,' Nanette said. 'Do you need me to translate?'

'*Non, merci.* I speak enough English. Please give me five minutes alone with the patient.'

Nanette made her way back to Jean-Claude and Mathieu and quickly explained the situation to them, before returning to see what the doctor said.

'Bed rest for the next twenty-four hours. Then check with a doctor again. No exertion.'

'How about flying? I'm booked to return to the UK in a couple of days?' Patsy asked.

The doctor shrugged his shoulders. 'Go to the clinic tomorrow and see what the consultant advises.'

Jean-Claude insisted on calling a taxi to return to the apartment, where he and Mathieu solicitously helped Patsy across the foyer to the lift. Once back in the apartment, Nanette saw Patsy into her room before joining the men in the sitting room.

Mathieu was holding a piece of paper, which he handed to Nanette. 'Florence left this note for you. Apparently, Zac has been ringing all evening.'

Nanette sighed as she read the housekeeper's message:

Zac Ewart needs to talk to you urgently. Would you please ring him at whatever time you return. Mathieu will give you the number if you don't have it.

'What on earth can be so important? I'll ring him in the morning,' Nanette said. 'I'm too tired and worried about Patsy right now.'

As Mathieu went to say something, Nanette held up her hands.

'Mathieu, my days of running after Zac are long gone. Incidentally, have you finished with the Vacances au Soleil papers yet?'

Jean-Claude shot his son a swift glance. 'What were you hoping to find?'

Mathieu shrugged. 'Just an address.'

'Did you find it?' Jean-Claude asked.

There was a barely perceptible pause before Mathieu shook his head. 'No. I'll get the papers for you now.' He went into his temporary office, returning seconds later with Nanette's envelope.

'I said I'd take Patsy some warm milk to help her sleep,' Nanette said. 'Shall I make us a nightcap too?'

Mathieu shook his head. 'Not for me. I've got a breakfast business meeting tomorrow, so, if you'll excuse me, I'm off to bed. Goodnight.'

'Can I get you anything?' Nanette said to Jean-Claude as the door closed behind Mathieu,

'No, thanks. I'll leave you to look after Patsy – and don't worry, I'm sure she and the baby will be fine. I'll see you tomorrow.'

'Thank you for a lovely evening, JC,' Nanette said. 'I really enjoyed myself. The best birthday for years.'

Jean-Claude gave her a gentle kiss and he was gone.

As the door closed behind him, the telephone rang. Quickly, Nanette snatched the receiver off its hook before the shrill noise could disturb everyone. She knew exactly who would be ringing her this late.

'Zac, stop pestering me...'

'I need your help, Nanette,' Zac's voice interrupted. 'I want you to go to *Pole Position* tomorrow morning, meet someone and put a package in the safe for me.'

'What? You ring at nearly midnight to ask me to do something trivial that your skipper can do?' Nanette said incredulously.

'No, he can't,' Zac answered quietly. 'You're the only person apart from me who knows a) where the safe is and b) the combination to it.'

'You mean the secret, personal one, in your cabin?' Nanette asked as realisation dawned. 'You've never changed the code?'

'No.'

'Can't the skipper simply put whatever it is in the main safe until you get back?'

Zac sighed audibly down the phone. 'No. If there hadn't been a problem with testing tyres, I'd have been there to deal with it myself. As it is, I'm unlikely to get back for some time. I'd rather it was totally out of sight. Five minutes, Nanette, that's all it will take.'

'You're not asking me to help with something illegal, are you?' Nanette demanded.

'Definitely not,' Zac replied instantly. 'If it makes you feel any better, I can tell you it's something to do with Vacances au Soleil.'

Nanette took a deep breath. 'OK,' she said reluctantly. 'I'll do it tomorrow.'

'Thank you. Eleven o'clock on board. You do remember the combination?'

'Yes.' As the combination was made up of her birthday date backwards, it was one she was hardly likely to forget.

'Thanks, Nanette. I owe you one.'

'If my returning memory is right, Zac, you owe me more than that,' Nanette said. 'When you get back, we need to have a serious talk. Goodnight.'

Quickly, before Zac could start to question her, Nanette replaced the receiver. She was determined to challenge Zac face to face, to see his reaction to her accusation. Now was not the time.

Tomorrow she would go to the yacht and do as Zac asked – but this was positively the last time ever she would do anything Zac Ewart asked her to do.

The next morning, Nanette took the twins to school before returning to the apartment and making Patsy some breakfast.

'You still look a bit peaky,' Nanette said. 'How do you feel?'

'OK, thanks, and I'm really sorry for spoiling your evening,' Patsy said.

'You worried me, but you didn't spoil the evening. I had a lovely birthday.'

'Did I hear the phone last night, after Jean-Claude had left?'

Nanette nodded. 'Zac.'

Patsy looked at her. 'And?'

'I'm going to collect something and put it in his personal safe on board *Pole Position* this morning,' Nanette answered slowly, knowing that Patsy wouldn't like it. 'Don't stress about it,' she added. 'It's not good for you in your condition. It'll only take five minutes mid-morning and then I intend to forget all about Zac Ewart until he gets back from Indianapolis next month.'

'Do you know what it is you're collecting?' Patsy asked.

'No. It can't be anything too large because the safe isn't that big,' she answered.

'Have you told JC or Mathieu what you're doing?'

Nanette shook her head. 'No. Mathieu has already left and I'm not expecting to see JC until this afternoon. I'll tell him then. What are you doing?' Nanette looked at her sister, horrified, as Patsy went to throw off the duvet.

'I'm getting up and coming with you, of course,' Patsy said.

'Oh, no, you're not. The doctor said bed rest for twenty-four hours, so don't you even dare to think about getting up,' Nanette scolded her. 'When I get back from putting whatever it is in the safe, I'm ringing the clinic to make you an appointment,' she said and tucked Patsy firmly back into bed.

Later that morning, she left Patsy with some magazines and strict instructions to take it easy and made her way down to the harbour.

Walking towards the yacht, she could see the gangway was raised, making access from the quay impossible.

Hadn't Zac told the crew he'd arranged for her to meet someone there? What would she do if the crew had all disappeared for the day and she couldn't get on board?

To her relief, as she got nearer, she saw Phil, the skipper, out on the starboard deck talking to someone on the next yacht. Seeing her standing at the stern, Phil raised a hand in greeting but didn't immediately move to lower the gangway and let her on board. Instead, he finished his conversation and took his time before pressing the button that would lower the gangway.

Nanette was sure he would never have dared to have kept Zac waiting, but he was clearly trying to make a point.

'Zac has asked me to meet someone here and—'

'I know,' Phil interrupted. 'He phoned me this morning.' He looked hard at her. 'I'm sure you are aware that the captain of a boat is the one held legally responsible for whatever takes place on board – regardless of whether he or the owner sanctioned it.'

'Yes, I know,' Nanette said quietly. 'All I can say is, Zac assured me last night, that it is nothing illegal he wants me to put in the safe, otherwise I certainly wouldn't be here.'

'Until this morning I wasn't even aware there was a second *secret* safe on board this yacht. It is something I should have been told about.'

'This is something you are going to have to take up with Zac.'

'Oh, I intend to,' Phil said. 'If you speak to him before I do, you can tell him that I'm seriously thinking of looking for another position – one where the owner treats me with the respect and trust I deserve.'

Nanette was silent, not knowing what to say.

'Cooee.' They both turned to see Evie standing on the quay. 'Hi, Nanette, haven't seen you in ages. How are you? Can I come on board please, Captain?'

Without waiting for a reply, Evie slipped off her high heels and walked along the gangway.

'I've got a package for Zac,' she said, rummaging in her tote and producing a medium-sized parcel.

'You have?' Nanette said, surprised. The last person she'd expected to be meeting was Evie.

'It's from Luc,' Evie explained. 'My ex-boss as of today,' and she held the package out to Phil.

Phil shook his head, declining to accept the parcel. 'Not me. Nanette is here to collect it – and put it somewhere safe,' he added.

Evie looked at the two of them, clearly sensing the tension, before shrugging her shoulders. 'Whatever. I've done my bit.'

'Thanks,' Nanette said, taking the parcel.

'Have you got time for a coffee?' Evie asked. 'When you've done what you have to do.'

'Love one. Give me five minutes to put this away first.' Nanette turned to Phil. 'All right if I go down below?' she asked.

'Be my guest – you know where it is,' and Phil moved aside indifferently.

Closing the master cabin door behind her, Nanette walked across the cream deep-pile carpet towards the en-suite bathroom. The luxurious bathroom with its marble and gold fittings had been spared refurbishment last year and was exactly as Nanette remembered it.

Kneeling down, she opened the vanity unit under the double marble sink and lifted out the white towels that were stored there. Carefully, she tapped at the front edge of the flooring shelf to loosen it before lifting it out and laying it on the floor.

Sitting back on her heels, she looked at the small dial previously hidden by the false cupboard bottom but now exposed in the recess under the sink. What was she going to find when the safe door opened? What secrets did Zac already have stashed away within the steel box?

Nanette took a deep breath. It had been a long time since she and Zac had devised the code. Remembering her birthday date backwards was the easy bit. Counting under her breath, Nanette concentrated on remembering the number of turns she had to make to the right and then to the left in between several of the digits. As she did the last turn to the right, she heard the satisfying *click* of the lock undoing and with a deep sigh of relief she pulled open the door.

The safe was empty – except for a handgun. Nanette stared at it, stunned. Since when had Zac found it necessary to have a gun on board? Sitting back on her heels, Nanette looked at the packet Evie had given her, wondering about its contents. She sat there for several minutes before coming to a decision and closing the door and spinning the combination lock.

The flooring shelf slid back in easily and Nanette replaced the towels tidily before shutting the vanity unit door, picking up her handbag and leaving the bathroom.

Evie was waiting for her in the stern and Nanette quickly called out 'Goodbye' to Phil, who was busy adjusting fenders near the bow, before following Evie down the gangway and back on to the quay.

'Shall we have coffee at the apartment?' Nanette suggested. 'Then I can introduce you to my sister, Patsy. Tell me, why is Luc your ex-boss?'

Evie sighed and glanced around before saying quietly, 'I think his business is in trouble. He's talking of restructuring, or he may give up altogether. Anyway, he's given me two months' pay in lieu of notice and told me he doesn't need me any more. He has promised to help me find another job if I want to stay in Monaco. Which I do.'

'Have you heard of any jobs going?'

'No. I've got an interview with an agency tomorrow, so I'm hoping they'll come up with something,' Evie said. 'Even if it's only temporary.'

Nanette glanced at Evie as a sudden thought struck her. Should she tell her about Zac needing someone for Vacances au Soleil? Though how could she possibly recommend a job with Zac when she suspected he was involved in something illegal?

She couldn't, she decided. So instead she said. 'I'll have a word with Jean-Claude if you like, he may know of something.'

'Thanks,' Evie said. 'I'm hoping something does turn up. I really like it down here and would hate to have to leave.'

As they walked back to the apartment, Nanette waited for the inevitable questions from Evie.

'Phil, the captain, told me you lived in Monaco before and were once engaged to Zac. Is that true?'

'Yes. It's not as if it's a big secret. Just something I rarely talk about to strangers. Every time I thought I'd mention it to you, the conversation veered off in a different direction before I'd plucked up the courage to raise the subject. I guessed that somebody was bound to tell you eventually,' Nanette said. 'Three years ago, my reputation was in tatters when I left and I had a hard time coming to terms with what happened. Telling someone new about the accident has always been difficult. Easier to keep quiet.'

'I can understand that,' Evie said.

'So, d'you still want to come up for coffee and meet Patsy?' Nanette asked as they reached the apartment block.

'Of course. Why shouldn't I? We've all got some sort of skeleton in our cupboards, haven't we?'

Nanette laughed. 'Come on up then and tell me and Patsy about your skeletons.'

* * *

The consultant at the clinic where Nanette had made an appointment for Patsy was thorough in his examination – and definite in his opinion.

'Everything seems fine now. I suggest you fly home as soon as possible in case the bleeding starts again. Leave it too late and perhaps the airline will refuse to let you fly. I think you will possibly deliver early.'

Leaving the clinic, the sisters decided to walk back to the apartment. As they strolled slowly along the embankment enjoying the sunshine and dodging the tourists, Nanette said, 'I'll ring the airline and change your ticket to an earlier flight. As much as I want you to stay, I think the consultant is right.'

Patsy nodded. 'Another twenty-four hours will be OK though, won't it? I really want to see the twins' school play tonight.'

'First available flight after this evening then,' Nanette said. 'Now, are you up for some retail therapy in Rue Princess Caroline before lunch?'

'Silly question, of course,' Patsy answered. 'I've got to make the most of my time here – besides, I must find a present for Bryan.'

'Good, but then you must get some rest before we go to the play. It's my afternoon to work for Jean-Claude, so I won't be around for a couple of hours. If you don't want to stay in the apartment alone, you can always come up to the villa with me.'

Patsy shook her head. 'I'll be fine. I'll probably sit on the balcony and snooze for a couple of hours. Shopping always tires me out even when I'm not pregnant!'

* * *

Once back at the apartment, Patsy went to sit on the balcony while Nanette telephoned the airline to change her flight. To her dismay, she was told the only flight with seats available was just eight hours before the one Patsy was already booked on – hardly worth the cost of changing.

Nanette glanced at her sister dozing happily in one of the wicker chairs on the balcony and decided to simply abandon the idea of getting Patsy home early. She still had at least two months to go and Nanette began to pray that the consultant's possible early delivery prediction fears wouldn't be proved true in the next few days.

Bryan, she knew, would be devastated if he wasn't with Patsy when she gave birth to their first child. How she was going to keep her own promise to be with her sister if the baby did come early after she went home was something she'd worry about later.

33

Leaving Patsy with strict instructions to rest until she returned, Nanette made her way up to Jean-Claude's villa that afternoon.

He was waiting for her in the garden and Nanette's heart skipped its customary beat like it did whenever she saw him. As much as she might tell herself not to rush things, she knew she was falling in love.

Standing in the circle of his arms as he held her tightly, she felt herself tremble with desire as he kissed her. Several moments passed before he released her with a sigh.

'How did the appointment with the consultant go?' he asked.

'Everything seems to be all right, although he thinks Patsy should go home earlier, but I can't change the flight – no seats available,' Nanette answered slowly. 'Haven't said this to Patsy, but now I'm worried that they'll refuse to take her anyway if we mention what's happened.'

'When does she want to go?'

'Tomorrow would have been ideal,' Nanette said.

'Excuse me a moment.' Jean-Claude punched some numbers into his mobile. As he began to talk in rapid French, Nanette wandered across to the terrace wall and looked down on the Mediterranean sparkling under the azure blue sky.

Jean-Claude joined her a few moments later. '*Voila*. Patsy flies tomorrow at fourteen hundred hours from Cannes-Mandelieu. I will drive you both there. You will arrange for her husband to meet her, yes?'

Nanette looked at him in amazement. 'How?'

'I have a friend with a private jet. He, like me, is happy to help,' Jean-Claude said. 'He flies to the UK several times a week on business and tomorrow he happens to have a spare seat.'

Nanette smiled. She'd forgotten how different the rich really were, with their private planes and expensive habits. 'I can't thank you enough, JC. And Patsy will be thrilled.' Impulsively, she reached up and gave him a kiss, before asking, 'Right, what do you want me to do this afternoon?'

'Nothing,' Jean-Claude said. 'Today I want to give you your birthday presents,' and catching hold of her hand he led her towards the garage where he kept his Lotus. 'I'm sorry it's a day or two late, but I wanted to show it to you in private,' he said, opening the door of a white convertible parked next to his treasured racing car. To Nanette's amazement, he handed her the car keys. 'I know you're ready to start driving again now, so this is here for you to use whenever you need it.'

'JC, I don't know what to say,' Nanette said.

'You don't have to say anything. Just put the keys in your bag so you have them when you need them.'

Jean-Claude reached into the car and picked up a small orange drawstring bag that was on the driver's seat and handed it to her.

'The car is something to make your life easier when you need to go places. This is your real birthday present from me, *ma chérie*.'

Nanette was quiet as she opened the bag she recognised as coming from the exclusive jeweller near the Casino. Inside the bag itself was a padded, silk-lined box.

Nanette caught her breath as she lifted the lid and saw her present.

'JC, thank you,' Nanette said, gazing in amazement at a watch nestling in the folds of silk. A classic Rolex Lady-Datejust in yellow gold. 'It's gorgeous. I've never been so spoilt. I'm over-whelmed.'

'Does the strap fit? We can have it altered if necessary,' Jean-Claude asked anxiously. 'Let me help you put it on.' Bent solici-tously over her wrist, checking it fitted correctly, he said quietly, 'It's wonderful to have someone special to spoil,' before taking her in his arms and kissing her.

As his lips claimed hers, Nanette abandoned herself to the delicious feelings swamping her and returned his kiss passionately.

34

'Well done, you two,' Nanette said as the twins came running towards her and Patsy, having been collected by Mathieu from the stage door of the theatre, after performing in their school play. 'You were both brilliant.'

'Wish Mummy could have been here,' Olivia said wistfully.

'I videoed all the bits you and Pierre were in,' Jean-Claude said. 'So Mummy will get to see you. She'll be home in a few weeks.'

'I took some photos on my mobile phone,' Patsy said. 'Here, take a look,' and she handed her phone to Olivia.

As the twins giggled excitedly over the photos, Mathieu asked, 'Would you two like to go for burgers as a special treat?'

'Can we go to that new one down in Fontvieille?' Pierre said.

'Sure, if that's OK with everyone else?' Mathieu said.

Half an hour later, as everyone tucked into gigantic portions of burgers and chips, Jean-Claude's mobile rang. With an apologetic 'Sorry' he excused himself and went outside to answer it.

He didn't say anything when he returned, instead concentrated on helping the twins choose a dessert, but Nanette sensed his mood had darkened.

It was late by the time they returned to the apartment and she expected Jean-Claude to say his goodbyes and go straight home. Instead, when Mathieu asked if he was coming up with them, he said. 'Yes. I want a word with Nanette.'

Nanette was puzzled, but it wasn't until after the twins were tucked up in bed and Patsy had said goodnight to everyone and gone to her room that he said anything.

'Have you seen Evie recently?' he asked, a strange look on his face.

'Yes,' Nanette said, immediately feeling guilty that she hadn't had time to mention the meeting on board *Pole Position* to Jean-Claude. Let alone the reason she was there. 'Patsy and I had coffee here with her the other day,' she added. 'I was going to ask if you knew of any PA jobs going. Luc has paid her off and she needs another job. Why do you ask?'

'It was Luc who rang earlier. He's a worried man. Don't know the ins and outs of things, but basically, he's in real trouble. He got caught up in a business deal that's gone wrong and now he thinks he's being made a scapegoat for others. Did Evie mention any of this when you met?'

Nanette thought about the packet Evie had given her and wished she'd had the chance to talk to Jean-Claude about it. She shook her head unhappily.

'Is this the Luc I think it is?' Mathieu asked as he came out of his room 'I'd heard his business was in trouble. Give Evie my number – I might be able to help.'

Jean-Claude rounded on his son angrily. 'Oh yes – get her to work with one of your criminal friends. At least it won't be Boris Takyanov now that he's had his application for a resident's visa refused.'

'How do you know that? It's not common knowledge yet,' Mathieu demanded.

'You'd be surprised at just what I do know – including your so-called business activities,' Jean-Claude retorted. 'For instance, I know that you and Zac Ewart had a meeting in Luxembourg recently. I also know you spent six hours in the *gendarmerie* three days ago. I know that Boris—'

'It's you, isn't it?' Mathieu said slowly. 'You're the one having me followed.' He shook his head. 'I can't believe my own father is spying on me.'

'Personally, I can't believe how easily my son has turned from successful businessman into a criminal,' Jean-Claude shouted. '*Oui*, I had you followed because I was worried and wanted to know what was going on so I could help you.'

Both men had forgotten Nanette and she looked from one to the other in dismay as father and son glared at each other.

Mathieu sighed heavily. 'I keep telling you I am not a criminal and don't need you to interfere.'

'Then stop behaving like one and tell me what's going on.'

'I can't. I've been sworn to secrecy. Besides, what you don't know, you can't tell.'

Jean-Claude stared at him. 'I can't believe that you've been stupid enough to get involved with something illegal. These people you're involved with won't hesitate to sacrifice you to save their own skins. What would happen to the twins then?'

Mathieu replied, 'Nanette's here to look after the twins. You, I have no doubt, would also make sure they came to no harm. Vanessa will be home in a few weeks and they will return to England. Meanwhile, I intend to see this through, whatever you say.'

Jean-Claude shook his head in despair and turned away from his son.

Mathieu moved as though to touch him on the arm and say something, before changing his mind and walking towards his room instead. His 'Goodnight' was almost inaudible and the door closed behind him, only to open a second or two later.

'Do me one favour: call off your private detective, please.' This time, the door closed on his words and stayed shut.

Nanette, looking at Jean-Claude's worried face, said gently, 'There's nothing you can do, JC.'

'I feel so helpless,' he said, clenching his fists. 'I want to shake him, make him see sense.' He smiled ruefully at her. 'You are right though. This thing has got to run its course, whatever the outcome. I can only pray that Mathieu comes out of it unscathed – whatever it may be.'

'Please don't be cross with me, JC, but there is something I should have told you a couple of days ago. Zac asked me to do something for him. I didn't want to mention it in front of Mathieu.'

Quickly, she told Jean-Claude about her visit to *Pole Position* and the package Evie had given her to place in the secret safe.

'Thank you for telling me. Your visit to *Pole Position* was the reason Luc phoned me. He was worried you were mixed up in something too. Do you know what was in this package?'

Nanette shook her head and bit her lip before saying quietly, 'No. And... and I didn't put it in the safe. There was a handgun in there and it frightened me. Zac never had guns on board before.'

Jean-Claude looked at her, surprised. 'What did you do with it?'

'It's in my room,' Nanette said. 'I'll fetch it.'

Jean-Claude turned the package over and over when she handed it to him.

'I suspect it's money,' Nanette said. 'But why would Luc give money – or anything – to Zac to put in a secret safe?'

Jean-Claude sighed. 'Maybe it's all part of his problems. I'd have sworn Luc was an honest businessman, but then I'd also have said Mathieu would never get mixed up with anything illegal.' He glanced at her. 'Was there anything else in the safe?'

'Only the gun. Zac never even owned a gun in the past,' she added quietly. 'Shall we open it?' Nanette asked, looking first at the package and then at Jean-Claude.

He didn't reply for several minutes and then slowly shook his head. 'Not here. I'll take it with me and put it somewhere safe. I don't feel happy with you having it here.' He sighed. 'It's late. Time I went home. I'll be here at about eleven o'clock tomorrow to drive Patsy to the airport. Goodnight, *ma chérie*.'

A gentle kiss brushed her cheek and he was gone, leaving Nanette feeling strangely bereft.

35

There was no sign of Mathieu the next morning before Nanette left to take the twins to school and his bedroom door remained firmly closed. When she returned, Patsy was out on the balcony enjoying her breakfast croissant and coffee.

'I'm going to miss this view,' she said. 'Can't believe in a few hours I'll be back on the farm.' She spread some marmalade on her croissant before adding, 'Lots of activity on *Pole Position* this morning. People coming and going.'

Nanette, helping herself to a cup of coffee, glanced up. 'What sort of people?'

'People in suits. Look, there's one of them leaving now.'

The sisters watched as a man carrying a briefcase appeared in the stern of the yacht with Phil. The two men shook hands and Phil waited as the man left before raising the gangway and disappearing into the main cabin.

'Hmm,' Patsy said. 'Wonder what that's all about.' She glanced over. 'Bit of a family ding-dong last night?'

Nanette nodded. 'Sorry if it disturbed you. Jean-Claude is getting increasingly worried about Mathieu. Unfortunately, I don't think there is anything he can do. Have you seen him this morning?'

Patsy shook her head. 'No. Florence said he went out very early.'

Nanette sighed. 'Part of me wishes whatever it is would all come to a head and hang the consequences – at least we'd all know where we were.'

Patsy stood up. 'Well, I'd better go and finish packing.'

'Need a hand?'

'No thanks. Might need Jean-Claude to carry the suitcase for me though, it's a bit on the heavy side.'

While Patsy finished her packing, Nanette stayed out on the balcony looking down thoughtfully at *Pole Position*. Just what had been happening earlier on the now deserted yacht? Something to do with Vacances au Soleil maybe?

Florence, busy cleaning the sitting room, had the radio on softly in the background and Nanette was gently humming along to a favourite song when Jean-Claude arrived.

'How are you today?' she asked, returning his hug and staying in the circle of his arms, concerned at the lines of worry she could see still etched in his face from last night.

Jean-Claude shrugged non-committally. 'I've been better, but I've done as Mathieu asked and called off the private detective.'

'Did he have any final information to give you?'

Jean-Claude glanced towards Mathieu's bedroom door. 'Is he here?'

Nanette shook her head. 'No.'

'Apparently Mathieu has had several meetings in recent weeks just over the border in Italy. The detective can't prove it, but he thinks Mathieu was recruiting people to join a business cartel.' Jean-Claude sighed. 'With Boris being refused a permanent visa, I'm afraid that Mathieu will attract more attention from the authorities and move up the list of undesirables. Who knows what will happen then?'

Nanette didn't answer. 'Did you open the package?' she asked instead.

'*Non*.' He shook his head. 'I thought we'd do it together when we get back. Now, is Patsy ready? We should really make a move. I've booked a table for an early lunch in Cannes before we go to the airport.'

* * *

Both Nanette and Patsy enjoyed the drive and the lunch Jean-Claude treated them to at one of the restaurants on the Bord de Mer at Cannes. It was 1:30 p.m. as they drove past the roundabout with the vintage prop plane that graced the entrance to Cannes-Mandelieu airport.

'Jean-Claude, thank you for a lovely last day. As for arranging this flight – I still can't believe that I'm going home in a private jet,' Patsy said.

After she'd checked in, Jean-Claude left the two sisters to say their goodbyes.

'You take it easy when you get home,' Nanette said. 'If Helen wants to spoil you – let her!'

'I will,' Patsy promised. She hesitated before continuing, 'Nanette, as much as I would like you to be with me, I will understand if things here make it impossible for you to come back when the bump arrives.'

Nanette hugged her sister. 'Fingers crossed, I'll make it. You've got a few weeks to go yet, so hopefully things will have sorted themselves out. Vanessa and Ralph might even be back. Now, your flight awaits. Ring me when you get home.'

Nanette left her sister to board the aeroplane and joined Jean-

Claude in the car park, where she watched the executive jet take off with the comforting feel of Jean-Claude's arm around her shoulders.

Settling into the car for the drive back to Monaco, Jean-Claude switched on the car radio as a news bulletin started.

'*A failed coup in South America has led to the arrest of a number of people in Columbia and Brazil. In a series of dawn raids this morning in a joint operation with Interpol, police have arrested a number of men in London and Monaco.*'

Jean-Claude and Nanette turned to each other in apprehension, both instantly thinking of Mathieu.

'*The arrested men, who include the Russian millionaire, Boris Takyanov, are being held in unnamed police stations. No further details have been given, but it is believed the investigation, code name Sunny Climes, is part of an ongoing inquiry into charges of fraud and tax evasion in Monaco and France.*'

Silently, Jean-Claude leant forward and turned off the radio before starting the car. Glancing at Nanette, he said quietly, 'I think we'd better get home as quickly as we can.'

36

Nanette was silent, scarcely noticing the kilometres flying past as she sat, immersed in her own thoughts, as Jean-Claude expertly negotiated their way back to Monaco along the A8 autoroute.

Jean-Claude had tuned the car radio into the Monte Carlo station frequency hoping to hear some more information about the arrests, but there were no further news bulletins before they arrived back in the Principality.

A worried Florence met them at the apartment door, hysteria in her voice as she said something rapidly to Jean-Claude. The only word Nanette caught and understood was 'Mathieu' and she looked on anxiously as Jean-Claude's expression became grimmer and grimmer before the housekeeper paused for breath.

'She thinks Mathieu's among the men who have been arrested,' Jean-Claude said, turning to Nanette. 'I must go and find out; see if there's anything I can do. I'll be back when I can.'

'I need to meet the twins,' Nanette said. 'I'll walk down with you.'

Leaving a clearly worried Jean-Claude at the entrance to the underground garage, Nanette made her way towards the twins' school, where Pierre and Olivia were already waiting for her in the playground.

The old port was busy that afternoon with yachts and boats continually making their way in and out of the harbour. Tourists strolled along the embankment taking in the atmosphere and trying to get a glimpse of the celebrities sunbathing on the decks of their large yachts.

Stopping to buy the twins an ice cream at one of the pavement cafés, Nanette watched hundreds of passengers as they disembarked from one of the large ships that spent the summer months cruising the Mediterranean and regularly berthed in the harbour.

Wandering back along the embankment they passed a deserted *Pole Position* – its gangway raised and the No Entry sign firmly in place. With Zac not due back until shortly before the French Grand Prix, the crew would be enjoying having time to themselves.

Briefly, Nanette found herself wishing she didn't have to wait so long to talk to Zac. She desperately needed to discuss her returning memories with him, tell him what she'd decided to do. She wanted to be free to get on with the rest of her life.

Stifling a sigh, she shepherded the twins across the road and back to the apartment, hoping to find Jean-Claude and Mathieu there. Florence, though, was still alone and shook her head when Nanette asked quietly, 'Any news?'

When the phone rang at eight o'clock that night, Nanette snatched it up instantly, hoping it was Jean-Claude.

'Hi, Sis,' Patsy's voice said.

'Oh, hi,' Nanette answered, trying to keep the disappointment out of her voice as she realised it wasn't Jean-Claude.

'Just ringing to tell you the bump is behaving itself and I'm home safely,' Patsy said.

'Great. You take care now for the next few weeks.' Nanette hesitated before adding, 'Patsy, can I ring you for a chat tomorrow? Right now I'm waiting for Jean-Claude to phone.'

'Is everything all right down there?'

Nanette crossed her fingers before answering. 'Everything is fine. I'll phone you tomorrow and we'll have a chat.'

Once the twins were settled and in bed for the night, Nanette wandered out on to the balcony, unable to concentrate on anything as she waited for news from Jean-Claude. Down below, Monaco nightlife was buzzing with its usual mid-evening intensity. Yacht crews were welcoming guests on board for dinner, glamorous couples were walking arm in arm along the embankment and groups of men and women were making their way into the various restaurants for an enjoyable evening with friends. The cruise liner Nanette had seen earlier, *Reine Soleil*, was slowly manoeuvring its way out of the crowded harbour, beginning its overnight journey to Corsica.

As darkness began to fall, the twinkling reflections of yacht and town lights in the harbour water seemed to Nanette to add a poignant romanticism to the familiar scene. A brief stillness in the night air, though, filled her with apprehension.

Unexpected tears pricked at the back of her eyes as she suddenly felt very alone and incredibly vulnerable for no real reason that she could fathom. She longed for Jean-Claude to come as she struggled to compose her thoughts.

A matter of minutes later, when he did arrive, Nanette surrendered herself totally to the joy of being held in his arms.

'You seem unhappy, *ma chérie*?' Jean-Claude said. 'Have you been crying?'

Nanette shook her head. 'Not really. I just felt sad and lonely for some reason. I'm better now you're here.' She stayed happily in the circle of his arms, glancing up at him. 'Now, tell me – is Mathieu in jail?'

'*Non*,' Jean-Claude said. 'I don't know where he is. I've contacted everyone I can, even people I wouldn't normally talk to, in the hope that someone would know something, but nothing.' He sighed. 'Maybe tomorrow we'll have some news.' He hesitated. 'I've brought the package with me,' he said quietly. 'I think we open it tonight.'

'Do you think we should?' Nanette said. 'I'm beginning to wish I'd just done as Zac asked and put it in his safe.'

'But, for whatever reason, you didn't,' Jean-Claude said. 'If we open it, it may provide a clue to what is going on. If not...' He shrugged.

'I think, whatever we find, I ought to put it in the safe before Zac returns,' Nanette said slowly, as she followed Jean-Claude into the sitting room.

'Does Florence have any rubber gloves in the kitchen?'

Nanette nodded. 'Do we really need gloves? I've already handled the package and so have you. Our fingerprints will be all over it anyway.'

'Yes, our prints will be over the outside of the package, but we have a legitimate excuse for that. It wouldn't be so easy to explain how your, or my, fingerprints happened to be on the inside.'

'I'll fetch the gloves.' Nanette said.

It was Nanette who pulled on the gloves when they turned out to be too small for Jean-Claude's hands.

Jean-Claude had placed the package on the table and they both looked at it thoughtfully for several seconds before Nanette picked it up and examined it.

'Look, if I pull this Sellotape off gently and open it carefully, I can reseal it and Zac need never know we've opened it.'

As she spoke, she gently ran her finger under the seal and carefully eased the package open. Nanette, biting her lip in worried concentration, felt her mouth forming an astonished 'oh' as she saw the contents slide out of the packaging: a piece of A4 paper with a handwritten list on it and two bottles of shampoo.

Nanette shook her head in disbelief as she looked at Jean-Claude and went to pick up one of the bottles.

'*Non*! Don't touch them,' Jean-Claude said.

Nanette looked at him, shocked. 'It's just bottles of shampoo, JC,' she protested.

'No, I don't think it's as simple as that,' Jean-Claude said. 'Leave the bottles for a moment and put the paper on the table where we can both see it.'

At first glance, it appeared to be a jumble of dates, some crossed through, with a single word – either Pepi or Cruz alongside, followed by two initials – RS or MW.

'The dates from April are each roughly a fortnight apart,' Jean-Claude said thoughtfully.

'The exception is May the thirteenth which is only a week after the preceding one. That's the only date to have Cruz and MW after it – all the others have Pepi and RS. Is there some sort of pattern here?'

'The crossed-out dates have all gone,' Jean-Claude continued. 'We're in the middle of June now and there are only two dates left, the twenty-fourth of June and then a gap to July the fifteenth.'

There was a short silence before Nanette said slowly, 'Think about it, JC. It's sort of following a Grand Prix timetable. The thirteenth of May was the day after the Spanish Grand Prix, the twenty-fourth of June is the day after the French GP and July the fifteenth is the day after Silverstone.'

Jean-Claude looked at her thoughtfully. 'Could that indicate Zac's involvement? Days when he would expect to be here? But what or who are Pepi, Cruz and what do the initials stand for?'

Mathieu's voice answered him before Nanette could speak. 'I can tell you that. Pepi is a crew member on the *Reine Soleil* and Cruz is on the *Mediterranean Wanderer*.'

Jean-Claude and Nanette spun round to see a dishevelled Mathieu regarding them tiredly from the doorway. Carefully, Nanette placed the paper on top of the shampoo bottles, forlornly hoping to hide them from Mathieu's view for some reason. Too late. He'd already seen them.

'Where did those come from?' he demanded.

'Never mind those,' Jean-Claude snapped. 'Where the hell have you been?'

Mathieu looked at his father. 'It's a long story that will have to keep until tomorrow.' He held his hand up to stop Jean-Claude's protestations. 'I promise, you and I will get together tomorrow when I will finally tell you everything I know.'

'Everything?'

Mathieu nodded. 'I promise. Now, will you please move that paper and let me see those bottles properly.'

Silently, Nanette picked up the paper.

'Where did you get these?' Mathieu asked again, as he looked at them.

Nanette hesitated before telling him. 'I was supposed to put them in a secret safe on *Pole Position*.'

Jean-Claude looked at his son. 'These bottles contain something other than shampoo, don't they?'

Mathieu nodded. 'I wondered how they were doing it. I had a good idea how the money laundering was being done but not the actual diamond smuggling.'

'Money laundering? Diamond smuggling?' Nanette said, looking from Jean-Claude to Mathieu. 'Zac?'

'Yes,' Mathieu answered. 'I guarantee, if you were to unscrew one of those bottles, more diamonds than you ever thought to see in your life would flow out with the shampoo.'

37

Nanette was returning from taking the twins to school the next morning when her mobile rang. Jean-Claude.

'*Cherie*, Luc has asked to meet me this morning. I'll come to the apartment as quickly as I can afterwards. Try not to let Mathieu leave before I get there.'

'I'll do my best,' Nanette promised, not sure how she could detain Mathieu if he decided to leave.

Mathieu was in the small anteroom he was using as a temporary office, working on his computer and listening to an international news bulletin through its speakers when she got back to the apartment. He glanced up as Nanette appeared in the doorway.

'I've brought you a coffee,' Nanette said, handing him a cup. 'Any news about Boris and the others?'

Mathieu shook his head. 'No. There's some trouble in Formula 1,' he said, as the radio bulletin switched to the latest sports news.

'*This weekend's French Grand Prix is under threat because of a problem with the tyres. Drivers are threatening to boycott the event over safety fears like they did in Indianapolis back in 2005. Our reporter spoke to current world championship leader, Zac Ewart, earlier.'*

Nanette and Mathieu listened as Zac gave his opinion on the problem before saying, 'I'm confident that it will all be sorted within the next forty-eight hours and I fully expect the cars to line up on the grid as usual for this Sunday's race – with me hopefully taking pole position.'

As the newsreader went on to the next item, Nanette turned to Mathieu.

'I just don't understand what made Zac get involved with Boris and all this illegal stuff in the first place. He earns so much money from his driving. I know he can't drive for ever, but he was going to build up Vacances au Soleil to give him a legitimate business to run when he quits driving. He doesn't need to do illegal stuff.'

Mathieu glanced at her. 'Vacances au Soleil *isn't* going to be a legitimate business. Zac intends it to be a front for more money laundering.'

'He asked me to work for him. He knows I'd never condone anything illegal,' Nanette protested.

'That's why you'd have been perfect. You'd have handled the day-to-day running of the business honestly, not realising you were spending money that Zac had come by illicitly.'

'When he was arrested, nobody would have believed that I was innocent,' Nanette said slowly. 'They would have assumed I'd been a part of the conspiracy.'

Mathieu shrugged. 'I guess so. As to why he got involved with all this – it's partly excitement, I think. Something to give him a kick when he loses the adrenalin rush of being able to drive at two hundred miles an hour. Also, it's good, old-fashioned greed.'

'Is that why you got involved – greed?'

Mathieu looked at her steadily. 'Do you really believe that of me, Nanette?'

'Three years ago, I wouldn't have believed it of Zac, now,' she shrugged, 'anything seems possible.'

There was a short silence before Mathieu spoke and then he ignored her accusation, saying instead, 'I thought my father would be here early this morning to interrogate me, I wonder where he is. Incidentally, is there something going on between the two of you?'

Nanette felt the blush spreading across her cheeks and knew denying there was anything between her and Jean-Claude would be silly.

'Thought so,' Mathieu said. 'He's a lucky man.'

'He rang to say he had to go to a meeting and would be later than he intended,' Nanette said. 'He was anxious that you might leave before he gets here.' She glanced at Mathieu. 'He's very worried about what you've got yourself involved in. That you are acting illegally. I hope you can reassure him when he gets here.'

'I certainly intend to explain how and why I got involved, but,' Mathieu hesitated, 'it's not over yet. There are still things I have to do. Whatever he says is not going to stop me doing them.'

Nanette took a sip of her coffee as she regarded Mathieu apprehensively. 'He's more likely to want to help than stop you,' she said. 'To try to prevent you ending up in trouble with the law.'

'Maybe it's time I let him get involved.'

Nanette felt her heart contract at Mathieu's words. The thought of anything happening to Jean-Claude filled her with dread. 'Mathieu—'

'Don't worry. I promise you I won't put him in a direct line of fire.'

Nanette heard the apartment door opening and went to greet Jean-Claude. She needed to feel his arms around her but wasn't yet ready to display her affection for his father in front of Mathieu. She returned Jean-Claude's gentle kiss quickly. 'We've been expecting you for ages,' she said.

'Luc needed to talk,' Jean-Claude answered. 'I'll tell you about it later. Where's Mathieu?' he asked anxiously. 'Not disappeared again?'

'Don't worry. I'm in the sitting room,' Mathieu called out. 'Ready to talk to you.'

'It's about time,' Jean-Claude said, looking at Mathieu expectantly.

'You know I've always kept in touch with Mama's relatives,' Mathieu said. 'Do you remember Uncle Sebastian?'

Jean-Claude nodded. 'Your mama's big brother. Had a restaurant in the centre of Paris for a long time. Didn't he retire a couple of years ago?'

'It was more a case of selling up while he still had something to sell,' Mathieu responded quietly. 'He was being targeted by a protection gang and he simply didn't have the strength to fight Boris Takyanov and his thugs any longer.' There was a short pause before Mathieu continued. 'When Boris turned up in Monaco, I knew it wouldn't be too long before he started his criminal activities down here. Anyway, I went to the police to put them in the picture about Takyanov in case the Parisian police hadn't passed on his details. I also offered my help in putting a stop to him.'

Mathieu looked at his father. 'I thought I owed Uncle Sebastian that, at least, but the police declined my help – until a few months ago. It was the main reason I couldn't do what Vanessa wanted and look after the twins in the UK,' Mathieu added, turning to Nanette. 'I had to stay here to become a part of the entourage that surrounds Takyanov.'

'The day I arrived and you'd been arrested – was that all part of the plan?' Nanette asked.

Mathieu nodded. 'The police were anxious for me to look like a criminal whom Takyanov would think could be useful to him, so they arrested me on some trumped-up charges. Paying my bail ensured that I had a reason to be grateful to him. His plan, as I suspected, was to muscle in on the local businesses and to run his international operations from here.'

'Luc told me this morning that Boris approached him initially when he first arrived in Monaco, wanting to invest in his business. He was angry when Luc refused,' Jean-Claude said. 'Somehow this year he got wind of the fact that Luc had cash-flow problems and offered to help. Luc says accepting his help was the stupidest decision he has ever made. The parcel Evie delivered to *Pole Position* and Nanette brought here was the last of several errands that Boris pressured Luc into running for him. He'd decided the only way out of Boris's clutches was to sell up and cease trading – rather like Uncle Sebastian, by the sound of it,' Jean-Claude said, looking at Mathieu.

'Did Evie know what she was delivering?' Mathieu asked.

'*Non*. Neither did Luc. When Evie told him Nanette had been there to take the package, he was worried that she was involved with Zac again and also Boris. The telephone call the other evening was to warn me.'

'Do you know how Zac got involved?' Nanette asked. 'He wouldn't have needed a business loan.'

Mathieu shook his head. 'You know Zac and I have been friends for – for ever really. When all this started, I had no idea he was caught up in it. I found it very difficult to spy on him. I kept hoping that he'd sort himself out and get free of it, but he's in too deep, I'm afraid. I'm sorry,' Mathieu said to Nanette.

She shrugged. 'Zac and I have some personal unfinished business to sort out, but he's no longer a part of my life.'

'Why didn't you confide in me before?' Jean-Claude asked quietly.

Mathieu sighed. 'Partly because I didn't want to involve you in case things got nasty, and' – Mathieu hesitated, before adding quietly – 'also because I know how wary you are about Mama's relatives. You'd probably have blamed Uncle Sebastian for getting me involved.'

Jean-Claude shook his head in protest. '*Non*.'

'Anyway, as I told you before, the police urged me to confide in no one,' Mathieu said. 'It was easier that way.'

'Does Takyanov still think you're a fellow criminal?' Jean-Claude asked. 'Even though you haven't been arrested this time?'

'*Oui*. Zac, too, trusts me – both as his friend and as a fellow conspirator. When he returns from the French Grand Prix, I have a feeling he intends to invite me to become more involved in his money-laundering sideline.' Mathieu bit his lip. 'The police have suspected a link between him and Takyanov for a long time, but now we have the proof he's involved in the diamond smuggling too. Surrendering my friend to the police is going to be one of the hardest things I have ever done.'

'Incidentally, what happened to the shampoo last night?' Jean-Claude asked, looking around as if he expected to see it still on the table.

'I meant to take it and keep it hidden until we decided what to do, but unfortunately your appearance drove it completely out of my mind.'

'I packed it up again,' Nanette answered quietly. 'It's in my room.'

'I think it's too dangerous for you to keep it here,' Jean-Claude said. 'The implications of you being found with it in your possession don't bear thinking about. Perhaps the time has come to hand it over to the authorities?' he continued.

Mathieu shook his head. 'I'd rather not just yet. With Zac in France for the Grand Prix rather than here in the Principality, it would only serve to complicate things. Best to keep it hidden until Zac returns and we can confront him with it. If you want me to look after it, I will,' he offered.

There was a short silence as Nanette looked from Jean-Claude to Mathieu.

'Personally, I think the best place for it is on board *Pole Position*. I really don't know what made me remove it,' she said quietly, shaking her head. 'At least if it's in the safe when Zac gets back, he doesn't need to know that I didn't do as he asked.' She took a deep breath and cut short both Jean-Claude and Mathieu's protestations. 'As I'm the one who took it and the only one who knows where the safe is, as well as the combination to open it, the responsibility to return it is mine.'

38

The city of Manaus was a huge shock to Vanessa. Ralph had told her it was one of the most isolated metropolitan areas in the world, but she was ill prepared for its vastness and the noise it generated.

As their boat drew alongside the floating dock, she stood up and looked around. Eleven hours ago, the boat had been moored in a quiet tributary with jungle animal sounds providing the background noise and happy, smiling natives helping them load the boat for the journey upriver.

Here, moored on the banks of the Amazon River itself, it was the raucous sounds of a modern industrial jungle that surrounded them as they stepped off the boat. It was hard to believe that this busy inland port was in the heart of the rainforest.

Vanessa gazed, fascinated, at the double-decked ferries and houseboats that were everywhere, crammed along the shoreline in front of ramshackle buildings on the water's edge. Dozens of large cargo ships were tied up unloading goods, others were taking sacks of coffee beans, rubber, and nuts on board; all, it seemed to Vanessa, in vast quantities. She glanced at Ralph.

'Do you think anyone is going to be interested in shipping the small quantities of produce Fruits of the Forest is going to have in the beginning?'

'Of course,' Ralph said confidently. 'We'll look for a small commercial shipper who is keen to expand and grow with the cooperative. No point in even approaching the big international boys in the beginning. We'll ask around tomorrow. Right now, let's get to the hotel.'

The hotel, a tall modern building ten minutes from the city centre, was blessedly cool after the humidity outside. Once they were registered, Ralph asked the receptionist to book a phone call to Monaco for them, and they went straight to their room.

When the phone on the bedside table rang, Vanessa snatched it up, only to be told the number wasn't answering and the receptionist would try again later.

'Perhaps by then we'll have a definite UK arrival date,' Ralph said, trying to ease her disappointment. 'Nick and Harry are going out to the airport later to try to book flights. Do you feel up to doing some exploring?' Ralph continued. 'Might as well see the sights.'

'Can we leave the touristy bit until tomorrow? What I really want to do is have a shower, something to eat and go to bed. I'm exhausted,' Vanessa said, trying to push her illogical worry about not being to get through to Mathieu and the twins away.

'Sure. In that case I'll go out to the airport with the boys. Do you want me to order you something from room service, or will you go down to the dining room?'

'A sandwich from room service would be fine.'

After her shower, Vanessa curled up on the double bed to eat her supper, revelling in the air-conditioned coolness of the room.

She'd forgotten during the last few months in the jungle what it was like to be comfortable and not continually damp with perspiration. While Ralph was out organising a flight, she'd use the time to write down the details of their return journey through the jungle in the diary, ready for the twins to read.

Ralph returned with frustrating news. 'I'm sorry, Vanessa, I know you're desperate to get home to the twins, but there are no direct flights available. We've got to go via the States. Even then we can't fly for seventy-two hours.'

Vanessa hid her disappointment. 'Can't be helped. Hopefully I'll get to speak to them tomorrow.' She glanced at Ralph, hot and sticky from his foray to the airport. 'Why don't you have a shower and then come to bed? It's far more comfy than the hammocks we've been using recently. We can actually have a proper cuddle.' Vanessa looked at Ralph, a half-smile on her lips.

'Now why didn't I think of that,' Ralph said, undoing his shirt and moving towards the shower. 'Give me five minutes and I'll take you up on that offer.'

* * *

The next morning, they were up early, intent on getting down to the docks to look for a shipping exporter willing to discuss handling the Fruits of the Forest produce. Vanessa also wanted to explore the Mercado Adolpho Lisboa, the city's oldest marketplace.

Their search around the docks for a shipping company proved fruitless. Nobody even had the time to speak to them, let alone discuss exporting Fruits of the Forest produce.

'Let's give up,' Vanessa said. 'I've a feeling it's going to be easier to organise it through a third party from the UK.'

Before returning to the hotel, they wandered through the vast ancient market thronging with locals buying their produce from the traditional stalls. The outside streets were packed with more stalls and souvenir sellers. Vanessa was delighted to find one selling the locally made woven bags and ponchos.

'Nanette will adore one of the bags,' she said. 'I'll get a couple of ponchos for the twins.'

Back in their hotel room, Vanessa booked another call to Monaco, crossing her fingers that this time she'd get through. Standing, receiver in hand, she listened to the ringing tone before shaking her head at Ralph.

'Still no reply. I don't understand it. Oh... hello Jean-Claude? Where is everyone? I was just about to hang up.'

Vanessa was silent as she listened to Jean-Claude for several minutes.

'OK. Will you tell Nanette I'll ring her tomorrow then with our plans? Yes, we've had a great time. Hope to see you soon. Love to the twins. Goodbye.' Vanessa slowly replaced the receiver before turning to look at Ralph. 'That was weird. Neither Mathieu nor Nanette were in the apartment. Nanette had taken the twins somewhere and he didn't know where Mathieu was. He assured me the twins are fine and looking forward to seeing me.' Vanessa sighed. 'Something is going on back there. I can just feel it.'

39

'Right, you two. Dry yourselves off, get dressed and go to the games room while I have a quick swim. Papa Jean-Claude will be here soon and then we'll have a quick snack before we go home.'

Nanette had taken the twins up to the villa on Sunday afternoon for a swim. To her disappointment, there had been no sign of Jean-Claude. Anneka had told her, '*Monsieur* had to go out for an hour. He asks that you wait for his return.'

Lazily floating on her back after completing a couple of energetic lengths, Nanette found herself thinking about Mathieu's revelations and the package currently concealed under her bed. Somehow she had to find the right moment to go inconspicuously to *Pole Position* and put it in the safe.

She heard the twins calling out 'Bonjour, Papa Jean-Claude,' and quickly swam to the steps and got out of the pool. Before she could pick up her towel, Jean-Claude appeared and took her in his arms.

'I'll make you all wet,' Nanette protested weakly, before she surrendered herself to his embrace. Several minutes passed before Nanette sighed and drew away. 'I think you'd better let me get dressed before the twins come demanding to be fed,' she said regretfully, giving Jean-Claude one last lingering kiss.

It was early evening when Nanette left to take the twins back to the apartment. Olivia and Pierre had already kissed their grandfather goodbye and were waiting for Nanette out on the terrace when Jean-Claude said, 'I've been thinking about the package. If you are determined to replace it – and I agree that would probably be for the best – I will come with you. I think tomorrow morning after the twins go to school, *n'est pas*? I will wait on the quay, while you go on board.'

Nanette hesitated before saying, 'Perhaps Mathieu ought to come with me instead. The police have involved him officially, whereas you...' Her voice trailed off.

'*Non*. I'm coming with you.'

Nanette smiled, before kissing him gently. 'OK. Thanks. Now, I'm going home to get the twins to bed and I think I might have an early night myself. I'll see you in the morning.'

When Nanette did go to bed, soon after the twins, she slept fitfully. She'd been convinced she was so tired she would have no problems sleeping, but the hot midsummer night air was stifling. Even the ceiling fan silently whirring away above her head was failing to keep her cool. It wasn't just the heat keeping her awake. Her mind was tossing and turning, too. All day Mathieu's words 'it isn't over yet' had been playing on her mind.

She knew Boris was still in jail, having been refused bail, and the latest rumour flying around Monaco was that Interpol had arrested his son. More arrests were expected to be made soon. Was that going to include Zac?

Mathieu had spent most of the day in the apartment on his computer after warning her and Jean-Claude that things were likely to come to a head soon and he intended to lie low for a few days.

Unable to sleep and sighing in frustration, Nanette got out of bed. Pulling on her dressing gown, she went through the silent apartment to the kitchen to fetch a glass of water. A dim light was shining under the threshold of Mathieu's door, everywhere else was in darkness. At least he was home tonight.

Returning to her room, she opened the curtains and pushed the balcony door open. The breeze from the harbour ruffled her hair but was too hot to bring any relief from the heat.

Glancing down at the harbour, Nanette was struck by a sudden idea as she looked at *Pole Position* gently moving on its mooring. The lights were on in the main saloon of the yacht – that had to mean only one thing: the crew, or at least Phil, the skipper, was still up.

Ten minutes – fifteen at the most – was all it would take to go down, put the package in the safe and return to the apartment. The quay was relatively empty of people, with only a few couples out, taking a romantic night-time stroll.

With luck, nobody would even notice her. She'd be able to tell Jean-Claude in the morning he needn't worry about accompanying her to the yacht. The package was back where it should be. She and Jean-Claude could no longer be linked to the contents.

Quickly putting on a pair of jeans and a dark top, she slipped her feet into her docksiders, before pulling the box from under the bed and taking out the Vacances au Soleil papers as well as the package. If the luxury holiday business was a front for money laundering, as Mathieu had said, those papers, too, would be better back on board.

Picking up her keys, Nanette quietly left the apartment and went down the marble stairs rather than take the lift. As quiet as it was at this time of night, the sound of its movement did drift through to the apartment and she didn't want to disturb Mathieu.

Once on the quay alongside *Pole Position*, Nanette was surprised to find that although the 'No Entry' sign was in place, the gangway to the yacht was lowered, so she simply unhooked the chain with its 'Private' sign and walked on board, before hooking it back in place. The door to the main cabin was closed and, as she opened it, Phil glanced up from the table where he was working on some papers.

'Hi. I just need to put these in Zac's safe,' Nanette said confidently, as she walked past him towards the master bedroom, willing him not to stop her.

Phil looked as though he was about to say something and then simply shrugged his shoulders and returned to his paperwork.

Nanette didn't bother to throw the light switch in the bedroom – there was enough light from the passageway for her to see her way across. In the bathroom, she pushed the door to as she switched on the mirror lights before kneeling down and moving the towels and lifting the under-sink shelf out.

Once again she concentrated on remembering the twists and turns between the numbers and breathed a sigh of relief as she pulled the safe door open. She was doing what she should have done originally – putting the package in the safe.

Another minute and she'd be on her way back to the apartment. Her actions froze as her gaze took in the empty shelf where the gun had been: there was only one person in the world who could have removed it.

The door behind her creaked. Slowly, she raised her head. A cold shiver ran through her as she saw the man reflected in the illuminated bathroom mirror.

Nanette watched, rigid with fear, as Zac Ewart casually

flipped off the safety catch before levelling the gun at her and asking, 'Why, oh why, did you have to meddle, Nanette?'

Night-time sounds of the crew moving about up on deck punctuated the silence as Zac regarded Nanette intently, the gun steady in his hand.

'What are you doing here?' Nanette forced the question out, her gaze firmly on the gun.

'Only five drivers were going to trust their tyres enough to line up on the grid. As none of them are anywhere near me in the championship, I decided I could boycott the race too, without it affecting my title chances,' Zac said. 'So, as I had some urgent business to sort out here, and my usual private jet was on standby, I decided to come home.'

'Do you intend on using that, or shall I put it in the safe too?' Nanette asked quietly, indicating the gun.

Zac looked at the gun as if he'd forgotten he was holding it, and shrugged. 'Might as well.' As he leant forward and handed it to her, he said, 'Don't worry, it's not loaded.'

Wordlessly, Nanette took the gun from him and put it in the safe.

'Why didn't you put the package in the safe the other day?'

Nanette swallowed hard. 'Couldn't remember the correct twists and turns between the numbers,' she said finally, hoping he'd believe her.

'Oh, and now you can. Came back to you in a flash, did it? Incidentally, I'll have the Vacances au Soleil papers if that's what's in the envelope. They don't need to go in the safe.'

Silently, Nanette handed the envelope up to him. 'You lied to me, didn't you, Zac, when you told me there was nothing illegal about the package?'

Zac shrugged. 'Did you open it?'

Nanette flushed but didn't answer.

Zac's eyes narrowed. 'You did. I trust you didn't go as far as using any of the contents? Or even showing them to anyone else?'

'Why would I show bottles of shampoo to anyone?' Nanette said, as innocently as she could. Nothing would induce her to tell Zac that Jean-Claude had been with her when she opened the parcel – or that Mathieu had also seen the contents and told her what they contained.

'Good. Well, go on, put it in the safe.' He watched as she carefully did as she was told and closed the door. 'Don't forget to leave everything tidy, will you?' he said, looking at the shelf and the towels on the floor, before turning on his heels and leaving Nanette alone in the bathroom.

Shakily, she carefully slotted the shelf back in position before reaching for the towels. Only a few more minutes and she'd be off the yacht and on her way home.

Nanette steadied herself against the cupboard as the yacht rocked unexpectedly on her mooring. That wasn't right. Boats didn't rock like that on their harbour moorings. Suddenly she registered the muted vibration of the boat's engines. *Pole Position* was underway. Terror flooded her body as bile rose in her throat and she realised the truth.

Leaving the towels on the floor and slamming the bathroom door behind her, she ran to the nearest porthole in the master bedroom. Monaco town lights were fading into indistinguishable specks along the shoreline. The walls that guarded the entrance of the harbour were disappearing from view as the yacht made for the open sea.

'Beautiful evening for a trip round the bay, don't you think?'

Nanette spun round to see Zac watching her lazily from the large king-sized bed.

'Turn the yacht around and let me off,' Nanette demanded.

Zac shook his head. 'Sorry, I can't do that. We have to talk.'

Nanette glared at him. 'If I'm not there to take the twins to school tomorrow morning, Mathieu will be worried.'

Zac shrugged. 'I spoke to him a few minutes ago. I told him you were spending the night on board with me.'

Nanette flushed angrily at the implication behind his words. 'If you don't turn around immediately, the first thing I shall do when I get back is go to the authorities and have you charged with kidnapping,' Nanette threatened.

'They'd just think you were a spurned lover – after all, you were happy enough to come aboard before. Besides, you did come aboard of your own free will. Phil will attest to that.'

Disconsolate and fighting back tears, Nanette stared at him. It seemed a long time ago that she had thought she loved this man. 'How long do you intend to keep me on board?'

Before Zac could answer, there was a discreet knock on the cabin door.

'The saloon is ready, sir,' the head stewardess said.

Zac turned to Nanette. 'You told me recently we needed a serious talk, so, shall we be civilised and do it over a meal?'

'Answer my question. How long?'

Zac sighed before saying slowly, 'As long as necessary. Now, shall we eat? I haven't eaten properly for hours.'

'I'm not hungry,' Nanette said.

'Suit yourself. You can talk to me while I eat.' Zac swung himself off the bed and walked to the saloon.

Two places were laid on the mahogany dining-table – crystal glasses, silver cutlery and candles in gold candelabra gave a gentle glow to the cabin. Champagne nestled in a silver ice bucket, while a CD of guitar music was playing softly in the background.

'Just like the old days again when we were together,' Zac said.

'Hardly,' Nanette snapped.

Zac poured a glass of champagne and offered it to her. When Nanette shook her head and turned away, he raised the glass in a mock salute before taking a long drink and then topping up the glass.

'Vanessa is due back soon, isn't she? Thought any more about working with me on Vacances au Soleil? We could be a good team again. I'll even make you a director if you want. I'm hoping Mathieu is going to join the company too, in the near future.' He moved across to the table and helped himself to a portion of smoked salmon.

Nanette, about to protest that Mathieu definitely wouldn't be joining him and that she knew Vacances au Soleil was a front for a money-laundering operation, stopped. Zac didn't yet know the part Mathieu was about to play in his downfall.

'The answer is still no, Zac. I won't work for you again.' She paused. 'Besides, I'm not entirely convinced you're not lying to me when you say it's a legal business.'

Zac regarded her steadily.

'You lied to me – to everyone – three years ago, about the accident, didn't you? So what's to stop you lying to me again?' she said, watching his face for a reaction to her words. 'I wasn't driving that night, was I, Zac? What I don't understand is why you lied? Why you ruined my life?'

In the silence that followed her words, Zac impassively forked some smoked salmon into his mouth.

Nanette felt her temper rising. How could he be so indifferent to what she was saying, to her feelings? He didn't care. Had he ever really cared?

'I remember driving to the restaurant,' Nanette continued softly. 'I remember the friends who were there. We all had a lovely meal and the champagne flowed. As it was my birthday, I drove us there and you promised to drive us home, so half a glass of champagne was all you drank.'

Nanette took a deep breath. 'I also remember coming out of the restaurant and finding it was raining – hard. The kind of wet weather you are renowned to like for pushing your car to the limit. I remember you getting into the driver's seat when we left the restaurant, a happy smile on your face. And yet, after the accident, you deliberately made it look as though I'd been driving when I was over the limit. When all the time it was you who lost control of the car when it aquaplaned.' Nanette held her breath, waiting for his reaction.

Zac sighed before finally looking her in the eye. 'Couldn't you just see the headlines in the *Nice Matin* – "Formula 1 Ace charged with dangerous driving"? So, when the *pompiers* arrived and assumed you were the driver as it was your car, I decided not to enlighten them.'

'It was very convenient for you then, that I lost my memory for so long, wasn't it? Couldn't speak up and set the story straight.'

Zac didn't reply.

'Is that why you didn't come near me again? Why you had me airlifted back to the UK? You were afraid that I would suddenly broadcast to the world that it wasn't me behind the wheel that night. It was a famous racing driver who had taken the coward's way out!'

'I did pull you out of the wreckage before it burst into flames. I deserve some credit for that, don't I?' Zac asked quietly.

'I saw the headlines calling you a hero for saving my life, and I owe you my thanks for that.' Nanette glared at him. 'But what you did afterwards was despicable, Zac. I was vilified and ostracised by my friends, sent away like I was contagious. I was labelled a drunken driver, charged with dangerous driving and lost my licence. The world thought I'd nearly killed you, when in fact it was you who nearly killed me.'

'The media would have crucified me, Nanette. I was at a critical point of my career – just changing teams – I didn't need the wrong sort of publicity. You, on the other hand' – he shrugged before giving her a sardonic smile – 'who was going to really care whether you lost your licence? You were just my girlfriend, no one special in the eyes of the world.'

As he stared her down, defying her to argue with him, Nanette knew that any lingering love she had once felt for Zac Ewart had just been bludgeoned to death by his callous words.

'Tomorrow I am going to start clearing my name,' she said defiantly.

'Why bother after all this time? Besides, who are people going to believe: a world-famous racing driver or a one-time office girl?' Zac hesitated before adding quietly, 'I did try once, Nanette, to set the record straight, but by then the police had done their paperwork and it was too late.'

'If you had any decency left, you'd come with me and make them acknowledge the truth.' Nanette gazed reflectively at Zac. Life on the race track was a serious business, not to be taken lightly, but away from the circuit, Zac had always had this cavalier attitude to life. It had been one of the things she'd found difficult to accept about him. Jean-Claude, she knew, would never have deserted her in her hour of need. That Jean-Claude would always be there for her, she didn't doubt for a single second.

'Nanette, what are you thinking? You're miles away. I remember you getting that dreamy look when we were together. Are you thinking about us?'

Nanette shook her head. 'Oh no, Zac. I'm not taking a trip down memory lane with you. I'm thinking about my future and you are staying firmly in the past.'

'Have you met someone else?'

'Yes,' Nanette said simply. 'Someone very special. Someone who truly loves me.'

Nanette didn't understand the pained look that crossed Zac's face, but she did realise that he clearly hadn't been expecting that answer from her.

There was a short silence, before he said slowly, 'I hope things work out for you.' He drained his glass of champagne before continuing quietly, 'My life changed after the accident too. The last three years have been difficult for me. There are different things at stake these days – that's why I can't suddenly announce I was responsible for the accident.'

'Things like your business deals with that criminal Boris Takyanov? You know, Zac,' Nanette said thoughtfully, 'I never had you down as a common criminal. How did that happen?'

Zac was silent for several seconds before saying, 'I stupidly got myself involved in something I shouldn't have. The next thing I knew, Takyanov made me an offer I couldn't refuse – didn't dare refuse,' he added quietly. 'Now I'm in too deep for him to let me go.'

'He's blackmailing you? Oh Zac, what a mess,' Nanette said sadly. 'Well, I can't see him doing much in the way of business from Monaco jail,' she added.

Zac spun round from the table where he was helping himself to yet more champagne. 'Takyanov's been arrested?'

'Hadn't you heard? Along with several of his so-called business associates. And his son in Brazil too.'

Zac pushed past her and opened the cabin door. 'Phil, turn around and take us back to harbour *now*,' he shouted.

Nanette heard the skipper's answering 'Will do', felt *Pole Position* change course and closed her eyes as her body relaxed. This nightmare would soon be over.

Unexpectedly, Zac grabbed her hand. 'I need some air. Come on, let's go out on deck and watch the lights.'

As Zac pulled her towards the yacht's bow, Nanette was struck by an irrational fear. Could he possibly be planning to push her overboard and claim it was an accident?

40

Dawn was breaking over a sleeping Monaco as *Pole Position* sailed towards the harbour entrance. Nanette, standing in the cockpit, felt an overwhelming sense of relief sweep through her body. She would soon be back on dry land.

A tense Zac had insisted they spent the entire return journey up on deck and now Nanette watched the harbour walls getting closer with unconcealed pleasure.

As Phil carefully positioned the yacht to motor slowly into her allocated berth and the crew tied the large navy fenders in place, Zac turned to her.

'I guess you and I are all washed up now. No chance of even remaining friends?'

'We were all washed up, as you put it, when you decided to lie about the accident,' Nanette said, watching Phil press the button to lower the gangway. 'I can never forgive you for that.'

Zac suddenly turned her to face him, gripping both her arms tightly.

'Stop it, Zac, you're hurting me.'

The pressure increased on her arms as Zac ignored her words and squeezed harder.

Nanette closed her eyes, willing him to stop inflicting pain, and waiting for him to release her.

'You think this hurts? Be warned, Nanette – it's nothing to what could happen. I made a mistake letting you take the blame for the accident and I'm sorry. Do one last thing for me: walk away from whatever you think is going on. Other people don't have my scruples – or share a past with you.'

The grip on her arms lessened and Nanette opened her eyes to see Zac staring at her intently.

'Goodbye, Zac,' she said. Trembling, she moved away from him towards the gangway, desperate to put as much space between her and Zac Ewart as possible.

Blinded by the tears that had started to run down her cheeks, she didn't see Jean-Claude standing on the quay until it was too late and she'd run into him.

'*Doucement, ma chérie,*' he said, gently enveloping her in his arms. '*Doucement.* I'm here now to take care of you.'

The gentle kiss he placed on her forehead wasn't enough for Nanette. She turned and looked at him before hesitantly kissing him on the lips. As she surrendered herself to Jean-Claude's passionate embrace, she was conscious of a statue-like Zac watching them with an unfathomable look on his face.

* * *

It was the swish of the curtains that woke Nanette and she blinked as sunlight flooded the bedroom. Jean-Claude had entered the room quietly and placed a tray of coffee and croissants on the bedside table before crossing to the window to open the curtains.

Nanette smiled sleepily to herself as she watched him. He'd been insistent she go to bed after he'd brought her back to the apartment early that morning.

'I'll take the twins to school if Mathieu hasn't returned. You get some sleep. Afterwards, you can explain exactly why you went alone to the yacht,' he'd said.

Nanette had done as she was told and gone to bed. To her surprise, within minutes she'd fallen into a deep dreamless sleep.

'What's the time?' she asked, sitting up as Jean-Claude placed the tray on her lap.

'One o'clock. How do you feel?'

'Fine.'

'Are you ready to tell me why you went alone to *Pole Position*?'

Nanette, about to answer flippantly, 'It seemed a good idea at the time', looked at his concerned expression and said quietly, 'I'm sorry, JC.' She stretched out a hand to gently touch his face. 'At least he didn't push me overboard as I thought he might do at one stage,' she said quietly.

Jean-Claude looked at her, horrified. '*Mon Dieu*. I kill him if he hurt you.'

'Any hurt Zac inflicted on me is now in the past. I have no intention of going anywhere near him in the future,' Nanette said, wearily. 'I'll tell you all about last night, but first I must get up. Give me ten minutes to shower and dress.'

'I wait for you in the sitting room,' Jean-Claude said, kissing her gently on the cheek as he took the tray. 'Take your time.'

Half an hour later, Nanette joined him on the balcony, where he was reading a newspaper.

'The charges against Takyanov are getting longer by the day,' he said, folding the newspaper. 'With more people being drawn into the net.'

'Is Mathieu around?' Nanette asked.

'No,' Jean-Claude shook his head. 'No idea where he's gone. Vanessa phoned while you were sleeping. She and Ralph arrive back in the UK at the end of the month. She wants you to take the twins over. She said something about her and Ralph taking them on holiday. Anyway, she's going to phone you this evening to discuss it.'

Nanette looked at Jean-Claude in dismay. She'd forgotten Vanessa's return would signal the end of her stay in Monaco.

Jean-Claude caught hold of her hands. 'You leave the twins with Vanessa and come back to me, yes? You will have some holiday due?'

'Patsy's baby is due soon. If I'm in England, I'll have to be there for that. Maybe afterwards? Where would I stay? Mathieu won't need me in the apartment without the twins.'

'With me, of course, at the villa, no question. Anneka will prepare the guest suite, and look after us.' Jean-Claude took her in his arms. 'It will be wonderful, *chérie*. Just you and me. Getting to know each other properly. We'll swim, relax, go to Italy.'

Nanette smiled at him. 'Sounds wonderful. Maybe by the time I get back, all this business with Mathieu and Takyanov will be resolved. Has Mathieu accepted your offer of help?'

Jean-Claude gave a shrug. 'Apparently there is not a lot I can do – simply wait in the shadows and be ready to make a move when he asks – *if* he asks.'

'Maybe that's for the best,' Nanette said. 'He's always said you must trust him; he knows what he's doing.'

'Which is more than you did last night,' Jean-Claude said. 'I couldn't believe it when Mathieu rang to say that Zac had told him you were spending the night with him.'

'I couldn't sleep and it seemed like an ideal opportunity to get rid of the package,' Nanette said. 'If I'd known Zac was on board, I certainly wouldn't have gone.' She looked anxiously at Jean-

Claude. 'You didn't believe the implication behind those words, did you?'

'No. I didn't believe you'd spend the night with him willingly – I was terrified that he would force you,' Jean-Claude said quietly.

Hesitantly, she began to tell Jean-Claude about the previous night's events. She glossed over her terror when she realised they had put to sea. Jean-Claude, she knew, would be furiously protective on her behalf.

'At least Zac has finally acknowledged the truth about the accident,' she said. 'He was driving that night. He lied to the *pompiers* and the *gendarmes*. My loss of memory was very convenient for him.' Nanette took a deep breath. 'I told him I was going to the authorities to clear my name. Although he reckons I'd be wasting my time because people won't believe me.' She bit her lip. 'Until last night I hadn't realised how deep the scars were – how much the past was damaging my present. I've decided not to try to clear my name. I will walk away from it. I need to relegate it to the past and forget it. Move on with my life. Leave Zac to live his.'

Jean-Claude took her in his arms.

'I can never forgive him for what he did, but it's not worth dragging it all up again,' Nanette said, as he bent his head to kiss her. 'You, Patsy and those who matter will know the truth and that's all that matters to me now.'

41

As the taxi pulled into the farmyard, the driver, a local man who knew Patsy and Nanette, nodded in the direction of a battered red Mini parked by the hay barn.

'Reckon you'm an aunty,' he said sagely. 'That's Dr Owen's car.'

'Reckon you could be right,' Nanette said, fishing in her bag for the fare.

Helen came bustling out of the kitchen. 'It's a boy,' she said, seeing Nanette. 'I've got a grandson, imagine!'

'Can I go up and see them?' Nanette asked impatiently. After dropping the twins off with Vanessa and Ralph, the journey to the farm had seemed to go on for ever.

'Doctor's with Patsy at the moment. Come into the kitchen and I'll make some tea. You can take a cup up to Patsy.'

It was half an hour before Nanette opened the bedroom door and peered round. 'Hi, Mum! Congratulations.'

Patsy, cradling her new son, smiled at her sleepily. 'Hi, Aunty. Didn't you time your arrival well, missing all the gory bits? Meet your nephew – all seven pounds, two ounces of him.' Patsy held out the tiny bundle and Nanette tentatively took the precious cargo into her arms.

'I'm sorry I didn't get here in time to be your birthing partner,' she said, taking the precious bundle and gently cradling her new nephew in her arms, she gazed at him in wonder. Was this the closest she was going to get to having a baby of her own? 'But it's your fault, baby boy, for being impatient and coming a week or two early,' she said. 'He's gorgeous. So much hair. Helen told me it was very quick. True?'

Patsy pulled a face. 'Midwife said that too. Most first babies take longer. All I can say is it was a very painful three hours.'

'Any names yet?'

Patsy shook her head. 'Helen is all for Hew Trefor.' She laughed at Nanette's expression. 'Apparently they're very old family names – Bryan's middle name is Hew. I fancy Dylan Robert.'

'The new granny is beside herself with joy,' Nanette said. 'I don't suppose she'll care what you call him, so long as she's allowed to spoil him. Dylan's a nice name.' Nanette smiled down at the baby boy.

'Bryan and I are hoping you will be a godmother,' Patsy said.

'I'd love to.'

'Good. Any ideas who you'd like to see in the godfather role?' Patsy asked innocently.

'I'm sure you and Bryan can choose someone suitable without my input,' Nanette said, laughing and refusing to be drawn on the question she knew Patsy was really asking. 'Shall I put Dylan back in his cradle?'

'Please. How long can you stay?' Patsy asked, watching as Nanette gently placed a cover over the sleeping baby.

'A few days. Vanessa and Ralph have taken the twins to Cornwall and I'm officially on holiday for the next fortnight.'

'Why can't you stay longer then?'

'I've promised to return to Monaco and spend the time with Jean-Claude,' Nanette said, blushing.

Patsy looked at her sister speculatively. 'Are you going to tell me any more?'

Nanette shook her head. 'Not right now. I'm sure you need your rest. I promise we'll talk later when you're up and about. I could do with some sisterly advice.'

* * *

It was two days later, sitting companionably under the shade of the horse chestnut tree that dominated the hidden farmhouse garden, sipping cold lemonade, with Dylan asleep in his pram beside them, before Nanette talked to Patsy about her worries for the future.

'I've got to decide what I want to do. Vanessa's come back fired up with enthusiasm for starting a Fruits of the Forest cooperative in Brazil. The twins are growing up and don't need a nanny twenty-four hours a day now, so she's offering me the job of helping her organise it – getting sponsorship, outlets, all the legal bits and pieces, you know the sort of thing.'

'Sounds like something you'd enjoy,' Patsy said. 'I'd guess there would be a few trips to Brazil and the Amazon too.'

'The thing is, the whole business would probably be based in the UK and...' Nanette sighed.

'Jean-Claude is in Monaco,' Patsy finished the sentence for her. 'Is it serious between you two?'

'On Jean-Claude's part for several weeks,' Nanette admitted. 'Now that my memory's returned and the whole Zac Ewart business has been finished with, I feel free to return his love. You

don't think the age difference – fourteen years – is too much?' she
asked her sister anxiously.

Before Patsy could answer, Dylan stirred in his pram and
Nanette got up to check on her nephew. Picking him up and
cradling him in her arms, she sat back down in the shade.

'Lots of people marry with that age gap between them. From
what I've seen of the two of you, you're perfect together. He
adores you and, no, of course he's not too old,' Patsy said. 'Might
be wise to check with him how he feels about babies, if you're
thinking of having a family with him. He might think, been there,
done that and just want you to himself.'

Nanette nodded thoughtfully. Patsy could be right, but she
was rather hoping that Jean-Claude would happily embrace the
idea of them having a baby together. From the way he'd spoken
about Mathieu and Amelia, she suspected he would be. But it was
a question only he could answer.

42

Nanette picked up a magazine and a paper from the newsagent in the departure lounge on Monday afternoon and settled down to wait for her flight back to Nice.

She'd enjoyed her few days with Patsy and baby Dylan but had missed Jean-Claude desperately. She smiled happily to herself – a few more hours and they would be together, with no responsibilities to worry about, just time to enjoy each other's company.

The newspaper was full of Zac's performance in the Austrian Grand Prix the previous day. He'd driven a faultless race and won convincingly, according to the reporter. His nearest rival for the championship had only managed ninth place, thus increasing Zac's lead substantially.

Nanette stared dispassionately at the photograph of Zac standing jubilantly on the podium, before turning to the women's pages. Zac Ewart was no longer a part of her life. She wouldn't waste her time reading about him.

Three hours later, she stretched her legs as the captain's voice crackled through the intercom of the 737.

'Welcome to the French Riviera. The temperature in Nice and along the Côte d'Azure is thirty-three degrees and the forecast is good for next few days.'

Collecting her suitcase from the carousel, Nanette looked through the glass windows towards the arrivals hall. As he'd promised, Jean-Claude was there waiting for her. She smiled happily and waved. Exiting the door from the final customs checkpoint, she walked towards him, looking forward to his welcoming kiss.

Surrendering herself to his arms, oblivious to the milling crowds, she sensed a tension in his body.

'Is something wrong? Has something happened to Mathieu?'

'*Non*, it's not Mathieu. Let's have a coffee before we drive home,' Jean-Claude said, taking her suitcase and leading her to the escalator to go to the fourth floor.

Seated at a window table of La Badiane lounge with its view out over the runways, Jean-Claude ordered two coffees before gently taking both of Nanette's hands in his.

'Zac drove home after winning the Austrian Grand Prix via his friends the Oliviers, breaking his journey and staying overnight with them. They have a farm up in the hills – do you remember them?'

Nanette nodded. 'They live near Entrevaux. We used to visit them a lot. Mathieu took the twins there fairly recently.'

'I have some bad news, *ma chérie*. Zac left there early this morning and got involved in an incident on one of the isolated mountain roads.'

'What sort of incident?'

'A car had overturned on a hairpin bend. A mother and baby were trapped inside. When Zac came on the scene, the only thing stopping it from tumbling down the gorge was a tree. Zac managed to pull the woman out before going back for the child.'

Jean-Claude was silent for a moment. 'As he was struggling to undo the baby seat, the car burst into flames.'

Nanette gave an involuntary gasp and covered her mouth with her hand. 'Did he get the baby out?'

'Yes, wrapped in a blanket. But Zac himself suffered third-degree burns. The doctors are very non-committal about his chances.'

Nanette turned and stared unseeingly as a plane landed and taxied down the runway, her thoughts in such turmoil, she barely registered Jean-Claude's next words.

'The thing is, *ma chérie*, I know things are over between the two of you, but in his delirious state, he's been crying out for you. Can you bear the thought of holding a vigil at his bedside?'

* * *

Nanette clutched Jean-Claude's hand tightly as they made their way into the Princess Grace Hospital in Monaco. They found Zac in a small private room, wired up to a large piece of apparatus that was emitting a series of steady bleeps. Nanette swallowed hard as she looked at the heavily bandaged figure in the bed, unable to see any recognisable features and thinking it could be anyone.

Quietly, Nanette approached the bed.

'Zac?' she said softly.

No response.

Nanette turned questioningly to the nurse making notes of a reading off the machine.

'I'm sorry,' she said. 'Monsieur Ewart slipped into a coma an hour ago.'

Nanette glanced across at Jean-Claude.

'Why don't you sit down here?' he said, pulling a chair towards the side of the bed. 'I'll go and find us some coffee.'

Sitting there, gazing at Zac's motionless body, Nanette felt the tears welling up. Through the years they had been together, she had become hardened every time Zac climbed in a racing car, to expect the worst. She'd always known it was a dangerous sport where fatal accidents occurred despite all the modern safety measures and regulations. She'd learned to live with that fear, keeping her worries to herself and never mentioning them to Zac. He was doing a job he loved and living his life the way he wanted to and she'd reasoned it wasn't up to her to stop him.

To see him now, lying here in a hospital bed because he'd helped someone else was a cruel irony. Nanette bit her lip, determined not to cry at the unfairness of it all.

Tentatively, with her fingertips, she gently touched his bandaged hand, hoping against hope that he would open his eyes. However much he had hurt her, however much he had reviled her, she had once loved this man.

'I'm here, Zac,' she whispered. 'Please don't die.'

Jean-Claude returned with coffee and a sandwich for her. Moving away from the bed, Nanette gratefully accepted the plastic cup of steaming coffee but shook her head at the sandwich he offered.

'Thank you, but I couldn't eat anything.'

A sudden discordant beep from the machine at Zac's side brought another nurse hurrying into the room, but seconds later the machine had settled back into its steady bleep, bleep.

The nurse shook her head in response to Nanette's worried look but didn't say anything as she left the room. Nanette gave a deep sigh as she moved back towards the bed, willing herself to think positive thoughts, and praying that Zac would be all right.

* * *

It was late evening before Jean-Claude persuaded Nanette it was
time to go home.

'You need to get some sleep, *ma chérie*. To eat something. If
there's a change in Zac's condition overnight, the hospital will
ring, and we'll come straight back, I promise,' Jean-Claude said.
'There is nothing you can do here.'

Glancing back as they left the room, Nanette sent a silent
prayer winging in Zac's direction. *Please, please wake up tomorrow.
I want you to know how brave we all think you were.*

The lights were on in the villa as they drove up and Mathieu's
car was parked in the driveway. Mathieu himself opened the front
door to them.

'How's Zac?'

'He's been in a coma since this morning,' Jean-Claude replied
quietly. 'What are you doing here? Do you have some news? A
problem?'

Mathieu shook his head. 'No problem. I wanted you to know
that Boris was finally allowed to post bail today and he's out on
remand. He's had to surrender his passport, of course, and must
report to the police every day.' He looked at his father. 'As far as
he's concerned, I'm still helping him, so the pretence goes on for
at least a few more days. I'm hoping that he's finally going to give
me the name of his contact in Brazil who organises the diamond
smuggling. I can hand the completed file over to the police then.'

'Does Boris know about Zac?' Jean-Claude asked.

'Yes. He's asked me to let him know the moment there is any
change. He says he and Zac still have some unfinished business.'

'The stuff I put in the safe!' Nanette gasped. 'Do you think it's
still there?'

Mathieu shrugged. 'Who knows? Maybe Zac moved it on

before he left for the French Grand Prix. The unfinished business could be something to do with setting up Vacances au Soleil.'

Patsy phoned that evening. 'I've just heard about Zac on the BBC. Is it really as serious as they say?'

'Yes,' Nanette managed to answer. 'JC took me straight to the hospital as apparently Zac was asking for me, but he was in a coma by the time I got there,' Nanette told her. 'It doesn't look too good, to be honest. All we can do is pray that he pulls through. I'm going back in the morning, but there's nothing I can do. I'll ring you tomorrow.'

* * *

Nanette spent a restless night in Jean-Claude's guest suite, unable to sleep, fearful that the phone would ring, summoning her back to Zac's bedside.

Early-morning sunlight was streaming in through the French doors of the sitting room when she went downstairs. Jean-Claude was in the kitchen, listening to the news on the radio and preparing a breakfast tray for her.

'After you eat, I take you to the hospital,' he said, pouring her a large mug of coffee.

Nanette smiled her thanks and cupped her hands around it. Information about Zac's accident was dominating the local radio stations' news bulletins and Nanette tensed as the voice of the woman he'd rescued came on the air. Praising his actions and calling him a hero, the woman sobbed with gratitude as she publicly thanked Zac for saving both her and her baby daughter and wished him a speedy recovery.

Silently, Jean-Claude leant across and switched off the radio. 'Breakfast, *ma chérie*, then we leave for the hospital.'

There was a small group of journalists hanging around the

main entrance to the hospital as they arrived. One of them clearly recognised Nanette, but a glare from Jean-Claude and a sharp warning '*Non*' stopped him in the act of pointing his camera at her.

Zac's room was full of doctors and nurses and a worried Nanette and Jean-Claude had to wait outside for some time before they were allowed in.

'Is there any improvement in his condition?' Nanette asked.

'Monsieur Ewart had a stable night,' a young nurse informed them, 'but he remains unconscious.'

Nanette sat by his bedside all day, leaving only for a short time when Jean-Claude insisted she needed some fresh air and something to eat.

It was early afternoon when Zac stirred briefly and returned the gentle pressure as Nanette held his hand. That hardly-felt squeeze filled Nanette with hope, but the rest of the afternoon passed without any further progress in his condition.

At eight o'clock, as Jean-Claude suggested they should think about preparing to leave for the day, Zac unexpectedly opened his eyes and looked at them.

Nanette felt her heart skip a beat as she smiled down at him. 'Hello, Zac.'

'Sorry. Shouldn't have lied.' The words were spoken so softly that Nanette could barely hear them. She bent over him, eager to catch his next words. 'Please forgive me.'

'Of course, Zac. It's in the past. Just get well.' Nanette glanced up as the machine started to emit a series of quick beeps and a nurse bustled in to check it.

'Would you mind leaving and coming back tomorrow please?' The tone of the nurse's voice suggested it was more an order than a request.

As she went to leave, Zac murmured her name, 'Nanette – thank you.'

Nanette smiled at him and shook her head. 'Thank *you*, Zac. There is one very grateful mother and baby out there telling the world what a hero you are.' Gently she lent down and placed a kiss on his forehead – the only part of his face that wasn't covered in a bandage. 'I'll see you tomorrow, Zac.'

Moving towards the door where Jean-Claude was waiting for her, she smiled again and mouthed 'goodbye'. She just caught the whispered words 'Be happy, Nanette' before Zac's eyes closed again.

Jean-Claude held her hand tightly as he quickly led her past the journalists still waiting in the foyer.

'Any news?' one called out.

'*Non*,' Jean-Claude answered shortly.

To Nanette's surprise, Jean-Claude didn't drive straight back to the villa, instead he drove down to Cap d'Ail and parked the car.

'Come on, a walk along the beach to blow the cobwebs away,' he said. 'You need some fresh air before we go home for supper.'

Strolling along with Jean-Claude's arm around her shoulders holding her tight, Nanette felt strangely detached from reality. The last thirty-six hours had passed in a blur. Only now was she beginning to fully comprehend what had happened.

Zac's delirious ramblings had taken her to his bedside out of compassion and in remembrance of their past love. Now, as the breeze off the Mediterranean ruffled her hair, she thought about that love. How Zac's actions had changed it – how she had changed in the aftermath of her accident.

'If – when – Zac comes out of hospital, he will still need a lot of care for some time,' Jean-Claude said quietly, interrupting her thoughts. 'Round-the-clock attendance probably.'

Nanette nodded. 'I'll find the best for him. We'll nurse him back to health. Thank goodness he can afford all the care and help we need.'

At her words, Jean-Claude stopped walking and turned Nanette to face him. 'You are going to help nurse him?'

'No, not nurse him, but I'll organise his day-to-day needs. He has no one else. He was an only child and his parents died years ago – long before he became a racing driver.'

Jean-Claude nodded thoughtfully. 'How do you think he will react to the scars he is clearly going to have? Modern plastic surgery can do so much, but I'd hazard a guess that Zac's good looks have gone forever.'

'He's never been a bitter man – arrogant and self-seeking, maybe,' Nanette answered slowly. 'I think once he knows the extent of his injuries, he'll get on with improving what he can and simply accept what he can't. He's always been very strong like that.'

'And you, *ma chérie*?' Jean-Claude gazed at her intently. 'How strong are you? How will you deal with a damaged Zac Ewart in your life?'

'JC, I can't just walk away from him.' The thought, *like he did to me*, she mentally squashed.

'I wouldn't ask you to. I just don't want you to be hurt again.'

'I won't be, I promise.' Nanette put a hand up and gently stroked Jean-Claude's face. 'Can I tell you something? Sitting at Zac's bedside, I thought about you and me and wondered how I'd feel if it were you in that hospital bed.' Reaching up, she kissed him. 'I couldn't bear it. I would really be hurting then.'

He hugged her tightly for several seconds before releasing her. 'Come on, let's walk.'

* * *

Dusk was falling as they returned to the villa. Mathieu met them at the door, his face serious.

'The hospital rang. Zac suffered a stroke shortly after you left. Nanette, I'm sorry, they did everything possible, but they couldn't save him.'

43

Nanette lay on the airbed, her fingers dangling in the cool water as she drifted aimlessly around the pool. Jean-Claude had urged her to go for a swim, but she simply didn't have the energy.

She'd felt so positive that evening, walking on the beach with Jean-Claude, watching the setting sun, believing against all odds that Zac was going to recover now he'd regained consciousness and making plans for his future care.

The numbness that had descended over her as Mathieu told them the sad news had drained her of all rational thought and energy. Only Jean-Claude's quiet, loving presence had kept her focused on the things that needed to be done.

Nanette knew that the F1 world would want to pay their respects to one of their own, but in the middle of a busy racing season, it would throw up all sorts of logistical problems for drivers and their teams to attend. Jean-Claude had helped her set up the small private funeral service for Zac that would take place tomorrow in the church at the cemetery. They'd announce details of the memorial service they planned to hold in December at the end of the racing season.

An unknown Monsieur Mille had phoned, wanting an urgent meeting with her that afternoon. Jean-Claude had been strangely reticent about the man, saying simply that the name seemed familiar, but he wasn't sure, and, as Monsieur Mille had declined to give details over the telephone, she'd have to wait and see what it was all about.

Reluctantly, Nanette paddled the airbed towards the pool steps. The mysterious Monsieur Mille would be here soon. She needed to shower and get dressed. Maybe she'd start to shake off this stupor after tomorrow when the saga of her and Zac would finally be laid to rest alongside his poor burned body.

* * *

Monsieur Mille, when Jean-Claude introduced them half an hour later, turned out to be a lawyer. Zac's lawyer.

'Mademoiselle Weston, I am here to offer my condolences and my services. I have to tell you that you are the only beneficiary of Monsieur Ewart's estate.' He handed Nanette a legal document and an envelope containing a set of keys.

A stunned Nanette looked at him in disbelief as Jean-Claude took charge and began to question him.

'There is no mistake. Monsieur Ewart lodged his Will with me three years ago, with the instructions that, in the event of his demise, I was to contact Mademoiselle Weston with the news and offer her my services.'

'It's just that three years ago...' Nanette's voice trailed off.

'I believe you had a bad car accident about that time,' the lawyer said. 'Monsieur Ewart was concerned for you.' He stood up and held out his business card. 'I will leave you to read Monsieur Ewart's Will. If you have any questions, this is my number. These things take time, but you will need to come to my office to sign papers – perhaps next month.'

Nanette stayed in the sitting room while Jean-Claude saw the lawyer out, her thoughts in turmoil. Why hadn't Zac changed his Will since then? Was it his way of trying to make amends? Or was it just a mistake on his part? Whatever the reason, it was too late now.

Her fingers were shaking as she unfolded the heavy document. There was no mistaking her name in bold letters six or seven lines down the page, identifying her as the beneficiary of Zac Ewart's estate. *Pole Position*, the apartment in Fontvieille – those were the keys the lawyer had thoughtfully put in the envelope – and Zac's bank account were now hers. Silently, she handed the paper to Jean-Claude when he returned.

'You're going to be a wealthy woman,' he said.

'I don't want all this,' she replied, looking up at Jean-Claude.

'I don't think you can refuse,' Jean-Claude said gently. 'Once you've signed all the legal documents, you can do what you like with it.'

'I'll give it away then. I certainly don't deserve it.'

John-Claude regarded her thoughtfully. 'The package you put in the safe – I think we should take a look and see if it's still there. I don't want you implicated in Zac's criminal activities simply because you now own the yacht.'

'I need some fresh air – shall we go now?' Nanette asked. 'Get it over with. I'll just get my bag.'

Nanette's mobile phone rang as they were leaving the villa. Vanessa.

'I just wanted you to know that I'm coming down for the funeral tomorrow. Mathieu is meeting me in Nice tonight and I've booked a room at the Columbus.'

'Are the twins coming too?'

'No. Ralph is taking them to his parents in the country for a couple of days. I thought they were a bit young – although Pierre in particular is terribly upset about Zac. I think he was looking forward to boasting that Zac was a friend when he won the Formula 1 World Championship.' There was a pause before Vanessa said, 'You coping? We'll have a long talk tomorrow.'

'Yes,' Nanette answered. 'I'm fine. There's a lot to talk about when you get here.'

* * *

The harbour was busy as Nanette and Jean-Claude made their way to *Pole Position*. As they walked, they saw *Mediterranean Wanderer* negotiating its way to a quayside berth, scores of cruise passengers lining her decks for their first look at Monaco.

Several police cars were parked along the embankment road, effectively blocking a lane of traffic. A loud blaring of car horns from exasperated drivers forced into gridlock competed with the noisy siren from the liner as it warned smaller craft to get out of its way.

Nanette nudged Jean-Claude. 'Isn't that Boris sitting at that café? Oh, and there's Mathieu.'

Jean-Claude followed her gaze. 'Wasn't *Mediterranean Wanderer* on Zac's list? Maybe Boris is waiting to meet someone. As long as Mathieu isn't doing his dirty work for him.' Jean-Claude gave an anxious look in his son's direction.

'Shall we wait and see?' Nanette suggested.

Jean-Claude shook his head. 'No. I have to do as Mathieu says and trust him. I still feel bad at the way I doubted him. Let's go look at the safe.'

Phil, the skipper, was alone on board and eager to offer his condolences to Nanette. 'It's hard to believe. Such a tragedy. Away from the racetrack too,' he said. 'Have you heard anything about what happens next?'

'The funeral is tomorrow – very low-key and private. We're planning a memorial service in early December,' Nanette answered, unwilling to tell Phil yet that she was the new owner of *Pole Position*. He'd find out soon enough. 'Remember those things I had to put in Zac's private safe? I need to see if they are still there. We won't be five minutes,' Nanette said, taking Jean-Claude's hand, compelling him to follow her into the master cabin, where she closed the door.

Kneeling in front of the cupboard in the bathroom, she took out the towels and the shelf. Carefully, she twisted and turned the number into the combination lock and pulled the door open. The package and the gun were still there.

A muttered 'Merdé' escaped from Jean-Claude. '*Désolé*. I was hoping that Zac had already moved the stuff on. OK, the gun isn't too big a problem – we can simply hand it in to the authorities. It's not illegal to own a gun. The package, though, does give us a problem. We certainly can't leave it here.'

'I'll put it in my bag, shall I?' Nanette asked. 'Take it back to the villa and talk to Mathieu. He may be able to suggest something.'

'*D'accord*,' Jean-Claude said, picking up the gun and making sure the safety catch was on before he slipped it into the inside pocket of his jacket.

Phil was waiting for them in the stem. 'Safe empty, then?' he asked, giving them a curious look.

'Yes,' Nanette said. He wasn't to know that it was empty because the contents were now nestling in her bag.

Passengers from the cruise liner were thronging the pavements as Nanette and Jean-Claude stepped ashore. Traffic along the harbour road was still at a virtual standstill and a large crowd was watching the *gendarmes* frogmarch somebody off the *Mediterranean Wanderer*.

Passing the pavement café where they'd seen Boris earlier, Nanette glanced around in time to see him disappearing into the crowd, with a thoughtful Mathieu watching him go.

Mathieu raised a languid hand in greeting as he saw them and walked towards them. 'Cruz has been arrested. I expect things to start happening now,' he said. 'You're looking very serious, Nanette. Has something happened?'

'We need you to come up to the villa,' Jean-Claude answered before Nanette could. 'We urgently need to decide what to do with a certain package.'

* * *

Zac's funeral service was as private as Nanette had hoped it would be. Altogether there were just nine people in the congregation to hear the vicar's eulogy of Zac's life and the brave actions that had taken it away from him.

The Oliviers had travelled down and were seated with the woman whose life and baby Zac had saved. Phil was there and Monsieur Mille slipped into a seat at the back. Mathieu and Vanessa sat behind Nanette and Jean-Claude.

Listening to the words of praise for a man who had been a part of her life for several years and who would continue to be a never forgotten presence by virtue of his legacy to her, Nanette found herself fighting back the tears. Silently, Jean-Claude handed her a handkerchief.

After the short service, everyone was invited back to the villa. The Oliviers, Monsieur Mille and the rescued woman all declined, citing various reasons, but Phil accepted.

'So, if the rumours are to be believed,' he said, awkwardly, as

Nanette offered him a drink, 'you're my new boss. Are you going to keep *Pole Position*?'

'Phil, I'm sorry, but it's too soon to know. I haven't decided what I'm going to do about a lot of things, *Pole Position* included. When I do, I promise I'll keep you informed. In the meantime, I'd appreciate you staying on as her skipper.'

Across the room, she could see Mathieu in earnest conversation with Jean-Claude and Vanessa, but it wasn't until after Phil had left and the four of them were alone that Nanette heard what they were talking about.

'Boris has had his bail revoked,' Mathieu told her. 'Once the police got Cruz into custody, he sang like a bird. Apparently, he was more than just a courier. He was able to supply missing contact names, routes and some other information the police needed. They didn't wait for Boris to do his daily sign-in – they rearrested him last night and got a judge to revoke his bail.'

'Did Cruz implicate Zac in any way?' Nanette asked quietly.

Mathieu shook his head. 'No.'

Nanette sighed before asking, 'What did you do with the shampoo?'

'Told the police where it had come from and handed it over. Don't worry,' he continued, seeing her anxious look. 'It won't be used as evidence. Seeing there are enough people willing to testify against Boris, now he's in custody and can't threaten them any more, I've "lost" my dossier on Zac's activities. I can't see the police bothering with a dead hero. I shall have to give evidence against Boris, of course.'

'Does he know yet that you were double-crossing him?' Jean-Claude asked.

'No. The police are keeping that little bit of information for the trial. I really hated deceiving you.'

'Now I know the truth, I have to say I'm proud of you,' Jean-

Claude said. 'You did the right thing. And I'm sorry I doubted you – I'll know better next time.'

Mathieu shook his head. 'There won't be a next time, I promise you. I'm just glad it's all over and I can get back to a normal life,' he said, looking at his father.

There was a short pause before Jean-Claude spoke again. 'Does getting back to a normal life mean getting more involved in my business as well as your own? I was hoping that we could combine them both, with me taking a sabbatical for a few months.'

'Shall we have a business meeting tomorrow morning and start to sort things out?' Mathieu said.

Jean-Claude hesitated. 'I was going to suggest I took Nanette down to Zac's apartment, but when we get back would be fine.'

'JC, don't worry about that,' Nanette said. 'I'll drive myself down. Leave you free to discuss business with Mathieu. Vanessa will come with me, won't you?' Nanette turned to her friend.

'Of course.'

'Are you sure?' Jean-Claude asked.

'Definitely. My convertible has been sitting in your garage far too long. It's time I got mobile again.'

Nanette knew unlocking the door to Zac's apartment for the first time and realising whatever it contained now belonged to her was going to be an emotional experience and would likely bring back a lot of memories, both happy and sad. Having Vanessa at her side as she discovered the contents of the apartment, in case she struggled to contain the tidal wave of sadness for the way Zac's life had ended that was lurking just below the surface, would be better than breaking down in front of the new man in her life.

44

The next morning, Nanette drove herself and Vanessa down through Monte Carlo towards Fontvieille and parked in one of the underground car parks near the circus tent.

'Do you mind walking to the apartment from here?' she asked Vanessa. 'You can tell me how the plans for the cooperative are coming on as we go.'

She winced as a particularly noisy helicopter came in over the Mediterranean to land at the shoreline heliport, just metres away from where they were standing.

'I'm still looking for sponsors for the first year. Flying down here for Zac's funeral was the main reason I'm here, but it isn't the only reason. I need to talk to you about Fruits of the Forest.'

Nanette looked at Vanessa and waited.

'I know you said you didn't want to be involved because you were going to be spending more time down here and I planned to run Fruits from the UK. Well, I've changed my mind. Ralph and I are going to relocate down here. He can work from anywhere, the twins like their school and seeing more of Mathieu – and, of course, both my business and the cooperative will benefit from the tax breaks Monaco can give. So, will you change your mind?'

'Oh, Vanessa,' Nanette said. 'I'm sorry, the answer is still no. Jean-Claude has plans for us to do some travelling together. I do know someone who needs a job though and who would be perfect. Evie. Her boss got caught up in all this smuggling business and she lost her job recently.'

'This Boris Takyanov certainly spread his business tentacles widely, didn't he?' Vanessa said. 'Unbelievable that so deep in the jungle, we should cross the same worldwide criminal organisation masterminded by Boris that Mathieu was investigating.' She shivered, remembering Ralph's accident. 'The only time I was truly scared was when the villagers accused us of putting the evil eye on them because of Boris's son's failure to honour their deal.'

'I find the fact that Zac got taken in unbelievable,' Nanette said. 'Trying to involve me in Vacances au Soleil to give it respectability was despicable.' She shook her head. 'I just took it as the final proof that he didn't give a hoot about me, but then, this happens,' and she looked up reflectively at the apartment building where they were now standing. 'So I realise he did care in his own way.'

The concierge welcomed them politely, pointed out which lift they needed to take for Apartment 210 on the twelfth floor and returned to tending the vast pots of lilies that graced the foyer.

Stepping out of the lift and inserting the key in the apartment door, Nanette shivered.

Vanessa glanced at her and asked, 'You okay?'

'I'm fine. Probably a reaction to the last few days. This whole Zac thing still feels unreal.'

'We don't have to do this today, do we?' Vanessa asked. 'You don't have to rush into sorting things out.'

'No, but I do need to make a start,' Nanette said, before resolutely turning the key. 'This is surreal,' she murmured, looking around the sparsely furnished sitting room. It was full of things she recognised from Zac's old apartment – things they had chosen together. The two white leather settees facing each other across the glass-topped coffee table, the music centre, the Persian rug, the grand piano from Zac's grandmother. She recognised too, the art work on several walls which had come from *Pole Position* when the yacht had been refurbished, It all brought back poignant memories of her time with him.

She brushed away a tear before walking across and picking up a silver-framed photo standing on the piano. It was one of Zac standing in the cockpit of *Pole Position* looking relaxed and happy.

'I've never thanked you properly for having the twins for me and coming back to Monaco,' Vanessa said unexpectedly. 'I know it was a difficult decision for you to return.'

'I'm glad I came. Getting my memory back, clearing things up between Zac and me – imagine how I would have felt if Zac had died and we'd never talked about the accident.' Nanette took one last look at the photo and gently replaced it on the piano before turning to face Vanessa.

'You did me several favours by going up the Amazon for five months.' Nanette smiled at her friend as she moved towards the master bedroom door. 'It's thanks to you I've now got Jean-Claude in my life.'

'The rainforest was such a great experience. I can't tell you how much it changed the way I look at things,' Vanessa said quietly.

Nanette barely heard her friend as she looked at Zac's bedside table. Two things had caught her attention. Yet another silver-framed photo – and this time Nanette couldn't stop the tears from coursing down her cheeks as she looked at it. Taken the night they got engaged at a party in the Automobile Club in Monaco, she and Zac were standing with their arms entwined in the traditional manner, toasting each other with champagne, her engagement ring sparkling in the camera flash.

She hesitated before picking up the small white box that stood alongside the photo. Surely not? The large square sapphire surrounded by diamonds glinted in the sunlight as she opened the box. Her engagement ring. The one she'd had couriered back to Zac from Devon when she'd realised he'd abandoned her. She snapped the box shut and replaced it on the bedside table.

'Do you think Zac's got any tea? I think we could both do with a cup,' Vanessa said. 'Come on, let's inspect the kitchen.' Gently, she led Nanette out of the bedroom.

By the time Vanessa had found and made a pot of tea, Nanette had stopped crying.

'I'm sorry. I thought I was all cried out over Zac Ewart, but apparently not.' She took a deep breath. 'Such a waste but life moves on. At least his reputation as a brilliant racing driver will remain intact. He'll never have to face the criminal charges that Boris and the others will.' Nanette took a sip of tea.

'This is a great apartment,' Vanessa said, looking around. 'Are you going to keep it and live here?'

'I'll probably sell it. Can't see myself living here somehow. If I keep it, I'll rent it out. Oh!' Nanette said, looking at Vanessa. 'Why don't you and Ralph make it your base when you move down here?'

45

After Vanessa had gone back to the UK and he'd had his business meeting with Mathieu, Jean-Claude insisted they enjoyed the few remaining days of Nanette's official holiday doing things together.

On the last day, they drove up into the back country and had lunch in a village square, sitting beneath the shade of an ancient plane tree. As the waiter placed their tomato and mozzarella salad starters in front of them, Jean-Claude glanced across at her.

'I'm so happy you decided not to rush back to the UK with Vanessa. I love having you around.'

Nanette smiled at him as he picked up her hand and squeezed it.

'Have you thought about what you are going to do with your legacy yet?'

'I've done nothing but think about it,' Nanette answered. 'There is one idea floating around in my brain I want to talk to you about.'

'Do you still want to give it all away?'

Nanette shook her head. 'No, that was a silly idea. I'll keep it, but I do want to do something useful with it if I can.' She poured herself a glass of water from the carafe the waiter had placed on the table before continuing. 'I was wondering about *Pole Position*. We could have some fun with her, or I could sell her and maybe invest the money. What do you think? Are you a keen sailor? Have to admit I'm veering towards selling her.'

Jean-Claude smiled. 'I have to confess, I'm not a lover of yachts. I have only to step on board one to have an attack of *mal de mer*. But any ideas what you'd do with the money? She's worth at least two million dollars,' Jean-Claude said.

'I hadn't realised she was worth that much, but that would be fantastic.' Nanette smiled at him hesitantly, trying to gauge his reaction to her next words. 'I was thinking of using it to sponsor Fruits of the Forest, for the first year at least, in Zac's name. Even if it's registered as a charity, it's going to need a large injection of cash to get it off the ground.'

'Not your conventional investment then?' Jean-Claude said, smiling. 'Well, it won't make you a fortune, but it would make a difference to many people's lives in the rainforest.'

'From what Monsieur Mille tells me, Zac's left me quite a large fortune – I don't need to make another one,' Nanette said quietly. 'Right, that's decision number one: next week, I'll find a broker and put *Pole Position* up for sale.'

Nanette stopped talking to watch a woman pushing a buggy with a sleeping baby and holding a little boy by the hand pass their table. Patsy's words about Jean-Claude not wanting a new family came into her mind.

'Decision number two?' Jean-Claude probed.

'If I'm staying in Monaco, I need to find somewhere to live. I don't want to live in Zac's apartment in Fontvieille; besides, I've already offered it to Vanessa and Ralph in the short term.'

'What is wrong with living at the villa with me?' Jean-Claude demanded. 'The guest room has never had a more welcome occupant.'

'I don't want to get in the way,' Nanette said. 'I was only supposed to be here for a holiday.'

'*Ma chérie*, you know how I feel about you. You will never be in my way. Maybe you move out of the guest suite, but you stay at the villa. That's decision number two dealt with.' Heedless of the other diners, Jean-Claude leant forward and gently kissed her. Nanette felt a glow of happiness spread through her body at his words and she responded to his kiss.

Later, as they were making their way back to the car, they passed the mother and her two children playing in the park alongside the church. The small boy miskicked his ball, which landed at Jean-Claude's feet.

Jean-Claude promptly kicked it back and for several moments he and the small boy had an animated kick around while Nanette talked to the mother.

'That took me back,' Jean-Claude said, when they eventually waved goodbye to the toddler. 'I used to play football with Mathieu years ago.'

'You obviously like children,' Nanette said.

'Before things went wrong with Amelia, I'd always hoped Mathieu would have a sibling.' Jean-Claude shrugged. 'I've always regretted that.'

'Well, it's not too late, is it?' Nanette said. 'I'm sure Mathieu would still adore having a half-brother or sister,' she teased, smiling at him.

A look of incredulous wonder crossed Jean-Claude's face as Nanette leaned forward and kissed him.

Nanette sighed happily; he'd given her the answer she wanted. Now she knew where her destiny was.

* * *

On the night of the Monte Carlo Gala for the Global Ocean, Nanette carefully slipped the wisp of pale-lemon chiffon that was her evening dress over her head. Hard to believe that she was still in Monte Carlo and actually going to the Gala that Jean-Claude had bought tickets for all those weeks ago. So much had happened in that time. Not least that she'd moved into the villa and was living with Jean-Claude and had never been happier.

The Gala came at the end of a few very busy weeks: overseeing the sorting out of Zac's affairs; selling *Pole Position*; helping Vanessa and Ralph move into the Fontvieille apartment and persuading Vanessa to let her use the proceeds from the sale of *Pole Position* to sponsor Fruits of the Forest for a year.

'Are you sure? It's an awful lot of money to be virtually giving away.'

'Absolutely positive. Zac bought *Pole Position* about eight years ago and I'm fairly certain it was with his winnings and sponsorship deals from that time, but who knows?' She'd shrugged her shoulders. 'If, and we don't know for certain how long Zac was involved with Boris, any of this money I have now inherited came from smuggling Brazilian diamonds or money laundering, then this is a way of giving it back legally.'

Nanette slipped her feet into her high-heeled gold sandals and did them up. Her Rolex yellow gold watch Jean-Claude had given her for her birthday was always on her wrist these days and she picked up her beaded evening clutch bag.

Jean-Claude was waiting for her in the sitting room. 'You look beautiful,' he said, taking her in his arms. 'The belle of the ball. Come on, the others are waiting. Let's party.'

Jean-Claude had invited Vanessa and Ralph to join them for the evening, and also Mathieu and Evie. Since Evie had started working for Fruits of the Forest, she and Mathieu had become friends and, to Nanette's secret delight, the two were rapidly becoming an item around the town.

The whole of Monte Carlo seemed to be in a festive mood that evening. Champagne flowed, people wined and dined and everyone was on their feet dancing for hours.

Towards midnight, she and Jean-Claude mingled with the other partygoers standing on the terrace of the casino in a brief pause in the festivities before the fireworks began. Vanessa and Ralph had managed to save them a good viewing position and Mathieu and Evie soon joined them.

Nanette, standing there with her friends and Jean-Claude's arm around her shoulders, looked around contentedly. Tomorrow she and Jean-Claude would be flying to a very different world when they left to visit the UK for Dylan's christening. Jean-Claude had been delighted when Patsy had phoned and asked him to be a godparent with Nanette and had been planning all sorts of surprises for the unsuspecting Dylan and his parents. Two contrasting worlds, but both now very much a part of her life again. One summer in Monte Carlo had proved life-changing in ways she could never have anticipated.

The whoosh of the first warning rocket and everyone looked skywards, except Jean-Claude, who gently drew Nanette towards him.

Surprised, she looked at him as he took both her hands in his. '*Ma chérie, je t'aime.* Will you please marry me?'

The sky exploded with thousands of silver stars in time with her heart as Nanette whispered a tremulous, 'Yes, please.'

Jean-Claude slipped a ring on her finger while more fiery flashes of gold, silver, red and blue filled the sky over Monte Carlo before showering down into the Mediterranean.

Surrendering herself to Jean-Claude's arms, Nanette knew

beyond all doubt that his love was her second, and true, legacy
from Monaco.

EPILOGUE

It is the second week in December and Monte Carlo is counting down the days to Christmas. Christmas lights are strung across streets and around windows, and decorated fir trees are everywhere. There are even rogue Father Christmases hanging from the windows and balconies of some apartment blocks. Casino Square is a mass of sparkling twinkling lights. The Christmas market chalets set up on the quay are busy every day and locals as well as visitors are enjoying the festive atmosphere while the sun shines in the pale blue winter sky and the sound of Christmas carols fills the air.

Nanette is in the bedroom she shares with Jean-Claude in the villa getting ready for Zac's memorial service in the Sainte-Dévote Chapel and thinking not only about the last few months but also about the past.

It is three years since she's been in the Principality at this time of year. When she was Zac's PA, the three weeks before Christmas had always been the highlight of her year. The F1 season had finished for three months, allowing the drivers time to relax and recuperate with friends and family before it all started up again in the New Year. She'd enjoyed spending so much uninterrupted time here in Monaco with Zac in those December weeks. They had been good times, with no indication they would ever end. But end they had, leaving her with such bittersweet memories. Today's memorial service would be her final memory of Zac Ewart and the way he had affected her life.

Organising today's event, to which everybody who was anybody in the F1 world was coming to pay their respects to a driver who would be forever remembered as one of the best drivers who sadly never won the championship but who had died a hero, had been harder than she'd anticipated.

Nanette sighs. She still has guilty feelings over her inheritance from Zac. She's done her best though, putting the money from the sale of *Pole Position* to good use in creating the Zac Ewart Trust fund which will benefit the new charity, Fruits of the Forest, that Vanessa has been busy getting set up. And like everyone, Nanette is pleased that Boris Takyanov has received a lengthy jail sentence and is safely behind bars.

A quiet knock on the door and Jean-Claude enters. 'The taxi is here, *ma cherie*. You are ready?'

'Yes, I'm ready,' she answers quietly. She has found the last few months difficult, even with the love and help of Jean-Claude, but she is definitely ready to face the world and remember Zac Ewart as the heroic man he turned out to be in the end.

She is also ready for her new life with Jean-Claude. Next week, they go to join Patsy and Bryan for baby Dylan's first family Christmas. Afterwards, in the New Year, she has a wedding to organise. Jean-Claude wants them to get married in the spring, something she is happy to agree to. It will have to be an early spring wedding, though, because she has a new secret she plans to tell him once the memorial service is over. A secret she is more than happy to share and one that she knows will be received with delight.

ACKNOWLEDGMENTS

One Summer in Monte Carlo was originally published under the title Follow Your Star and I've enjoyed revisiting the story, tweaking and lengthening with extra scenes and chapters.

Thanks to 'Team Boldwood' particularly to my editor Caroline Ridding with her indispensable advice and input, and to copy editor Jade, and Rose the eagle-eyed proof reader, for their invaluable input to making the story the best it could be.

Editing this book in the lockdown of 2020 meant that life was strangely empty of social contact for months so huge thanks must go to my online friends – both the virtual and the Real Life ones – for the chats, the spirit raising memes and for just being 'there' on my computer whenever I needed a boost.

Heartfelt thanks too, go to my readers who enable me to carry on doing a job I love. Receiving e-mails from readers saying how much they've enjoyed a book I've written is truly wonderful.

Love,

Jennie

MORE FROM JENNIFER BOHNET

We hope you enjoyed reading *One Summer in Monte Carlo*. If you did, please leave a review.

If you'd like to gift a copy, this book is also available as an ebook, digital audio download and audiobook CD.

Sign up to Jennifer Bohnet's mailing list for news, competitions and updates on future books.

http://bit.ly/JenniferBohnetNewsletter

Explore more gloriously escapist reads from Jennifer Bohnet.

ABOUT THE AUTHOR

Jennifer Bohnet is the bestselling author of over 10 women's fiction novels, including *Villa of Sun and Secrets* and *The Little Kiosk By The Sea*. She is originally from the West Country but now lives in the wilds of rural Brittany, France.

Visit Jennifer's website: http://www.jenniferbohnet.com/

Follow Jennifer on social media:

f facebook.com/Jennifer-Bohnet-170217789709356

y twitter.com/jenniewriter

O instagram.com/jenniebohnet

BB bookbub.com/authors/jennifer-bohnet

ABOUT BOLDWOOD BOOKS

Boldwood Books is a fiction publishing company seeking out the best stories from around the world.

Find out more at www.boldwoodbooks.com

Sign up to the Book and Tonic newsletter for news, offers and competitions from Boldwood Books!

http://www.bit.ly/bookandtonic

We'd love to hear from you, follow us on social media:

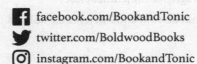

facebook.com/BookandTonic

twitter.com/BoldwoodBooks

instagram.com/BookandTonic